The
DAYS LOST

SHANNON McCRIMMON

Published by Shannon McCrimmon
www.shannonmccrimmon.com
www.facebook.com/shannonmccrimmonauthor

Cover Design: Popcorn Initiative • www.popcorninitiative.com
Cover Illustration: Sheila Lutringer • www.flavortint.com

For Daddy

"Lost time is never found again." Benjamin Franklin

PROLOGUE

He jerked Ellie off of the floor and wrapped his arm around her neck narrowing her path for air. "Your fate is sealed." He held his gun up to her head. She tried to fight him off. "I wouldn't do that if I were you." He squeezed harder. She gasped, choking for air. Blood pounded in her ears. The air in her lungs was withering away, and everything around her was turning darker and darker. The nightmare she had over and over again had become her reality.

CHAPTER 1

Ellie rolled out of her bed and rummaged through the pile of laundry that was sprawled all over her bedroom floor. She couldn't tell what was clean or what was filthy and picked out a pair of gray shorts and a lavender sports bra, held them up to her nose and sniffed. Both had a fresh scent, and Ellie deduced that these two items were in fact a part of the elusive clean pile. She searched for a matching pair of socks but came up short. One light pink sock—a mishap from washing reds with whites—and one stark white sock, made their way onto her bare feet.

She tugged on her sports bra, ensuring that it was snug and fit tight against her small chest. Her tanned stomach was covered in tiny goosebumps. The brown hairs on her arms stood up. The cool mountain air managed to creep into her parents' vacation house in Western North Carolina—a place Ellie would call home for her entire summer vacation.

She laced up her scuffed pair of Nike's and walked into to her bathroom, turning on the faucet and splashing ice cold water onto her face. She blinked a few times and picked up a hand towel off of her bath room counter, using it to wipe her face. She gathered her damp hair and tied it up into a pony tail. Shorter pieces fell on and around her heart-shaped face, and she grabbed two hair clips to pin back the loose, dangling hairs. The weight of her thick tresses felt heavier than usual. A trim was in need—that was obvious from the split ends—and she planned to cut it herself later that night. The idea of sitting for hours in a beauty salon having her hair coifed, sprayed, or cut into the latest style wasn't something she preferred. Ellie liked things simple and without any fuss.

Elisabeth "Ellie" Morales was not a star athlete by any means.

She wasn't that girl—the one who participated in every single sport. In the back of her senior yearbook there was one lone caption next to her name: Cross Country Team 9th -12th grade. She couldn't pitch a fast ball or score a goal, and her eye-to-hand coordination skills were subpar at best. But there was one thing that she could do—and do well—and that was run. With her long stride and slim build, Ellie had the perfect frame to run long distances. She could zip past others with little to no effort while they struggled to catch their shallow breaths and bring their pulses to a steady and safe beat.

To say that Ellie was a runner was an injustice to the amount of skill she had. Ellie could *run*. And that's what she did. Every day. Rain or shine. Hot or cold. It didn't matter. Every morning, as if it were a ceremonial religious act, she followed the same ritual: get up just as the sun was rising, put on her pair of Nike's, and shoot out the door with her legs in motion and her cadence in perfect rhythm, and run, run, run.

Her shelves at her home in Coral Gables, Florida were cluttered with trophies and medals from various races, most of which she placed first, and on that rare occasion, second place. The second place medals were hidden in the back behind the large trophies, blue ribbons, and fake golden medals. But it wasn't about being the best, or about winning. She enjoyed the freedom it gave her, the peace of mind.

She bent forward and touched the round silk floral rug. Her fingertips glided against the smooth surface, and she wanted to stay in that position forever. The stretch felt oh-so-good. It always did. Her muscles were were sore from the long run she had gone on the day before, and the day before that, and so on. She shot up and took a hold of her left foot and brought it to the back of her thigh. She squeezed hard—a warm tingling sensation came over her. She let her foot drop to the ground and then grasped firmly onto her right foot, mimicking the same move. Her fingers loosened their hold on her foot, and it slowly touched the floor again.

She searched her room, wondering where her dog, Bosco, was. He never left her side, and she knew the only reason he would was if table scraps were involved. Bosco was supposed to be the family's dog, but really he was hers, and everyone knew and accepted that fact.

"Bosco!" she hollered.

Nothing.

"Bosco!" she shouted again.

A loud thump startled her. She spun around to see what the noise was. Again, another thwack. And then two more. She charged over to the wall, hearing the pounding of a fist beating against it.

"It's the butt crack of dawn Ellie, shut up!" yelled her younger brother, Jonah, from his room next door.

"How do you like this?" She balled her hand into a tightly clenched fist and hammered it several times against the wall while laughing devilishly. She continued to torment him a few more seconds. He mumbled a sassy, curse word filled response, and she did it one more time just to aggravate the tar out of him.

"You'll pay later!"

"I'm so scared." She snickered.

Bosco charged into her room and immediately leapt onto her bed. Ellie dashed over to her bed and plopped down next to him. "Hey boy. You ready for a run?" She stroked the top of his wiry, furry head. His long tongue stuck out, and his tail wagged back and forth.

"Guess that's a yes," she answered, noticing his tail in motion. "Come on." She tapped the bed and jumped off as Bosco eagerly followed.

***

Ellie and Jonah had the standard sibling relationship: insult, argue, physically fight, and then hug it out. There was a three year age gap between them. Jonah was fifteen and would be a junior in high school in the fall. Ellie had just graduated and would be transitioning to college.

Even though Jonah grated on Ellie's nerves, no one else was allowed to pick on him. No one. She defended him more than once in her lifetime. He was mouthy, and often made snarky comments to guys twice his size, saying more than he should given his small stature. Jonah liked to test people—to see how far he could take things, and once he knew, he'd go all the way.

When Jonah was in the second grade, he got into a shoving match with Robbie McReynolds, a chubby, mean kid who enjoyed picking on anyone smaller than him—which was a majority of their elementary school's population. Jonah had shoved the big ogre and spewed out "You're so stupid you got locked out of a convertible car with the top down!" When Robbie saw the other kids laughing at him, he grabbed Jonah by his shirt collar, and pushed his scrawny body hard against the pavement telling him that he was dead. Ellie saw Robbie's cavity stricken teeth were gritted and his hands were balled into tight fists about to find their way to her brother's face. She took off her heavy backpack filled with text books and violently swung it at him, striking him directly on the right side of his plump freckled face. She proceeded to yell at him and told him not to touch her brother or she'd hit him again.

It was rare for any student at their elementary school to be suspended, but Ellie was the exception to that rule. Five entire days. That was her penance for defending her brother—for giving the school bully a taste of his own medicine. Even though she received lectures from her parents about the cons of fighting (although Ellie suspected her father was proud that she stood up for her brother) and was on restriction for several months, she thought it was worth it. She loved Jonah, and no matter what, they stuck together.

***

Her house smelled like strongly brewed coffee. Ellie's dad, Miguel, had made cafe con leche which Ellie often referred to it as "sweet nectar of the gods." A can of Cafe' Bustelo and a cobalt blue jar filled with sugar sat on the granite counter top. The stove top espresso maker was still on the stove next to a sauce pan that been used to boil his milk. It was too sweet for her to drink, especially before a run, and she'd only indulge in having a cup on very special occasions. She thought it was ironic that a heart surgeon who saw corroded arteries on a daily basis, would drink liquid sugary sweetness every single morning without any second thoughts. He wasn't a health fanatic and never preached nutrition to Jonah or Ellie. Ellie was secretly thankful. Her friend, Delia, had very strict parents who counted calories and refused to have sugary foods of any sort in their household. Needless to say, after a few lackluster meals, Ellie stopped going over to Delia's for dinner. Food in the Morales family was about enjoyment, and Ellie was glad she had a healthy perception when it came to food and her body.

He sat slumped at the breakfast table, reading the newspaper, and his hands were cupped around his ceramic coffee mug—one that Jonah had made in art class. It was dented in the middle and the handle was lopsided. He was up earlier than usual. Dark circles shadowed his charcoal eyes. He looked up at Ellie, pursed his lips and then shook his head.

"What?" Ellie said.

"You're essentially naked. Go put something on."

Ellie looked down at her lavender sports bra and baggy running shorts. She yanked on the elastic waist band, pulling them up to cover her exposed navel. "I'm wearing the same thing I always do."

He mumbled something to himself, got up from the table and abruptly left the room.

Ellie glanced down at Bosco and then shrugged her shoulders. "Someone got up on the wrong side of the bed this morning," she whispered. She headed toward the front door, wrapped her hand around the dull bronze knob and pulled.

"Ellie, wear this," her dad said, coming from behind her.

She turned around and saw the gray fleece jacket he was holding. "Papi," she whined. "I'm fine. Once I start running, I'll get hot anyway."

"Just wear it." He stared her straight in the eye, and his voice was unwavering. She could tell he wasn't asking; he was telling.

Ellie took the jacket and begrudgingly put it on. The warm, dense fibers did feel good against her cool skin, but she wasn't about to share that bit of information with her father.

"Thank you," he said said with a subtle "I told you so" smirk. "Stay on the trail," he added in a stern, fatherly voice. "I don't like you running alone in those woods. It's dangerous."

"I've run on the trail a million times. Anyways, I'm wearing my compass." She pointed to her wrist, tapping on her watch with its built-in navigation system. It had been a gift from him two Christmas' before.

"Take your phone with you," he said.

"I can't get a signal with my crappy phone," she moaned and added, "I'll be fine," trying to reassure him. "See you in a few hours." She flew out the door before he had time to respond.

"Be careful!" he shouted as she ran down the gravel driveway and toward the woods.

CHAPTER 2

Ellie stood at the entrance to the hiking trail near her home. Her hands were already numb and her teeth chattered uncontrollably. She exhaled, watching her warm breath dissipate into the thick, frigid air. She carefully zipped up her hoodie, thankful that her father had been so perceptive.

"Guess he was right. We're not telling him though, are we boy?" she said, rubbing her palms together.

Summer weather in the North Carolina mountains was unpredictable—one day it could be a scorcher, the next day a frosty, bitter cold day. Even though it was early June, it didn't feel like summer to Ellie. She was accustomed to the same temperature throughout each season: warm and humid with a gentle, tepid breeze coming from the Atlantic Ocean.

That was part of the appeal when Ellie's parents had purchased the house. They wanted to experience a change of seasons. They made promises, that they'd visit the home in the fall to see the leaves, in the winter to have a possible white Christmas, in the spring to see tulips and other flowers bloom—flowers that were rare to them because they didn't stand a chance in the brutal Florida sun— and in the summer to enjoy a break from the Florida heat. But it seemed that they only managed to visit a few times over the years.

Tucked away on acres and acres of mountainous land with stunning views of the Blue Ridge Mountains and in the most remote area of Western North Carolina, their two-story timber frame vacation home was picturesque. Surrounded by trees, rhododendrons, and mountain laurel, it was the type of house featured in home décor magazines for award-winning design. It was richly painted in earthy colors that complimented the natural surrounding environment. The exterior was lined with pieces of tree bark, emerald green window sashes and ruby red shutters. Inside there was a feeling of warmth with douglas fir wooden beams crisscrossing the high vaulted ceilings, walnut hardwood floors, lodge style furniture, and a large stone fireplace—so grand that it caught everyones eye when they entered the home. It was a true masterpiece—and one created by Ellie's mom, Laura.

Nothing inside was garish or gaudy. There weren't any useless dust-collecting knick knacks, dead animal heads showcased, or generic paintings from some retail outlet. Her mom had refused to allow anything of that sort to be in a home of hers. Decorating was her forte. It was what she had gone to college to study, and everyone else in the family was forbidden to put in their two cents about the décor—not that any of them cared to or had an opinion anyway. They were content—as long as they had a place to to lay their head at night, the rest of the house could be an atrocious mess for all they cared.

They planned to stay there all summer. It was unusual for Ellie's dad to take so much time off from his job as a surgeon—he loved his job as much as his family—but it was his last option, his only choice. Her mom passed away six months before, and when she died, their family unit was severed. Her dad was desperate to sew it back together. He thought a lengthy stay in the mountains would help them all get away from the overt reminders of his children's mother—from all that made the grieving process even more of a hurdle to overcome. Ellie, obsessed with running, would do nothing else, and refused to talk about the elephant in the room. Jonah incessantly pestered Ellie and his father, vying for a fragment of their attention. Trying to hold it all together took every ounce of strength her dad had left in him, and it was starting to show. His youthful, handsome face, once a blank canvas, was now shadowed with black circles under his dark eyes and lines that covered his entire forehead. His black as coal hair was turning various shades of silver. And he no longer sat up straight, his shoulders were constantly hunched.

Since Ellie was just like him, he knew how she was coping. If he was struggling to keep afloat, he knew she was in the same condition, and he only had so many life preservers. Jonah was Ellie's opposite. He was more like his mother, analytical and logical, and this outlook made his grieving process unique. Still, even when Jonah reached out, he received nothing in return from his sister or father. They kept their dark feelings hidden, and discussing the matter was out of the question.

Ellie and her mom were as opposite as any blood relation could possibly be. Ellie was more like her father—headstrong and stubborn. A tomboy since she was born, Ellie wanted nothing to do with the girly, prissy things that her mother had relished. She had tried to feign interest when her mom talked about going shopping or getting manicures, but she had a terrible poker face and her mom knew she could not care less.

Ellie had to learn too early in her life that you never know what you have until it's no longer within your reach. Looking back on all of those times that she sighed, rolled her eyes, and replied in typical adolescent fashion, "okay," to her mother as if it were the worst possible thing she would have to do, she regretted it. Every single minute of it.

As she ran, Ellie replayed the last conversation she had with her mother over and over again. Like a broken record, the words they spoke repeated themselves in her mind. *Why did she argue with her mom about going Christmas shopping? Why didn't she just go? Why did she have to be so difficult about it?*

*****

"Ellie, let's go Christmas shopping together. You and me only. We can grab some lunch afterwards," her mother said.

"Oh come on, Mom. The mall is packed full of people. You know I can't stand crowds," she complained.

"Help me pick out your father's gift," she had said and nudged her. "Come on. It'll be fun."

Ellie sighed heavily. "Can't one of your friends go with you?"

"They could. But I'd rather spend the day with you."

"Do I have to go?" she groaned.

"No, Ellie. I just thought you may want to." She touched Ellie's cheek, forcing a smile. "It's okay. You don't have to go if you don't want to."

"We'll go some other time, Mom," Ellie said, making a promise she'd never be able to keep.

*****

Her last words to her mother echoed in her head as she ran through the forest. Instead of thinking about starting college and all of the excitement centered around beginning a new chapter in her life, Ellie's thoughts were centered on her mom and all of the regret she had about their last conversation. She wished more than anything that she could have one more day with her. She'd go Christmas shopping and have lunch, just to hear her mother laugh and see her smile again. She'd ask her questions that she needed the answers to, hug her and tell her that she loved her, tell her sorry for being so selfish, and ask her if she'd ever forgive her for not being the daughter she so desperately wanted.

The ground was soft and wet from the rain the night before, and sprinkles of mud and dirt splattered sporadically on her legs and all over her worn tennis shoes. She needed a new pair but was too superstitious to buy any. This pair had helped her place first place in the state championships, and she couldn't just toss them out in the trash. They were her good luck charm.

Her shoes stuck to the mucky ground, the mud seeping into each and every tread. Her pony tail bobbed against her back. Most people would turn around complaining that this was horrible terrain for running. Not Ellie. Not ever.

Droplets of water from wet leaves fell onto her hair. The air was cool and still moist. She could see her breath as she exhaled. The more she moved, the more she sweated.

She ran to the beat of the music—to the pounding of the drums and the strumming of the electric guitar. The volume on her IPOD was set high—the way she liked it.

"You'll go deaf!" her mother had warned her more than once. She figured if she was going to lose her hearing, better that she do it from life's enjoyment than let it pass by only to lose her hearing naturally as she grew old.

A branch scraped her cheek, causing a sharp, stinging pain. She touched her face with the tip of her finger. It was smeared with blood. She wiped her face again—this time with her palm—and trekked ahead.

The path was well marked for hikers and runners—with painted strips of bright blue on various trees letting hikers know that they were in fact on the trail and not lost in the woods. No one was daring enough to venture out this morning. Only those serious about exercise would head out on a day when the air was nippy and the ground was still saturated. She should have felt afraid running alone out in the middle of the woods on a deserted trail, but she didn't. Her mind was focused on running. It was her coping mechanism.

An hour had passed, and she still wasn't tired. Bosco started to fall behind—his tongue hung out. She came to a stop and turned around to face him. She peered down at Bosco. His breath was rapid. "We'll rest here a while, okay boy," she said, touching his head reassuringly. Bosco was no longer as spry as he used to be.

The forest was thick with pine trees—large and formidable. She stared up and saw the sun peeking its way between the branches—a ray of sunshine beamed down to the ground and cast a warm sunny glow.

She plopped down on the moist ground leaning against the rough bark of the tree trunk. She could feel each and every groove poking into her back. Her shorts felt damp from sweat. Green moss covered one of the long exposed roots. She traced her finger over it, feeling the soft texture. Bosco lay down next to her and closed his eyes, falling fast asleep. Ellie scrolled through the playlist on her IPOD and chose a softer, more mellow tune.

The sun continued to shine through the trees and found its way to them. The warmth was welcome. Birds chirped and flapped their wings high in the sky. A stream of water flowed in the distance. Ellie felt at peace. This was her idea of Zen.

She kept nodding off and on, her eyes half closed, and she was almost completely asleep. Almost. Bosco's loud bark startled her from her lethargic state. He stood on all fours and charged toward something. His loud constant growl echoed throughout the maze of trees.

Ellie frantically shot up.

"Bosco!" she shouted. "Bosco!" she hollered again, this time louder and with more authority.

He ignored her and continued heading away from her—toward something—whatever that elusive "something" was. She ran after him, trying so hard to catch up. He veered left, then right, and then dashed through a creek of water. Water splashed all over the place. Ellie followed, and her shoes were soaked the instant she stomped into the frigid water. An intense feeling overcame her, and her feet were numb within a matter of seconds.

She yelled again, "Bosco. Stop!"

He hurried up a steep incline, panting and short of breath, and then glided down the hill continuing to run despite the strain. He wouldn't stop. It was like he was being pulled, and nothing would make him quit. Not even Ellie.

Ellie watched as Bosco disappeared behind a broad and bulky rhododendron bush. Everything behind it was camouflaged. If he hadn't run through, and if she hadn't stooped down to the ground and moved the branches to peer behind it, she would have never known that it blocked an opening to a cave.

She crawled, pushing the branches out of her way so that she could enter. Fortunately, these weren't thorny like those nasty raspberry bushes. The ground was ice cold and getting through the small opening was a tight fit, even for someone as slim as Ellie.

"*Woof, woof, woof!*" Bosco's bark echoed off the cave's walls.

Ellie raised her arms above her head trying to decipher the size of the cave. She was enveloped in nothing but darkness. Her teeth chattered and tiny goosebumps formed all over her. It was much more brisk—the temperature had dropped at least ten degrees.

There was ample room, more than enough for her to stand up straight. She slowly got up off of the ground, and stumbled through, searching for a way out. A beam of light shined in the distance. Ellie breathed a sigh of relief. She wasn't claustrophobic, but the idea of being stuck in a cold, dark space with hardly any clothes on wasn't high on her bucket list. She followed the light until she had reached the exit on the other side.

She squinted her eyes, and cupped her hand above them, trying to block the sun's blinding light. Everything looked white and blurry. Her eyes were in shock, and it took them a moment to adjust.

Bosco ambled to a weeping willow tree that had sprouted near the edge of a beautiful emerald green lake. He wasn't barking anymore. The lake separated two massive rock walls. She had entered a gorge—and it didn't remotely resemble any other part of Western North Carolina. This topography was unique to the area— like something you would see out west or in Western Canada, not in the south and definitely not in North Carolina. She took it all in—the granite walls that soared to the sky and shimmered from the sun, and the dazzling lake of water that was like nothing she had ever seen before in her life—it was like liquid jade. It was majestic. The water lapped against the sandy, rocky shore. Ellie treaded in Bosco's direction, confused by his erratic behavior.

Even though the slow beat of drums and the strumming of a guitar blared through her ear phones, another sound was much more prominent and it made her stop still in her tracks. It was the most enchanting music she had ever heard—like an angel in heaven singing. She took off her headphones, unstrapped her IPOD from her left arm, and turned it off.

The tune was an unfamiliar one—something from another time—long, long ago. It was a song Ellie didn't recognize. She listened intently to the beautiful, serene sound. She was completely mesmerized by his voice. Bosco's tail was wagging, and he was staring in awe at the source of the harmony—as if he was hypnotized too.

He continued to sing and gathered wood off in the far distance and across the body of water, unaware that he was being watched.

Ellie thought he was dressed in an odd way: long chestnut colored pants that resembled uniform trousers, suspenders strapped around each broad shoulder, and a button down shirt in a muted color. His brown hair was unkempt and shaggy—as if it had been cut by a child. He had some facial hair, not too much, but just enough to show he was indeed a man and definitely not a boy. She was curious and tried to get a closer look at him. She failed to notice the large tree branch in front of her and stepped on it, snapping it in half.

The stranger's singing ceased. He dropped the wood from his hands and looked around, suddenly aware that he was not alone. His posture changed; it was much more tense and threatening, and his jaw was clenched tight. He placed his hand on his hip, touching something. Ellie couldn't see what it was but thought it might be a weapon.

Ellie back peddled quickly, hoping that he wouldn't see her, afraid that she had trespassed into a forbidden territory. Bosco barked in response to Ellie's anxiousness, and the stranger looked directly in their direction. Even though they were more than a hundred yards away from each other, she could feel the iciness of his stare. Within a split second, Ellie spun around and bolted in the opposite direction with Bosco trailing behind her.

CHAPTER 3

She raced through the woods and made her way home within record time. She ached all over and felt edgy. She bent over and placed her hands on her knees; her breath was still uneven and ragged. Jonah met her outside carrying a basketball in one hand and slapped her hard on her head with his other. She grimaced but didn't have the energy to fight back. Under normal circumstances, she'd knuckle him in the stomach or poke him in the ribs in retaliation.

"You look like hell," he said and dribbled the ball. "You were gone forever."

She stood upright, shooting daggers at him with her dark brown eyes. "I wasn't gone that long."

He laughed and threw the ball upward toward the basket.

Ellie deliberated telling him about her experience in the woods. She didn't know what she would say, or even how she would explain it, because she had no idea what had just happened. She watched as Jonah shot another basket, and she folded her arms against her chest. At that point she noticed the IPOD wasn't strapped to her left arm like normal. In all of the chaos, she had left it, and now she wondered if she should try to get it back. She felt a pang of fear. Going back seemed like a bad idea. The entire encounter gave her a strange mix of emotions—wary and yet warm all over. It was as if his voice had called her and Bosco, and it was the most beautiful sound she had ever heard.

"Wanna play?" Jonah waved his hand in front of Ellie. "Earth to Ellie." He dribbled the ball and bounced it her way.

Her reflexes kicked in, and she caught the ball with both hands. "You sure you want to play me? I always beat you, Shrimp." Her breath had come back, and her pulse had reached a steady rhythm.

"Quit bragging," he said with annoyance. "I can think of a million things I beat you at, Ellie. Let's see," he counted on his fingers, "chess, checkers, grades. What was your final class rank? Top thirty-five percent." He let out a laugh. "What's mine again? Oh let's see, number one!" He raised his eyebrow and smirked.

"Quit being a sore loser," she said, letting his insult roll off of her shoulders. She knew it was his one defense mechanism, and she'd let him have it. "You just can't stand the fact that I'm a better athlete than you, which isn't saying much. Poor Shrimp," she teased. "Come on let's play."

Jonah would probably become a member of MENSA by the time he graduated from high school. Ellie was smart but not brilliant like him. His high intellect made things very difficult for him in high school. Socially, he just didn't fit in. Communicating with his peers was a struggle, and finding people on his same level was even more of a hurdle. Ellie knew what he went through. She witnessed how he was seen as odd and often ridiculed by dumb jocks who taunted him to improve their own low self-esteem. She hated that she wouldn't be there to protect him next school year. He wasn't frail, and he wasn't weak. Jonah could definitely fend for himself. She knew this about her younger brother, but she worried he would blurt out one of his insults to the wrong person, and she wouldn't be there for him. The protector in her wanted to be there to make sure he was going to be all right. With her mother now gone, Ellie felt compelled to take over that role.

Ellie lunged forward and threw the ball into the basket. "One to zero." She bounced the ball up and down against the concrete driveway, relishing having the upper hand.

He moved toward her and tried taking the ball from her. Ellie's elbow shot up, blocking him. She threw the ball over his head and into the basket again. "Two to zero," she quipped.

He sighed in frustration and then grabbed the ball from her. "It's on now," he said.

"I'm shaking." She playfully shook her knees.

Bosco's surge of energy came back and he ran between them, begging for attention. Ellie bent down to pet him dotingly. "You're a good boy aren't you?" she cooed.

Bosco wasn't a pure breed or a champion dog of any sort. He'd never be in the Westminster or complimented by strangers for being cute. He was a Heinz 57, a mutt with DNA from a variety of breeds. He struggled to learn tricks and rarely came to anyone on command, even Ellie, unless bribery in the form of food was involved. But his temperament was as sweet as honey, and he loved unconditionally. Those two qualities outweighed all of his faults.

No one knew his exact age. Their veterinarian speculated he was eight, which in dog years meant he was in his mid-fifties. Sometimes Ellie would find him running around the house, jumping on furniture, or wrestling with a toy. Other times, he was content being lazy, sleeping his day away.

Ellie always wanted a dog, and it seemed that everyone she knew had one. Her dad said that they cost too much. He didn't want to waste his money on vet's bills, food, and other things he said weren't necessary. To Ellie's dismay, her mom agreed. And so, Ellie lived thirteen years of her life without canine companionship.

Bosco came to be a part of Ellie's life by happenstance. Some would say that he and Ellie were drawn to each other. That he found her by magic. Out of all of the houses in Ellie's large neighborhood with its identical ranch style homes, he chose their front lawn to claim as his new home. No matter how much her dad protested and told him to scram, Bosco was just as unbending in his ways as he and Ellie were and refused to be scared off. Her dad would charge out to the front yard, shoo him away, only to find him stretched out on his front lawn, basking in the sun the very next day.

The first day Ellie saw the mangy, thin mutt with his ribs protruding and patchy, wiry hair, sprawled in her front yard waiting to be petted, she felt an instant connection and a deep desire to help the poor nameless dog. She snuck food out from the kitchen and turned on the watering hose so he could drink. She just couldn't brush him off and ignore him. Plus, he was so dang sweet—giving her sloppy kisses and nuzzling close to her to show his gratitude. He was the dog she had always wanted.

Ellie had already named him by day two. And within a few days her mom caved, coming out with her to feed him, play with him, and shower him with kisses and pats on the head. Despite her dad's earlier protests, the dog gradually won him over too, leaving him to agree to keep him as their family pet. It only took one week for Bosco to wedge his way into the Morales family.

***

The entire house smelled like a variety of spices and herbs: cilantro, oregano, and cumin. The sweet scent of banana and citrus complimented the rich aroma. Her dad had cooked Ellie's favorite meal: twice fried plantains, because frying them once wouldn't suffice; black beans and rice; Mojo roasted pork; and of course, flan. Ellie loved flan. It was her favorite dessert. Jonah said it tasted like snot, to which her reply was always the same. "How do you know what snot tastes like, Shrimp?"

Ellie's dad would never be able to cook Cuban food the way he preferred it—the way his mother had. She passed away long ago, and his was the only Cuban food he would eat. Even though there was a plethora of Cuban restaurants in Coral Gables, and it would have satisfied his craving for authentic Cuban cuisine, he always made the same complaint: "Why spend so much money at a restaurant when I can cook it at home for half the price?"

Born in Havana, Cuba in 1966, Miguel Morales lived in Cuba only fourteen years before he fled by boat to the United States with his father, mother, and masses of others who were seeking the same thing—freedom. The journey was a difficult one. Confined to cramped quarters, jostled by violent ocean waves and temperamental weather, Ellie's dad and his family sat hunched in a corner of a small boat surrounded by a group of strangers. Over heated, dehydrated, and full of trepidation, they all wondered if they were ever going to step foot on American soil.

It was an experience he tried not to think about, and he rarely if ever discussed it with anyone. Rekindling painful memories was something he never did. The past was the past. Once something happened, he looked forward not backward because he believed that living in the past would hold him back. Leaving his country and traveling in unsafe conditions across the unpredictable Atlantic Ocean and being forced to adjust to a new country and a brand new culture, was one of the most difficult experiences he ever had.

Acclimating to a new country and a new culture proved to be a challenge. He had to quickly adapt, or he would flounder. Trying to fit in at school and speaking little English made things even more difficult. He learned to absorb himself in the new culture.

Earning an education was his way out of poverty, and he studied religiously with little to no time for socializing. Going to college was what mattered most to him and his parents. But he was not just a bookworm. He was a skilled runner and could zip past anyone who raced him.

It was one day as he ran around his school's track in PE class that he caught the track coach's eye. He was so fast and could outrun anyone on the track team. There was no way the coach was going to let talent like his go to waste. He instantly became a member of the team. He had the sense to know that having brains and brawn would be his first class ticket to college. A small private liberal arts college later offered him a full scholarship, and he eagerly accepted.

A proud man, he loved his family and believed it was his duty to support them. That's what his father instilled in him, and that is what he hoped to instill in Jonah. Some would say he was "old school" with his strict rules and traditionalist views on life. He believed in hard work and that as a father he should be able to provide for his family. He knew that studying medicine would allow him to afford the luxuries he so badly wanted. It was during his residency that he met Laura Marshall. The moment she stepped into the hospital elevator with him, he was smitten. All it took was a quick glance at her, seeing her beautiful porcelain skin and yellow wavy hair, and after receiving a simple smile from her bright red lips, he was hooked. The last thing he needed was to fall in love. He had school to worry about, but the smile led to a conversation, and before he knew it they were dating. She was everything he wanted in a woman: beautiful, smart, and self-sufficient. She was confident and sure of her self. He couldn't help but fall in love. They were married within a year, and Ellie was born within the first year of the marriage, and Jonah was born three years later. Losing her was the worst thing he had ever dealt with in his life, and it made every other obstacle up to that point seem like child's play.

"Help me set the table," he said to Jonah and Ellie. Jonah took a spoon, scooped a heap of black beans and rice and placed it in his mouth. He playfully swatted him on the arm. "Wait until dinner." He grabbed a new spoon and stirred inside of the pot.

"You need more salt," Jonah said to him.

He pursed his lips, mumbled something in Spanish, and poured more salt into the pot.

Ellie stood next to him and inhaled. "Smells good," she said to her dad.

He gave her an appreciative smile. "What happened to your cheek?" He noticed the red mark that was etched across her olive skin.

"A tree branch ran into me," she said.

"You're supposed to duck." Her dad chuckled.

Ellie took the spoon and grabbed a heap, placing it in her mouth.

"Ellie," he moaned. "Now I know where *he* gets it from." He indicated by moving his head in Jonah's direction.

"He gets it honestly," she said and grinned.

Ellie had heard her dad tell her on more than one occasion that her smile reminded him of her mother's, the way her eyes danced when her lips curled up. Ellie knew without a shadow of a doubt that her father *loved* her mother. After years of marriage, they acted like newlyweds to which Jonah and Ellie would moan and say "gross" whenever they would kiss or show any type of affection toward each other. Her parents had hoped that she and Jonah would have the same kind of relationship when they married. Neither she or Jonah had ever been involved in a serious relationship. They both went on dates, and Ellie even dated the same boy for a few months, but it never grew beyond that. She just didn't seem too concerned with having a serious boyfriend. This was a relief to her dad. He wasn't ready to let go of his daughter just yet.

Ellie may have acted like her father and had his doe brown eyes, coal black hair and tanned, olive complexion, but she inherited her mother's heart shaped lips and delicate jaw line accentuated with high cheek bones. Ellie was a nature girl—naturally attractive without all the frills. She would never be as stunning as her mother had been, and she could not care less. Sure she wanted to be considered pretty, but it wasn't a top priority for her. There were more important things to think about. Her mother had always preached the importance of inner beauty—that intelligence and a kind heart were what mattered most because "your looks will go away when you get old and haggard but a big heart won't wither." Even though her mom knew that she was attractive, she never had the vanity associated with it.

They finished their dinner. It was Ellie's night to clean up, which she dreaded. Scrubbing pots and pans, putting dirty dishes away in the dishwasher, and cleaning counter tops were chores that she loathed. Tidying and straightening weren't things she did well, either. If it involved heavy labor, she often disappeared and was no where to be found for hours on end stating that she had to use the restroom or she didn't feel well—really lame excuses that no one bought but didn't dispute, either.

"Wipe the counters, okay," her dad said, tilting his head to the side and giving Ellie a knowing look. Ellie refrained from rolling her eyes and knew that what her father asked of her was not a stretch. She hadn't planned to wipe them.

Some would call her a slob, and she was repeatedly reminded that her future college roommate may not be so keen on her nasty habits which included leaving bowls of cereal and other dirty dishes in her bedroom, a constant unmade bed, and having baskets full of laundry that she would dig through to grab clothes to wear only to place them back in her hamper.

"If we get salmonella, it's on you," Jonah added to Ellie, and she flipped him the bird, mouthing a curse word to him in Spanish. Ellie spoke Spanish, some would say poorly—her dad had made sure that she and Jonah were able to communicate with their grandparents, and he wanted to pass down a part of his culture to them. To his dismay, Ellie had mastered and was quite accomplished at knowing every single bad word or phrase in the Spanish dictionary. In the world of high school, phrases like "eat shit and die" were common. In a predominately Spanish speaking school, being able to say it in Spanish was critical.

Ellie put the dirty dishes into the stainless steel dishwasher, turned it on, and began to clean the granite counter top. The hum of the dishwasher put her in a trance. She wiped back and forth and got lost in the motion. Seeing the natural stone reminded her of the gorge—the enormous walls that sparkled in the sun. Her mind wandered, and she started to picture him. She was curious and wanted to go back to see if he was there. She argued that she wanted her IPOD—that was why she had to go back. It had nothing to do with him. Running without music would be miserable and was simply out of the question. And so it was decided. She would get her IPOD even if that little voice in the back of her mind told her to stay away.

CHAPTER 4

Ellie had forgotten to close her blinds the night before, so the sun lit up her entire room. She would never get used to the sun rising so early. It was only a little after six o'clock in the morning, and she was already wide awake and raring to go. She shot out of bed and grabbed a pair of hot pink running shorts and a neon yellow sports bra. She purposely chose the atrocious ensemble. After a near scuffle with a trigger happy hunter the year before, Ellie learned to dress in bright colors to avoid being a mistaken target.

She pulled the bra over her head and slipped into the shorts. Her worn, grungy Nike's laid on the floor with a trail of dirt surrounding them. A pair of socks laid on the floor next to the shoes. She picked them up, inspected to see if they were clean, put them on her feet, and laced up her shoes.

She opened the top drawer to her dresser and took out a half used bottle of body lotion. She opened the cap, closed her eyes and took a whiff, smelling the sweet scent of vanilla. For just one minute she thought of her mom and then closed the cap, placing the bottle back safely in her dresser. Her dad had neglected to throw her mother's bottle of lotion out, and Ellie snuck it into her room the moment she discovered it. Her memories, and things like the lotion, were all that she had left of her mother.

She headed out of her room while Bosco followed. Her dad lay asleep on the living room couch sucking in air and breathing out like the hum of a John Deere tractor. He'd grow quiet, whistling away some air, and then the loud snoring sound would come back. Ellie tip-toed near him, trying not to wake him. This had become routine—him sleeping on the couch. Since her mother died, he hadn't slept well and had claimed the sofa as his new place to rest his head at night instead of sleeping in his own room, which Ellie suspected reminded him too much of her mother. The faint scent of Estee Lauder's Beautiful still lingered on her winter clothes that hung in the master closet. The first week they had arrived, Ellie sat in that closet for more than an hour quietly sobbing, enveloped in her mother's scent, painfully aware that it too, would soon disappear. She hadn't been back in that room since.

Ellie understood her father's lack of sleep. For months she lay awake tossing and turning, trying to close her eyes and sleep, but the pain was overwhelming. Her mother was always on her mind. Constantly.

Three to four hours a night—that was the extent of shut eye she had since her mother passed away. As with all things, it would take time, and Ellie longed for the day when she could get a good night's rest and when her chest wouldn't feel as if it were caved in.

She opened the refrigerator door and gulped down several swigs of ice cold water. A chill came over her and her sensitive teeth temporarily hurt from the instant shock. "Brain freeze," she whispered to Bosco. One lone bottle of water sat on the top shelf. She grabbed it, and moved toward the front door.

A wave of warm air welcomed her. It was crazy hot outside—a complete contrast to the weather from the day before. North Carolina summer weather was consistently inconsistent. This day was proof of that. The cool breeze had all but dissipated. The sun was already unleashing its fury, and it had barely risen above the horizon.

"Geez. It's like Florida hot today," she complained to Bosco. She wiped the beads of sweat that had formed on her forehead. She yanked on her pony tail and cursed her thick hair. She was tempted to stomp inside the house, grab a pair of scissors and cut the darn nuisance off. This thought had occurred to her on more than one occasion. Having long hair was such a pain—especially when it came to running.

Bosco looked up at her waiting for her next move. His tongue hung out and was covered with dribbles of spit from salivating. "You sure you wanna go, boy?" She knew that he couldn't answer, although she swore he understood her when she spoke to him. He took a few steps forward. "That's what I thought," she said and started moving.

The air was thick and humid, and she was perspiring all over. Her legs and arms were drenched. She could hear her feet pounding the soil as she made each swift step. Running without music was like hiking in the woods without a compass.

"This sucks," she said to Bosco.

A murder of crows hovered above her, flying from one tree to the next, stalking her as she made her way through the hodgepodge of greenery. Their irritating calls echoed throughout the woods. Squirrels scurried on the ground in search of food. It was irritating—running without the strumming of an electric guitar or to the rhythmic beat of drums and hearing the calls of nature instead. She wanted to hear the poetic lyrics of her favorite songs.

"I can't wait to get my IPOD back," she muttered under her breath. Her arms swung in motion, and her legs kicked it up a notch. She was in a hurry even if common sense told her to turn around and forget about the stupid IPOD.

"No way," she fought with herself. "It's mine, and I won't be scared off." She thought about how she must have looked—like a mad woman talking to herself running in the brutal heat. "At least

I'm not answering myself," she said, and then realized that was exactly what she had just done. She grew silent and trekked onward.

Ellie crawled through the same cave she had been in the day before. The drop in temperature was welcome. She walked slowly, her arms stretched out before her, moving as well as she could without any light guiding her along the way. "I can't believe I forgot to bring a flashlight," she berated herself out loud. Bosco refrained from barking and continued to trail her.

As she exited the cave and entered the gorge, the emerald lake glistened, and the massive granite walls shimmered from the sun. She squinted her eyes. Bosco headed to the weeping willow tree and rested underneath it, avoiding the sun's rays. It was one of the few shady spots. She scanned the area—taking it all in— and wondered if *he* lived there. Did he call someplace near there his home? Had he been a camper who had claimed this beautiful hidden place for an overnight stay? She knew if she were camping, she would do the same. It was remote and far away from heavy foot traffic and throngs of tourists trying to "get in touch with mother nature." Ellie hated that about campsites. It wasn't camping if a hundred other people had set up their tents within close proximity to yours. And don't get her started about campsites with hot showers or the RV's. She loathed them all. To her, using a generator while camping was cheating—you might as well stay at a Holiday Inn.

She hadn't been camping in a long time, perhaps seven or eight years. Her dad used to load up the car and drive the family up to the mountains for a week long trip—away from the hustle and bustle hectic city life. That's what he liked most about going to the mountains—that it was away from everything, and a small part of it reminded him of Cuba.

After several camping excursions, her parents decided it was time to buy their dream vacation home, and they hadn't been camping since. Ellie missed it. She yearned to sit around a lit fire with them all—laughing, eating, and enjoying the simple things in life. That was what camping was all about—simplicity. And the smell—there was nothing Ellie loved more than having her wardrobe full of the fresh scent of campfire. She thought about asking her dad and Jonah to go camping—more for nostalgia's sake than anything else. She wanted to rekindle that little piece of her past—a part that was full of pure bliss, before life's heartache stepped in.

Bosco closed his eyes and fell fast asleep. "You're supposed to be helping me, boy," she said to him. "Fat lotta help you are."

She walked around searching for her IPOD. It had to be around there somewhere. She hadn't gone very far that day—just in that general area and behind the tree so that she could spy on the man with the intense eyes. She rolled her eyes at her last thought.

I sound like a girl from those cheesy romance novels. Get a grip, Ellie, she thought.

She searched the ground—nothing but dandelions and wildflowers in pink, purple, and yellow. Monarch butterflies fluttered their wings, rested for brief moments on the tips of flower petals, and then flew off in another direction. She stalked over to the tree and poked Bosco so he would move. She wanted to search the ground around it, but Bosco refused to budge and rolled over on his side. "Nice," she said and sighed.

This was strange. The IPOD should have been easy to find. It wasn't like finding a needle in a haystack. She hadn't walked very far the day before, and she knew that was where she had dropped it. "Where can it be?" She squinted her eyes and tapped her fingers against her chin, pondering what to do next.

"I was there, there and there," she said and pointed. "IPODs don't walk. Unless...." she started. She scowled and said, "Unless it was taken. Of course." She threw her hands up in the air and kicked the ground in annoyance, specks of dirt flew everywhere. Buying another IPOD was simply out of the question. She bought this one with money she had saved from baby-sitting. Her dad didn't believe in giving his children things that he thought were useless and unnecessary, and to him, an IPOD met that criteria. Clothes, food, and shelter were all a child needed. She had to beg him for a cell phone, and when she finally received one, it was a prepaid phone with limited minutes.

"You get one hundred minutes each month. Use more, you pay for them yourself," he had told her.

"I might as well write letters to my friends," she complained.

"Good. That's cheaper than using a phone," he said.

Her blood was boiling, and her ears were turning three shades of red—a telling sign that Ellie was furious. "You may have beautiful eyes, but you're a slimy thief!" she hollered and then felt ridiculous for shouting this absurd statement.

Bosco stood on all fours, and his ears pointed up. He heard something.

"What is it?" she asked him.

Her heart began to beat in an erratic rhythm. A dark thought overcame her. If he was a thief, then he wasn't a good person. If he wasn't a good person, then he probably wasn't someone she needed to be all alone with out in the woods. She had no idea if he was around or not, but she wasn't about to wait around like a sitting duck to find out.

She started to move out of the gorge and toward the cave. Bosco barked and ran in the opposite direction.

"Bosco!" she yelled.

He ran around the lake to the other side—to the place where "the thief" had been the day before. Ellie's stomach turned. Her palms were clammy, and her heart beat faster and faster. She had no choice. She had to chase him.

CHAPTER 5

"Darn you, Bosco," she mumbled between shallow breaths.

Bosco charged through the dense forest of evergreen trees, mountain laurel, rhododendron, and raspberry bushes. The thorny branches pricked Ellie's arms and legs.

He leapt over a fallen tree trunk and continued on his quest. Ellie tried to catch up. He was so fast and so intent, and she was heading so deep into the forest. She was immersed in a sea of trees and had no idea how far she had gone, but from the feel of her sore feet and her heaving chest, she knew she had traveled far.

Bosco finally came to a complete halt— standing on all fours and completely hypnotized—as if a magnetic force made him stop. She came up behind him and was about to give him a stern lecture, but something kept her from doing so. She heard the same angelic voice singing another unfamiliar tune. His voice joined others— almost as beautiful as his—but not quite. Nothing compared to his voice. A soprano and an alto sang along with him. His was the perfect pitch and met both of their tones in the middle, creating an impeccable harmony. It was enchanting and pulled at her to walk further—to explore and see where these voices were coming from. She knew she should turn around and bolt like a bat of hell, but she couldn't. She just couldn't.

She walked as quietly as she was able, careful not to make too much noise, and followed their voices. They were getting louder which meant she was getting closer. The forest was less dense, and it was easier to move without having her arms and legs cut from nasty raspberry bushes. *Were they some kind of traveling musical group that performed in grungy honky tonk bars and camped while they toured?* she wondered. Ellie's imagination went wild. It always did. Her mother had told her on more than one occasion that she had an overactive imagination.

Trees were cut down and created a clearing in this one area. Two log cabins sat beyond the clearing in the middle of the dense forest encompassed by rows of pine trees. The cabins appeared as if they had been built hundreds of years ago, but the wood wasn't weathered. They were primitive looking—like the type of log cabins she saw in black and white photographs of pioneers claiming their plot of land and making this part of America their new home. Built with precision and not ostentatious like so many other cabins, these were simplistic.

She moved a branch out of her view so that she could stare at the sight in front of her. She covered her mouth with her hand to muffle the sound of her heavy breathing. Everyone told her she was noisy. Jonah called her "Thunder Foot" because she clomped around the house like a horse and stomped hard on the floor anytime she moved.

Everything else was eerily quiet—as if the entire forest had shut itself down to listen to this impromptu concert. The sounds of squirrels rustling through plants and wildflowers, birds chirping, and other animals scurrying about were all muted. Ellie had turned off every other noise so that she could focus solely on this alluring song. Bosco was as enthralled as Ellie. How could he not be?

A funnel of smoke circled the air, whirling up to the clear blue sky. There wasn't a cloud to be seen. *Maybe they're circled around a camp fire singing tunes and roasting marshmallows?* She could smell the burnt wood and game cooking over a hot fire. It permeated the air. She walked gingerly, touching the pine logs—each cut and placed precisely. Whomever had built the cabin was an expert

She crept to the ground and hovered on all fours—dirt
r short unpainted fingernails, and her knees turned three
black and brown. Bosco was smart enough to stay put in
his ⌐ spot and leave Ellie to her own devices.

"If they're axe murderers, I guess I can count on you," she
grumbled, looking over at her supposed tough dog. "Watch dog,
my ass," she added. She continued to crawl until she reached the
end of the cabin wall. She stopped and peered around the corner.
She knew she shouldn't spy. First of all, she was rather inept at it,
and secondly, she had no idea who these people were or if they
would hurt her.

Ellie liked adventure, and even though she was intelligent
and had more common sense than most people her age, if an
opportunity arose to do something fun, she'd do it. She had no
qualms about "borrowing" (as she liked to phrase it when she told
the story) several rolls of toilet paper from her church bathroom and
skipping Sunday night mass so she and her friends could roll their
youth leader's home. It was done in jest. Ellie and her friends loved
their youth leader and wanted to play a prank on him. A phone
call from a busy body church member to her parents telling them
they had a thief for a daughter changed things. Ellie had to pay the
church for the toilet paper she took, and she spent Homecoming
weekend grounded and cooped up inside her bedroom because of
her impetuous nature.

She knew by the sound of his voice that it had to be "the thief,"
and when she got a closer look and saw the fire reflected in his deep
set eyes, her heart sped up. Never had a boy aroused this kind of
reaction. *He's a thief*, she thought. *Not someone I should get all googly-
eyed over.*

A group of people sat around the lit fire. They were dressed peculiarly, rustically: the women wore long skirts that reached their ankles, with button down tops in gingham prints; the men were dressed in long wool trousers and suspenders. Ellie wondered if it was a part of their band's costumery or maybe they were traveling gypsies.

An older woman with a long white braid that reached her plump waist played a fiddle—the bow moving back and forth in gallant and spirited fashion. She tapped her foot against the ground, bouncing her legs up and down in perfect rhythm to the lively music. A young woman, maybe Ellie's age, and an older man, maybe her dad's age, sang in unison while "the thief" took the lead. He stood with one foot on a tree stump, tapping it up and down, and plucked at his banjo strings with his fingers. Another man sat on one of the tree stumps circling the fire and tapped his large feet against the dirt, slapping his knees in unison to the beat of the music. He wasn't singing, but he evoked the same liveliness and spirit the others had.

There was something cooking over the fire. Ellie couldn't decipher what it was, but it smelled good. The heavenly aroma filled the air. Her stomach grumbled. She hadn't eaten breakfast, and she was tempted to go over there and invite herself to their little pow wow.

Yeah. That'd go over well. Hi. I'm spying on you, and I'm hungry. Oh, and I think you have my IPOD. While I'm here, can I get that back?

She continued to stare at them, wondering who they were and what brought them there. She tried to be inconspicuous, hiding as well as she could. All it would take would be for one of them to turn around or for the Thief to look in her direction, and she would be discovered. She continued to listen to them sing, envious of their abilities. Ellie was tone deaf and couldn't sing in tune. Not one note. When she was a little girl, her mother placed her in piano lessons thinking it would help her musical ineptness, but it only magnified the problem. Ellie lacked musical talent.

The song abruptly ended. The older woman and boy placed their fiddle and banjo down next to them. The older woman spoke to the group. She had a southern accent—but it didn't sound anything like the locals in the area. R's were evident in most of her words and certain vowels were over emphasized.

She could hear the wood crackling from the fire. A few dishes clanked, and they began to talk all at once. They acted like a family—familiar and comfortable with each other. She would have stayed there and watched them eat, but her plans were interrupted.

Bosco barked. At what, she had no idea. She quickly turned her head in his direction and snapped, "Bosco!" She glared at him, hoping that it would shut him up. He barked again, which drew everyone's attention in his direction.

They all grew quiet—not a sound could be heard with the exception of the popping embers. "I'll go see what it is," the Thief whispered.

There was nowhere for Ellie to hide. He'd have to walk her way, and she'd stand out like a sore thumb with her gaudy fluorescent clothing.

"Grab the rifle," the older woman ordered.

Time to get the hell outta here, Ellie thought, and she jumped up. She could hear the Thief's footsteps. Consumed by fear, every sound amplified one hundred percent. Each step he took sounded like a giant walking: *boom, boom, boom.* His feet hammered the earth, and she knew it was only a matter of time until he saw her. Until she was exposed. She'd be dead before she experienced anything in her short life.

She swallowed and tried to muster the last ounce of courage she had left in her. *I can do this.* She had to do it; she didn't have any other choice.

She ran as fast as she could toward Bosco, who saw her frantic expression and felt her nervous energy. Ellie breathed hard and heavy—her heart was beating uncontrollably. She could feel the Thief closing in on her. She wanted to turn around and see how close he was to her but knew that doing that would only make things worse.

Look ahead, Ellie.

Thorny branches grabbed at her skin, cutting her all over. The forest was beating her up, but that was the least of her worries. Ellie felt like she was in one of the lame horror movies that Jonah liked to watch. The girl is always chased by the villain. And then the girl always trips and falls and helplessly screams while the crazy person stabs her to death. Only this was real life, and Ellie was running to save hers.

She reached the lake and wondered if she would have enough adrenaline to make it home. She'd have to run this pace for another grueling hour. It felt like an unrealistic mission, and she was starting to taste defeat.

She did the one thing she told herself she wouldn't—she turned around. He was running out of the woods and toward her. They were within a hundred feet of each other. Their eyes locked, and then he dropped his rifle. She didn't know if he was clumsy or trying to tell her something. His posture changed, and he formed a strange expression. He looked at her like she was a freak. Ellie wasn't sure if he was still a threat.

Neither one of them moved. Ellie didn't want to, and neither did he it seemed. She tilted her head to the side, studying him, trying to make out his features. He mimicked her in return, analyzing her. The sun was facing her and clouded her vision. Still, even if he was illuminated in a sea of light, she could feel his intense eyes staring into hers. If he was dangerous, she was in serious trouble.

Bosco growled, and his teeth were tightly clenched. Ellie spun around. A chestnut colored snake with a tan and pink pattern slithered within inches of her. It's distinctive yellow tail was pointed up—an indication it was a newborn. It was ready to bite, and its venom could be deadly no matter what age it was.

Ellie swallowed nervously. "Copperhead," she whispered. She looked down at her feet in horror. Its fangs were so close to her leg she could smell it— the scent of cucumber filled the air. Ellie knew it was only a matter of seconds before the snake struck her. Bosco was trying to protect her, but the more he barked and growled, the more irate the snake became.

It seemed as if it all happened in slow motion. The snake's fangs clung onto her ankle and wouldn't let up. The venom instantly shot into her. A burning sensation came over her, and Ellie roared in pain. Anyone within a mile could hear her horrific cries. She cursed in Spanish and screamed again. It was excruciating. The snake had accomplished its mission and slithered under a nearby rock. She peered down at her ankle and grimaced. It was swelling by the second. The heat was unbearable—it was as if she had just stuck her leg in a pot of boiling hot water. She thought cool water would be a reprieve and hobbled toward the lake. She felt warm all over, and her vision was skewed. She gazed down, and the ground appeared as if it were moving. Things were spinning. She swayed back and forth, and it was getting more difficult to maintain her balance. Everything was fading to black, and then she passed out. Her body slammed against the ground.

The Thief ran over and stood by Ellie, staring at her in wonder, and then he looked at Bosco, almost as if he were trying to get permission for what it was he was about to do. Bosco wasn't barking and watched as the stranger took off his shirt and wrapped it tight around the upper portion of her thigh, creating a tourniquet. Ellie opened her eyes, only slightly, and jumbled her words together.

"Shh," he whispered. "We're going to take care of you," he said soothingly, trying to keep her calm. Her saw her leg, what damage the snake had done, and he knew what could happen if he didn't act fast.

Ellie looked into his gray eyes as the sunlight beamed behind him, creating a halo effect. *Was he an angel? Was this the afterlife?* She tried to focus, but her vision was getting worse and everything around her was becoming dark again.

CHAPTER 6

He carefully scooped her up off of the ground and slung her as gently as he could over his bare broad shoulder. He moved fast, hoping it wasn't too late. Her leg was swelling. The venom would poison her blood if it spread any further.

She bobbed against him as he made his way through the thick brush, the pointed thorns scratching his skin. Ellie was passed out, completely unaware that her frail life was at stake and now in his hands. Bosco trailed behind them, barking from a strong case of nerves.

He could see the smoke hovering about the trees. Their voices were becoming louder and more clear. He knew this meant he was almost there. He breathed a sigh of relief. His granny would know what to do. She'd know how to save the girl.

They all at once stopped what they were doing and rushed to his side.

"What in the name of heaven?" his granny said.

His breaths were short and raspy. "She," he inhaled deeply, " was bit by a copperhead."

The rest of the group surveyed her leg, struck with horror by the sight of it. "We need to get her inside," his granny said.

He followed his granny and stepped inside one of the cabins with Ellie slung over his shoulder. There were five twin beds covered with patchwork quilts lined up in a row against one of the walls. A small table and five chairs sat on the opposite side, and a stacked stone fireplace centered the room. There was no kitchen, no bathroom, no other furniture. The cabin was bare of anything else. It was used for sleeping and eating indoors and nothing else.

The knotty pine wood floors creaked and moaned as he made

each step. He placed her down as carefully as he was able on one of the beds and looked to his granny for guidance. The old woman scrutinized Ellie's leg, assessing the damage the snake bite had done to her.

"Sam, get me some of them tobacco leaves."

He ran out of the cabin as soon as she asked. The rest of the group stood around helplessly waiting for Granny to direct them. Granny prodded Ellie's leg. It was puffy and had turned a blueish color, and it was hot. Burning hot.

"What can we do, Granny?" Sam's younger sister, Virginia, asked.

"Get me my kit," she said.

Virginia headed outside to the other cabin. She came back carrying Granny's box full of homemade remedies. She hurried over to her, holding onto the box, as Granny sifted through it.

Granny took out a glass bottle full of coneflower powder. She poured some in another glass bottle. "I need water," she told them.

The older man in the group, Caleb, hobbled over to the wooden table and grabbed a large jug of water that sat on top.

"Pour some in here." Granny pointed.

He did as he was told, pouring the water carefully. Granny shook the mixture together. It was a creamy, pasty consistency. She placed the bottle back in the box.

"We'll need that in a skinny minute," she said to Virginia.

Sam ran back inside the cabin. The tobacco leaves were draped over his arm. Granny peered at Sam's leather sheath. "Lemme have your knife," she said.

He pulled his long speared point Bowie Knife out of its sheath and gave it to her. The handle was sterling silver with a German silver cross guard etching. It was in impeccable condition—no wears and tears—maintaining its original luster.

She barely cut into the infected area, pricking it ever so slightly, just enough to perforate the skin and allow the tainted blood to be released. Blood oozed out of Ellie's leg.

She was too far gone to react to the sharp blade invading her body. She tossed a little and moaned.

Ellie could hear their voices. She could feel their presence. She couldn't keep her eyes open. Her blood pressure had dropped considerably. She was so tired and just wanted to sleep.

Granny squeezed Ellie's skin together, forcing more of her blood to come out. She hoped that the tourniquet Sam had created would keep the deadly venom from reaching the rest of her body. The puffiness deflated a little, but it was nowhere near being healed.

"Virginia." She motioned for the filled bottle.

Virginia gave her the pasty mix. Granny scooped it onto the palm of her hand and applied it to Ellie's open wound. She patted the area, smothering it with the paste. Globs and globs of it covered that part of her leg.

"Sam, help me wrap 'em leaves around her leg," Granny said.

Granny lifted Ellie's leg allowing Sam to wrap the leaves around it.

"We gotta wrap 'em tight," Granny said.

She pulled a ring of burlap out of her box, cut a few long strands with Sam's knife and wound them around Ellie's leg. The tobacco leaves and paste pressed hard against her wound.

"We'll change her wrappin' in a few hours. We need to put a cold cloth on her to keep a fever from a comin'," Granny said. "Take that cloth," she gestured to Sam, "and put it in that thar pot with some vinegar and water."

Sam grabbed one of their copper pots and mixed some vinegar with their jug of cool spring water. He carried the heavy filled pot over to his granny. She pulled out the rag and wrung it, and then placed it on Ellie's forehead.

"We'll need to keep changin' this. It needs to stay cold," she said to the group. "You'uns take turns takin' care of this girl." She looked down at Ellie with a peculiar expression. She frowned and said, "I hope she makes it. She's got some 'splaining to do when she wakes up."

***

Sam volunteered to take the first shift. He watched over her like a hawk, waiting to see if she awoke. He changed the cloth when it grew warm and rewrapped her leg and reapplied the poultice when time called for it. Ellie continued to sleep, waking every now and again for a brief moment, and then closing her eyes once more. The venom had fatigued her.

Sam took the cold cloth off of her forehead and soaked it in the copper pot. He wrung it, and placed it back on her forehead, moving a strand of hair away from her cheek.

"Who do you think she is?" Virginia said to Sam. He hadn't heard her come in and quickly removed his fingers from Ellie's rosy cheek.

He scratched at his mop of brown hair and squinted his eyes. "Don't right know. She's the same girl I saw yesterday that left that strange device."

"Think she can tell us anything?"

Sam shrugged his shoulders. "Don't right know that either, Virginia." He looked down at Bosco who was sleeping on the side of the bed. "Her dog sure loves her. I couldn't get him to stay outside."

Virginia squatted down and patted Bosco gently on the head. Bosco opened his eyes for one second and then closed them again. She stood back up and moved closer to Sam.

"He's sweet isn't he?" she said. "I sure wish we had a dog."

"You know we can't have a dog. It'd only call attention..." his voice trailed off.

She sighed. "I know," she said and paused for a moment. "I miss home."

"Me too."

"When do you think it'll be over?"

He shrugged his shoulders again. "Maybe she can tell us some news," he said, gesturing to Ellie.

"It's been so long, Sam."

"Don't fret, Virginia. We'll hear something soon," he said.

"I hope so."

***

Their whispering voices jarred Ellie from her deep slumber, but she continued to keep her brown eyes shut and lay there eavesdropping on their conversation.

"She's dressed right strange," Granny said.

"Think someone stole the rest of her clothes?" Virginia asked.

"Could be," Granny answered. "She ain't wearin' nothin'."

Virginia scrunched her face. "She's in her bloomers."

"We'll put a shirt on her. It ain't proper for them to see her like this," Granny said, motioning to the men in the group.

"It all don't seem right. She showed up, and you found that strange device," Caleb said to Sam. "You ever figure out what it is?"

He shook his head. "Not yet. Me and Moses have been tinkering with it. Never seen anything like it."

Moses nodded his head in agreement.

"I don't trust her," Caleb said. He folded his arms against his chest and looked down at Ellie incredulously. Even though her eyes were closed, she could feel the coldness of his stare.

"Look at her." Sam gestured to Ellie. "She's thin as a stick, and she don't even have a weapon on her. I doubt she's a threat," he said.

Ellie grew uneasy. She couldn't understand why they would call her IPOD a "device" like it was some new form of technology or refer to her outfit as "strange." They were the ones who dressed weird, with their *Little House on the Prairie* clothing. And call *her* a threat? *She* was the one who was chased with a rifle. Well, she didn't trust them either; but she was in no position to do anything.

Her body ached all over. It was as if she had been stretched from head to toe beyond elasticity. Each breath she took felt constricted, like a ton of weights had been stacked on top of her chest and were slowly being pressed down on her one weight at a time. And her leg felt like it had been engulfed in flames. She was so weak, and it was hard to stay awake and listen to them. She began to drift back to sleep again.

"That don't mean nothing. She could be one of *them*," Caleb argued.

CHAPTER 7

Sam sat in a chair close to Ellie as she lay asleep. He hummed quietly trying not to wake her. Bosco rested at his feet entranced by Sam's voice. The afternoon sun cast a beam of light into the otherwise dark room. He peered over at her, checking to make sure she was all right, and went back to looking at the nothingness in front of him, continuing to hum.

The sound of his voice beckoned and woke her. The yellow glow in the room and the sound of his ethereal tone made her think she was dreaming. She mumbled something, breaking Sam from his deep thoughts. He jumped off of the chair and leaned over her.

"What'd you say?" he asked.

She opened her eyes further; her vision was skewed. Her eyelids felt heavy, and wanted to close shut again, but she forced them open. She could see the shape of him standing over her. She looked down at her chest and saw she was wearing a brown long-sleeved button-down shirt. It smelled like campfire. She took a whiff and flickered a grin from the reminder of pleasant memories.

"I'm thirsty." Her throat was dry, and she had croaked like a frog when she said it.

"I'll get you some water," he said, walking to the table. He grabbed the water-filled jug and carried it over to Ellie. She struggled to lift her head—even that was a strain.

"May I?" he asked, gesturing to Ellie.

She whispered "yes," and he placed the palm of his hand behind her head, gently moving her forward. His thumb barely grazed the back of her neck.

He held the jug close to her lips, and she sipped. The cool liquid felt good as it went down her parched throat. She drank and drank and drank, until her belly was full and she couldn't any longer.

Ellie thanked him with her eyes, and he moved the jug out of her way. She laid her palms against the bed and pushed, trying to lift herself up. She fell down after one failed attempt and sighed in frustration. She felt like a weakling—a real wimp.

"Here," Sam said, placing his palm behind her head once more, moving her forward. He propped her pillow up and indicated for her to lean against it.

She got a whiff of his sweet and spicy scent—a mix of chicory and cloves.

"Better?" he asked.

"Yes." Her eyesight had returned to normal, and she was able to get a better look at him.

"Good," he said, his lips curled up into a crooked smile. The right side of his mouth went up higher than his left, and there was a tiny gap between his two front teeth.

She thought Sam's deep, husky southern drawl was like melted milk chocolate—sweet and delicious, the kind you want to savor and let linger on the tip of your tongue. He was younger than she originally thought and definitely good looking. If someone asked Ellie Morales to describe what handsome looked like, not cute or hot but distinguished looking complete with flaws that were still flattering, she'd say it was him—that it was this man that stood in front of her.

Ellie studied his face, noticing a few creases near his eyes. She wondered how old he was.

He can't be more than a few years older than me.

He was bigger than she thought—tall, but not too tall, and muscular— a full grown man, not the type of boy she would have gone to high school with or even see at college in the fall. And his eyes. Ellie wanted to swim in them. They were the most unique color—gray and blue swirled together— like an earthy slate.

"I'm Samuel Gantry," he said and bowed.

He waited for her to offer her name.

Who bows?

"Oh, sorry," Ellie finally said. "My name is Elisabeth Morales. But everyone calls me Ellie." Her voice still sounded scratchy.

"Ellie suits you." His expression was both warm and welcoming, and it made her feel at ease. "I'm called Sam." He stood at the edge of the bed. "Mind if I sit here?" he asked, motioning to the bed.

"Yeah. Go ahead," Ellie said, surprised by his manners. Most guys wouldn't have asked. Most guys didn't dress the way he did either.

She rubbed her tired eyes and yawned. "How long have I been asleep?" She figured it had been an hour or two at the most.

"Five hours," he answered.

"Five hours!" she said frantically. "I need to call my dad. He and my brother are probably going crazy. Can I please use your phone?"

Sam gave her a perplexed look and didn't answer her.

"Can I use your phone?" she repeated.

He scratched at his head and scrunched his face. "I'm not real sure what you're asking me for," he said.

Ellie folded three of her fingers against her palm, leaving her thumb and pinkie finger up in the "hang loose" gesture. She moved her hand up to her ear and tried mimicking the shape of a phone, hoping this would spark some sort of recognition. She didn't know how else to convey what a phone was. This was an entirely new concept for her. *Who didn't know what a phone was?*

"You know, to call people," she said.

"We don't have nothing like that," he said. She could tell he had no idea what she was talking about.

"You don't have a phone," Ellie said in disbelief. *It's the twenty-first century, who doesn't have a phone?*

"No," he answered. He leaned forward and tilted his head to the side, looking at her. "You sure you're feeling all right?"

"I'm fine but I've got to get home." She pushed against the bed, attempting to get up. She was far too weak and fell back down. "Ugh!" she groaned.

"You need to rest," Sam said, rushing to her side. "That copperhead nearly killed you." He held onto her arm and lifted her back up. His grip was firm yet gentle at the same time.

"I really need to talk to my dad," she pleaded. She closed her eyes and let out a deep breath "He can't deal with this right now. He's probably going crazy with worry. If he thinks something happened to me..."

Sam leaned closer. "Can I do something?" he asked.

She opened her eyes and looked at him. "No." She sighed. "Thank you," her tone softened, and she gave him an appreciative smile. He seemed nice, and she couldn't be rude to him just because he was technologically inept.

He didn't have a phone. Everyone had a phone, even senior citizens had a landline. Her grandmother even had a smart phone. She heard about religious sects where technology was forbidden. She figured he had to be a part of one of those groups.

She lay there thinking. They had her IPOD, and it had email capabilities, but she needed WiFi. And, if they didn't have a phone, they definitely didn't have wireless internet. Perhaps a neighbor did?

"Do you have a neighbor who has a phone?" She didn't even bother to ask about the internet.

"No. We are the only ones out here," he said. "I don't right know what you mean by a phone."

"It doesn't matter," she mumbled. She decided to give up trying to describe what a phone was to him. If they were Amish, they wouldn't have a phone, the internet, or electricity for that matter.

"How'd you find us?"

"My dog, Bosco, heard you singing."

"Oh," Sam said, his face became ruddy. "I sing a lot."

"It sounded pretty," she blurted, and her cheeks turned scarlet. She hoped that he would think that it was from the snake bite and not from him.

"Thank you," he said and paused for a moment. "Do you live near here?"

"Kinda. Well...not really. I was running, and Bosco took us off the trail," she started.

"What were you running from?" he interrupted, his voice edgy.

She laughed, thinking he was joking. But his serious expression told her otherwise. "I jog everyday for exercise," she explained.

"Exercise? Exercise what?"

"You know, working out. I have to stay in shape so I don't get fat or die from a heart attack at the age of forty. You work out, don't you?"

"Work out?" he repeated with a puzzled expression. "You mean do we have chores?"

"No." She sighed. "Like do you lift weights or jog?" She noticed his broad shoulders and the accentuation of his muscles from the tight fit of his shirt sleeves.

His fingers rubbed against the sparse brown hair on his face, and he stared at her peculiarly. "Where are you from?"

"Florida."

His eyes grew wide. "Florida," he said. "You're from Florida?"

"Um. Yeah." She didn't understand why he said "Florida" like it was the far end of the Earth. Like he was saying she was from Mars.

"I didn't think anyone lived down *there*," he said.

Ellie replied defensively, "Oh, just about a billion people."

"There ain't that many people living down *there*."

Again, he referred to Florida like it was the middle of nowhere. "According to the US Census there are."

He ignored her last snippy comment and asked, "How did you get here?" He crossed his legs and placed his hand under his chin, mimicking Rodin's "The Thinker."

"We drove," Ellie said.

"You drove a herd of cattle?"

"No," Ellie answered slowly as if she were speaking to a child. "We drove in our car."

"Car?"

"It's an SUV if you want to be literal about it," she said.

"What's an 'SUV'?"

"It's a sport utility vehicle," she answered and then stared at him skeptically. "Are you Amish or something?"

"We're Methodist. But what does my religion have to do with anything?" He squinted his gray eyes.

"'Cause you're all *Little House on the Prairie* around here," she said and read his expression. It was like she was speaking a foreign language. "I know about the Amish way of life. My mom was from Pennsylvania Dutch country," she explained.

"You're momma is from the north?"

"She was," her voice lingered. Speaking about her mom in past tense was too painful for her.

"Why are you in North Carolina?"

"You ask a lot of questions, don't you?" she said with a tinge of exasperation. She was tired, and playing twenty questions the moment she woke up wasn't what she had in mind.

"Just trying to figure you out. You came from nowhere, and we're all curious about you." His gaze met hers.

"We're here on vacation," she answered, purposely leaving out the details of what they were vacationing from. So far their little excursion had been a disaster. No one was healing—their wounds were still open—and now things were taking a turn for the worse. Ellie worried her that father was going nuts thinking that she was dead somewhere in the forest.

"Vacation?"

"Do the Amish not vacation?" she asked. "I mean, does your sect of the Methodist church not take a vacation every now and again?" she corrected. "You know, take time off from work?"

"That's something rich folk do," he said to her. "'Sides, it's not the safest time to be gallivanting around this part of the country."

"That's being a bit paranoid isn't? We're not at Def Con 1 status," Ellie said.

He stared at her in the oddest way. "You Floridians sure do talk strange."

"I could say the same of you," she mumbled, but he heard her anyway.

"You're down right sassy, ain't you?" he said and laughed; his gray eyes danced as he said it. He was amused by her, which irritated her.

He got up off of the bed and stared down at her. "I'll be right back. I'm getting the others." He left the room before Ellie had time to reply with a snide comment.

CHAPTER 8

She pushed down on the mattress; it didn't feel like the one she had at home which was firm with a little bit of cushion. She sunk down further, to the point that she could feel the wooden planks spaced apart every half a foot. She ran her fingers across it and took a whiff, smelling the pine straw and other earthy elements.

No pictures were hung, just one log after another filled the walls. The room was bare and lacked any sort of decoration. Ellie looked down at the hard wood floor, noticing there wasn't even a rug.

"Bosco," she called.

He placed his two front paws on the bed, his tongue hanging out. She patted him with slow, light taps. Never had she felt so constricted. Her muscles were aching. It was like being run over and over again by a bulldozer, and the heat coming from her leg was intense.

"You're a good boy," she said in a low voice. Bosco sat back down on the floor next to her.

Sam entered the room; four people trailed behind him. They stood at the edge of her bed and looked at her. She felt like an animal on display at the zoo.

"Ellie, this is my granny." He pointed. The waistband of Granny's long skirt fell below her large, sagging breasts. Her white-as-snow hair was bound in a tight, long winding braid and fell to her broad hips. She nodded quickly with a blank expression. Not the evil eye, frown, or smile. Nothing. Ellie couldn't read her.

"And my sister, Virginia." He gestured. Virginia gave a warmer reception than her granny. She smiled, attempting to make Ellie feel at ease and welcome. Ellie was immediately drawn to her and thought if circumstances were different they'd probably become friends.

Ellie noticed that Virginia had the same gray eyes as Sam but not his chocolate brown hair. Hers was a golden blonde, and her complexion was milky white, not tinted a caramel bronze like his. She was striking and had a perfect figure, a true natural beauty—the type of girl all the guys at Ellie's school would have hovered around vying for a minute of her attention. She went over to Bosco and petted him. He nuzzled closely to her, begging for more.

"He likes you," Ellie said to her, feeling a little jealous that she had been so quickly tossed to the side.

"I like him," Virginia replied, continuing to stroke the top of Bosco's furry head. "He's right cute, ain't he?" She giggled.

"This is my uncle Caleb." Caleb formed a scathing scowl at Ellie. A wooden crutch was pressed into his right underarm. He wobbled a little and then steadied himself, trying to balance on one foot. Most of his right leg was missing, and his pant leg was tied into a knot just below his right knee. He resembled Sam with the same angular jaw and gray eyes. His hair and beard were a salt and pepper mix. More salt than pepper.

"And this is Moses," Sam said. Moses stood taller than the rest of the group. Much taller. And he didn't look like the rest of them with his dark cocoa skin and black–as –night hair sticking up on his head.

Ellie noticed a plethora of scars crisscrossing his dark arms. He grew self-conscious as she stared at them, and he rolled down his sleeves. She quickly averted her eyes and looked back at Sam, hoping that she wasn't being rude. Her mother had always told her not to stare at people.

"Moses can't speak," Sam told her.

She glanced back at Moses. He peered down at the ground and avoided making any eye contact with her. He seemed embarrassed about it, which made Ellie feel bad for him.

Granny approached Ellie. "Mind if I look at your here leg?" It wasn't a question. She had already begun poking and prodding at Ellie before she could answer her.

To save face, Ellie answered a firm "No," which fell on Granny's deaf ears. Answer or no answer, Granny was going to do what she wanted to.

"Lemme have your knife," Granny told Sam.

Ellie gave a frightened look, wondering what she was intending to do with his knife.

He handed it to her. Granny cut the burlap and gave him back his knife. She began unwrapping the tobacco leaves. A white pasty consistency covered Ellie's ankle and calf. Granny stuck her finger in the poultice and pushed it to the side, trying to see the exact spot where the snake had struck. The area was no longer blue in color, but red and still a little puffy. Most of the swelling had gone down. The snake had left its mark: two tiny holes were permanently carved into her leg.

"Gettin' better," Granny said and looked up at Ellie. "You're lucky Sam found you when he did. If he hadn't, you'd be on death's door." There was no mincing words with Granny. "Sam says you're from Florida."

"Yes," Ellie answered.

"But you're all the way up here in the holler?" she probed.

Great. More interrogation. "That's right," she said, not quite sure what a holler was. She assumed Granny meant the mountains. North Carolina wasn't that far from Florida. She didn't understand why they were making it into a big deal.

"Don't seem right for a girl to be wanderin' around the forest by herself," Granny said and smacked her lips.

"You and my dad would get along well," Ellie said with a hint of sarcasm. "Speaking of which, I really need to get home or he's going to call out the troops to look for me."

"Is he in the Army?" Granny asked, and then looked at Sam and Caleb with concern.

"No," Ellie said. *What's up with everyone being so literal?*

"But you said..." Granny started.

"It was a figure of speech. My dad tends to overreact and worry too much," Ellie explained. *Especially since my mom died*, she wanted to add.

Granny rubbed her chin and squinted her small, pale blue eyes. The skin sagged, resembling the neck of a turkey. "Sam said you talked real queer."

Nothing but irony crossed her mind, but instead of responding with a sarcastic comment, Ellie said, "I really appreciate you guys taking care of me, but I really should be getting home."

She shifted her body and sat with her legs dangling over the bed. Her leg throbbed and moving so abruptly made her a little dizzy. White spots floated in front of her eyes. Bosco got up and stood next to her feet. His warm fur brushed against her clammy skin.

"We still don't know much about you. Don't right know if we should let you leave," Caleb said, staring her down.

Ellie's heart raced. "You can't make me stay here. That's kidnapping," she quickly retorted, trying to keep her voice firm and not quaking like her heart was. She was going to crumble.

"She's right, Uncle Caleb," Sam chimed in. His eyes met Ellie's.

"We can't make her stay here."

"Fine. Don't listen to me." He threw his hands up in the air. "When we're all caught 'cause of this jasper" he pointed aggressively in Ellie's direction and glared at her, "and sittin' in a prison or worse, don't blame me."

Ellie held up her hands in a surrender position. "Look if you guys are hiding from the police, I won't say anything. You saved my life, and I'm really thankful for that. The last thing I'm gonna do is turn you all in," Ellie said. "Promise," she added.

"'Course she'll say that. We can't trust her," Caleb said.

"Calm your horses, son," Granny said and stared intently into Ellie's eyes. "Something tells me you're bein' truthful."

"I am," Ellie said.

Caleb sighed heavily.

"You got a breathin' problem, son?" Granny said.

"No ma'am," Caleb answered. Even if he was a grown man, he was intimidated by his mother. Most people were, including Ellie. Granny was one not to be reckoned with.

"You need to give us your word you won't tell anyone you saw us," Granny said to Ellie.

"I won't tell a soul," Ellie said, and internally kicked herself for saying "I won't tell a soul." It sounded so cliché. "I won't tell," she said. Whomever they were running from wasn't her business nor her problem. She wanted to leave and get home to Jonah and her dad. And whatever they did that made them run away from the police, she didn't want to linger there any longer to find out.

"Sam, take her to where you found her." She looked at Ellie and asked, "Can you make it home the rest of the way by yourself? We can't risk Sam being out too long."

"Yes," Ellie answered quickly.

"Sam," Granny said, looking in his direction. "Take the rifle with you."

Ellie's heart skipped a beat. *Why did they need to take a weapon with them?* She didn't want to ask, and she figured they weren't going to tell her anyway. The room was filled with evasiveness.

"I don't need it. I have my knife." He tapped the handle of his Bowie knife.

"You certain?" Granny asked.

"It's no different than when I go and find fire wood," he said. "I'll be safe."

"Be sure your daddy puts a poultice on that thar leg," Granny said to Ellie. She scanned her leg one more time. "It's still swelled."

Ellie didn't even bother to mention that her father was a doctor, and he'd probably load her up with antibiotics the moment she was home. For once, Ellie was being prudent about her choice of words. "I will. Thank you," she said.

Sam came over to Ellie and took a hold of her hand, helping her up off of the bed. She noticed his veins protruding below the surface of his skin. His muscles were tight and firm. The hairs on his arms were golden blonde.

"Ready?" he asked.

She glanced down at both of their hands. They were still touching, and Ellie swore she felt the tiniest spark. He noticed their hands and let go.

"Yes," she said and walked precariously, slowly and with more caution than she normally did. She looked at them all and said, "Thank you. I mean it. Thank you."

Granny nodded once in recognition to Ellie's appreciation.

Caleb continued to glare at her as if she were a criminal, grunting under his breath, and Virginia patted Bosco on the head once more, giving Ellie a hug before she left. Moses handed Ellie her IPOD.

"Thank you," she said to him. He blinked his eyes and curled his lips upward into a slight smile. Ellie and Bosco followed Sam out of the cabin and into the forest.

CHAPTER 9

Sam walked side-by-side with Ellie, moving with her at a leisurely pace. It frustrated her to no end. She hated being the one who was slowing the group down—moving about like a turtle. She was always in the lead—at least when it came to running. Her leg hurt, and the pressure was mounting on her foot with each and every step she made.

"Do you need to rest?" Sam asked, mindful of Ellie's slight limp. She shook her head. "No. I'm good." She smiled, thankful for his concern. They walked in silence for a while, listening to the trees blowing from the wind, to their feet stomping against the leaves— crunching after each step— and to the birds making their calls high up in the trees. The air was thin and less humid than it was when Ellie had begun her run. It was a clear, sunny day, with few clouds hovering up in the bright blue sky.

Sam broke the silence. "What is that?" He gestured to the IPOD strapped to Ellie's arm. The headphones were draped around her neck.

"It's an IPOD," she said and saw his fuzzy expression. Of course he wouldn't know what that was either. "It plays music," she explained.

"That's not possible."

Ellie abruptly stopped and Sam followed suit. "Sure it is."

"How?"

"Well... I'm not very technological so I can't get into the logistics. It just does," she said. "Here." She handed him the ear phones. "Put these on." She pointed to the inside of her ears.

He did as she instructed. She turned the IPOD on and scrolled through her library trying to find the perfect artist to play. If this was going to be the first time he'd ever hear music from an IPOD, she wanted to make sure it was epic.

Ellie felt about music the way she did about running. She swore if she had lived in the 1980s, her shelves would have been stacked with record albums. As it was, her IPOD was almost at capacity and encompassed an impressive library with more than ten thousand songs.

Music was one of the few things she and her mom had in common. Her mother was crazy about music. She could hear the beginning of a tune and tell you the name of the song, the band that sang it, and the year it was released. If ever there were a music trivia champion, she would be its queen. Her record collection filled the spare room at their house in Florida, and Ellie often put a vinyl record on the record player, sat down on the floor, and listened to the music playing for hours. Her taste was as eclectic as her mother's: country; old school rap; alternative; reggae; Motown; blue grass; the list went on. She hated bubble gum pop, and boycotted all music in this genre, stating it was trivial crap with stupid lyrics that meant nothing. Ellie's music library ran the gamut.

Her mom loved to create her own playlists, and made special CDs for lengthy car trips. Ellie relished the surprise, noting that her mother was quite astute at finding the perfect song to play for each pivotal moment during their trips. Cross the state line of Georgia and Charlie Daniels', *The Devil Went Down to Georgia* played. Drive on the winding Blue Ridge Parkway and the Fleet Foxes' *Blue Ridge Mountains* blared on the CD player. It was serendipity at its best. She timed each song perfectly.

During the summer of her freshman year, Ellie went to camp in north Florida. A nine hour drive from Coral Gables, her mom knew she'd need eight special CD mixes designed especially for their trek to the panhandle—everything from Fleetwood Mac, Coldplay, and Marvin Gaye a part of the variety. They sang along to every song, citing the lyrics verbatim. It was just the two of them on the road with their music. When Journey's *Don't Stop Believing* played, the volume was turned up at its loudest and they sang their hearts out until the song ended. Her mom hit the replay button at least three more times, and they continued to sing along until their voices became hoarse.

Ellie associated music with memories or vice versa. If she heard a song, it'd relate to a life event. Sometimes pleasant. Sometimes sad. She swore she'd never listen to The Cure again. That was her mom's favorite band, and every single song painfully reminded Ellie of her. It was unbearable for her to hear Robert Smith's voice without picturing her. But Journey she could handle. It was a good memory, too happy to store away or forget about. Ellie made a point to listen to *Don't Stop Believing* every single day at the beginning of her run. It was her ritual, her way of saying good morning to her mother. Their time together on that road trip was lucid and fresh when the song played, and it made her mother alive again.

Ellie clicked the play button, and the music started. Sam heard the piano keys introducing the song, and Steve Perry's unique voice passionately sang about love and never giving up. The volume was set high, and it startled him. He jumped in response to the myriad of sounds flowing all at once. She turned the volume down and gave him a reassuring look.

"Listen," she said. She wanted to pat him on the arm for encouragement but decided that would be way too forward. The whole experience was surreal for her. Never in her life would she have thought she'd be teaching a grown man about the ins and outs of an IPOD.

He smiled and tapped his foot on rhythm to the beat of the music, getting completely lost in it. His gray eyes brightened, and his grin grew wide.

"You like them?" Ellie said, noticing his reaction.

He nodded and continued to move to the music. He listened to the song in its entirety, and hummed along with the band, capturing a few of the song's lyrics and singing with the chorus. Once it was over, he handed her back the headphones.

"That was amazing," he said.

"It's one of my favorite songs," she said, feeling like she had just exposed a part of herself to him. He had no idea how much that song impacted her, how much it meant to her. "I listen to it every day."

"But how can you hear them on there?" He pointed to the IPOD. "They're not here with us." She could tell he was struggling to understand, to take it all in.

"I don't know what to tell you. You just can," she answered vaguely, feeling like those people who give the answer "he just does," when asked "how do you know God exists?"

"That doesn't explain how I could hear them through that device." He pointed to the IPOD again, his face contorted from confusion.

"Like I told you, I'm not a tech guru."

"You sure do say the strangest things." He gave her that familiar look of amusement again. This time Ellie wasn't irritated.

He studied her, making Ellie aware of how bad she must have looked to him. Her hair was a matted mess, complete with tangles and in need of a good shampoo and brushing, and she hadn't taken a shower. She was covered in dirt and grime, and she was certain she stank with all of Granny's homemade remedies seeping into her skin. Her leg was the size of a bowling pin, and she had cuts all over her. A literal mess. That's what she was. The more she thought about her shoddy appearance, the more self-conscious she became. She couldn't understand why she even cared what he thought about her. For all she knew he was on the run from the cops, or crazy, or from a strict religious order that would forbid their relationship anyway.

"Right back at ya," she teased and lightly punched him on the arm. She quickly retracted it, feeling embarrassed by her overt flirty and too familiar behavior.

She started walking and muttered, "Awkward, Ellie," forgetting to keep her thoughts to herself.

"What was that?" he asked, catching up to her.

She glanced in his direction, feeling a little flustered. "Nothing." Ellie wondered if Sam noticed everything. He seemed to when it came to her anyway.

"I can't quite figure you out," he said, staring at her in wonder. "None of us can."

"There isn't much to know. I'm an open book, and really, I'm not that thrilling." She wished she was exciting, like one of those people with fascinating stories to tell about going on adventures overseas and engaging in other shenanigans. But so far, her life had been pretty dull. The loss of her mother shook it up, but not in the way Ellie had imagined or wanted. She still sought adventure and yearned to stray from the monotony of her humdrum life—to really get out there and live.

"You are to us. Matter of fact, you've caused quite the

commotion within our family, especially with Uncle Caleb." He laughed and then asked, "When did they invent that device?"

She crinkled her forehead and bit on her lip. "I'm not sure. I know it's been at least ten years."

"Ten years?" he said in disbelief. "And this is something only readily obtainable in Florida?"

"No," she said, thinking he used the strangest vocabulary words. "I'd be willing to bet you could buy this in the far corners of the Earth so long as you had wifi."

"Wifi?" he repeated.

Ellie saw she was confusing him even more. "Wireless Internet," she explained.

"I don't..." he started.

She flicked her hand up, stopping him. "It's fine. Let's forget I mentioned any of it, okay?" She paused for a moment and took a deep breath. "I need to rest for a minute." The walk was wearing her out.

"Take all the time you need," he said and meandered over to a tall pine tree, leaning against it.

Ellie carefully sat down on the ground with her legs against her chest, her arms folded over them. She touched her sore leg, feeling the puffy, tough, leathery skin. Normally it was soft and smooth, but the snake had affected its texture. It felt hard but sensitive to the lightest touch. She inhaled, taking a whiff of her shirt sleeve. The campfire scent reminded her of better times. She could feel Sam staring at her and looked up in his direction.

"Is this your shirt?" she asked.

"Yes." His voice was low, and every now and again, he would look around, checking his surroundings, like he was afraid they were being watched.

She started unbuttoning it. "I'll give it back."

"No. You keep it."

"But it's yours."

"I have others. I don't wear it much anyhow."

The right side of his mouth moved upward. Ellie liked his crooked smile for its imperfection and authenticity. He leaned down and grabbed a long stick of wood. He took out his knife from his leather sheath and began whittling away at it, peeling off a layer of bark. She could tell it was something he had done before, the way his hands moved and the lack of concentration he seemed to need while doing it.

He started to hum quietly, and then the hum turned into a soft melody. His tone was impeccable—a perfect pitch. It was a melancholy tune—sung with an underlying sadness. Ellie wondered if it was because Sam was so talented or because deep down he evoked the same despair the song's lyrics spoke of.

Bosco closed his eyes, in a daze from hearing Sam's silky voice. Ellie swore she had never heard anything more beautiful yet more compellingly sad. His voice was like a drug to her—she wanted to swallow it whole. She knew she'd probably never see him or hear him ever again, and that made her feel a tinge of sadness. She didn't know what it was about him that pulled at her so. She didn't know him, and for all she knew he was in serious trouble— trouble that she didn't need to involve herself with. But his eyes said something else, and for that, Ellie found it hard to let go.

With a lot of effort, Ellie tried hoisting herself up off of the ground. Sam stopped singing and offered to help her, but Ellie insisted on doing it herself. "I've got it," she said, but Sam ignored her and assisted her anyway.

"Thanks," she said, catching a slight smug expression on his face. "I had it," she added.

"I know, but I'd be remiss if I didn't offer you my assistance."

"Let's go," she responded, ignoring his formal boarding school vocabulary. Her English teacher would be impressed with his SAT words even if he did speak with poor grammar.

"All right," he simply said, and they trekked ahead.

Neither of them spoke the rest of their journey together. Both of their minds were swimming with thoughts—Ellie wanted to get home, to see her dad and Jonah. She peered over at Sam and could tell he was perplexed by it all.

Ellie could see the emerald lake in the distance. This meant that their time together was coming to an end. They trudged on, moving toward the sandy shore and finally coming to the entrance of the cave. They both stopped and looked at each other. "Guess you have to turn back now," she said.

"Yes. I 'spose so," he answered. "Are you certain you'll be fine on your own?" His concern for her was sincere and heartfelt. Ellie knew there was no way he could be some bad guy on the run.

"I'll be fine," she said.

"Well, it has been a pleasure Miss Ellie," he said; his strong southern drawl seemed especially prevalent at that moment.

"Thanks," she said. "For saving my life."

"You would have done the same for me."

"Please tell your family how much I appreciate their help."

"They know, but I'll tell them for you."

She wanted to hug him goodbye but second guessed herself. Instead, she held out her hand intending to shake his. Sam wound his fingers around her petite hand and bent over—his lips gently touching it—and applied the lightest kiss. Even though she thought it was odd for him to kiss her on the hand like they were in some Victorian movie, she was flattered by it and felt a warm tingling sensation, and she wasn't one to be easily swayed.

"Please be careful."

"I will. Bye, Sam," she said and headed into the cave with Bosco trailing behind her. Goodbyes were not her thing; they were too permanent.

She walked for another hour, stopping to rest a few times. The first thing she was going to do when she was home was take a long, hot shower and then lay down on her bed for days and days. If her father had anything to say about it, she'd probably have to go to the hospital instead. His overzealous concern for her well-being would sky rocket once he saw the shape her leg was in and learned what had happened to her.

She finally found her way home. As she exited the trail and slowly moved up her steep driveway, she saw blue flashing lights blinking in constant motion. Two men in uniform stood next to a police car. One spoke with her father while the other wrote things down on a note pad.

She saw Jonah standing next to her dad. He saw Ellie first and nudged him hard on his arm.

"Dad," he said. "It's Ellie!"

He quit speaking to the police officers and looked in the direction that Jonah pointed. He and Jonah ran toward Ellie, almost toppling her over. Their arms circled around her, holding her in a tight embrace.

Her dad kissed the top of her head and placed his palms on her cheeks. "Look at you," he murmured. He grabbed her again and pressed her tight against him. Ellie didn't fight his affection. She needed it. His forehead was wrinkled with worry. "Do you know how worried we've been? When you didn't come home yesterday, I thought the worst."

"Yesterday?" she said. "How long have I been gone?"

"Over a day and a half."

CHAPTER 10

"A day and a half? Are you sure?" Ellie asked.

When she had woken up, Sam told her that she'd been out for five hours, and by her estimation, the most she could have been gone was seven to eight hours. Not a day. And definitely not a day and a half.

"What happened to you?" her dad asked; searching Ellie's face, he grimaced seeing the cuts she had all over her. "Where have you been?"

"Bosco and I were taking a break from the run and I was bitten by a copperhead," Ellie lied and pointed down to her slightly swollen calf. "It snuck up on me."

He bent down to inspect it. He touched her leg carefully, examining it, and then stood up. "You definitely need some antibiotics to be on the safe side, but otherwise it doesn't look too bad." He realized he was in doctor mode and added in a fatherly tone, "You're a mess." He touched her face again, his brown eyes on the verge of tears.

"Guess we can close this case," one of the police officer's said, interrupting them. "Miss, we're happy you made it home okay," the police officer said to Ellie. "Sir, I'm sure you want to spend time with your daughter now that she is home." He tipped his hat and sauntered back to the police car, his partner in tow.

"Thank you," her dad said to them and turned back, looking at Ellie. Ellie swore he had aged five years overnight. "If anything had happened to you," his voice trailed off. "What exactly happened?"

"I told you, I was resting from my run and got bitten by a snake. I passed out for a while. I'm not sure for how long." She scratched at her head in contemplation. "When I woke up, I couldn't move too well. So I laid down for a while and tried keeping my leg elevated. When the swelling went down and the pain wasn't as bad, I made my way back home." She hoped that since she was mostly telling the truth, he wouldn't be on to her and ask more specific questions.

"You were in the woods all night by yourself?" he said with worry. "How long were you passed out?"

"A while. It was dark when I woke up," she lied. "Besides, I wasn't by myself, Bosco was with me."

"Thank God nothing else happened to you. Copperheads can be deadly, Ellie. You're lucky it didn't kill you." He looked down at her leg again and analyzed it. "Your leg looks good if it was a copperhead." He looked back up at her. "Are you certain it was a copperhead that bit you?"

"I'm guess I'm not one hundred percent sure," she answered. Ellie knew it was a copperhead that bit her, but this was her chance to get him to stop asking so many questions. If she told him the truth, he'd question why her leg did look good, and she didn't want to tell him about Sam or his family. She only ever told her father the truth, and lying to him was the last thing she ever wanted to do. But telling him the truth would betray the people who had kept her alive. And she just couldn't do that. The law would dictate that she turn them in for whatever it was they did. But sometimes things just weren't black and white; sometimes things were gray. You just had to go with your gut, and Ellie's gut told her that these people needed to stay protected, that maybe they weren't the bad guys. She could feel her heart pounding, and she wondered if she was giving anything away. She couldn't keep a straight face to save her life. Fibbing wasn't something she was good at doing.

He shook his head in disbelief. "Those damn woods. I've never liked you running on that trail. No more, Ellie. You hear me. No more!" He was emphatic.

"Dad," Ellie said. "I'm fine. Look." She pointed to her leg again. "It's not that swollen and it looks a lot better than it did a while ago," she said, being evasive about time. She wanted to say a few hours ago but now distrusted her sense of time as a whole.

A day and a half?

"I could easily be attacked by an alligator or some crazy lunatic at home in Florida," she said.

"The odds of that happening are highly unlikely," Jonah said.

She rolled her eyes at him, and he smiled. He was baiting her. It was his screwed up way of telling her that he missed her.

"I should have never let you run on that trail to begin with," her dad said, shaking his head.

"This," she pointed to her leg, "could have happened anywhere. Snakes are everywhere in North Carolina. I bet we have a dozen around this place," she argued.

"Why are you so stubborn?" It was a rhetorical statement.

"Because you are," she answered.

He sighed and smiled at his daughter. She was his mirror image. He wrapped his arm around her. "I'm just glad you're home."

"Me too."

***

Ellie tore off her clothes as soon as she entered her bedroom and threw them on the floor. She let the water run for a while, allowing steam to invade the room. It was scalding hot—just the way Ellie liked it. She entered the shower and stood under the shower head for what seemed like forever.

She finished bathing and rummaged through her things, searching for her flannel pajamas. She put them on, combed her wet hair and found her way to bed.

"Ellie," her dad called, tapping on the door.

"Come in," she said and sat up in bed.

Her dad entered, with Bosco behind him. Bosco charged past him and leapt onto her bed. He smelled like a bouquet of roses.

Ellie felt his clean, shiny coat and put her nose up to his brown fur, taking a whiff. "You bathed him?"

"He was filthy," he said, standing near her bed.

"I think I was dirtier than him."

"Yes. I believe you were. I don't even want to see the shape your bathroom is in." He looked in the direction of the bathroom and then back at her. A trail of mud led from the bedroom door to the bathroom.

"Don't worry, I'll clean it tomorrow."

"Promises. Promises," he teased.

"I will," she said defensively.

Jonah entered the room, carrying a plate of flan. "Are you hungry?" he asked.

She was famished. She hadn't eaten in hours.

Hours. Evidently it's been a day and a half.

She nodded enthusiastically. "Bring it over here, Shrimp."

He handed her the plate, and she consumed it within a matter of seconds.

"Oink. Oink," Jonah kidded.

"Is there more?" she asked, searching his empty hands.

"Yeah, Miss Piggy. Let me go get the pan. You can just eat from that with your hands," he said.

"Okay," she said. It sounded like a reasonable idea to her. It was done in Medieval Times; why couldn't she do it right there and then?

"I was joking, but if you insist," Jonah said and left the room.

"He was really worried about you," her dad told her reassuringly.

"I know," Ellie said and smiled.

He sat down on the edge of her bed and looked at her, his eyes showing concern. He ran his fingers through her wet, conditioned hair, touching her dotingly. "We thought the worst, Ellie. You don't know how relieved I was when I saw you."

She had a lump in her throat and tried hard to fight back the tears. "I know," she whispered.

He gave her a tired smile. "I'm just so glad you made it home. Please stay off that trail," he said it with desperation, and Ellie felt guilty. She'd try. For him she'd try, but she couldn't imagine a day without running. It was a part of her, and deep down she wanted to see Sam again.

Jonah came back into the room carrying the pan of flan. He handed the pan and a fork over to Ellie. She sat the pan down on her lap and began eating heaping serving after heaping serving. She was devouring it like there was no tomorrow. Never had she felt so hungry.

"You need to eat a real meal," her dad said. "Not just dessert."

"I'll," she said, food in her mouth, "start with dessert and work my way backwards to the main course."

"Let me get you something to drink and a sandwich." He got up and stood at the doorway. "I love you," he added, taking one more look at her.

"Love you too," she said, her mouth full of food.

Jonah pulled up a chair and set his feet on Ellie's bed. "How long were you passed out?" he asked.

"Don't know," she said, licking her lips, savoring the deliciousness from the flan she had just stuffed her face with.

"Must have been for a while," he said. "I didn't think a snake bite could knock you out that long."

"I guess it did," she said, trying to sound indifferent.

"You're hiding something." He tilted his head to the side and gazed at her suspiciously.

"No, I'm not." She stiffened.

"Whatever." He shrugged. "You know Dad's never gonna let you run that trail ever again."

She shook her head. "He'll budge after a few days. I could've been bitten anywhere. Look in our back yard, Shrimp. There's probably a gazillion snakes."

"He hasn't slept since you've been gone."

"I figured. Have you?" She saw the beginnings of dark circles under his hazel eyes.

"Yeah. Sure." His eyes shifted down and to the left.

"You haven't." She punched him lightly on the arm. "You missed me."

"I missed Bosco. Not you," he said, trying to keep his face straight and even, without a sign of emotion.

"Say that again, and look at me," she commanded, tickling the ball of his foot.

"No." He jerked and kicked it away from her.

"You can't," she taunted.

"Okay. Fine." He sighed. "I missed you. Are you happy?" he groaned.

She gave him a smug look and then leaned forward, her arms open for a hug. "Shrimp, I missed you more." He met her halfway, hugging her tight.

"Who's shirt were you wearing when you came home?" Jonah asked, breaking himself from their embrace and looking at Ellie.

"Oh it was something I found on the trail on the way home," she lied, looking him in the eye and consciously ensuring that she did not shift her eyes.

"It looked clean. At least compared to the rest of you."

"I think it belonged to a camper. Probably someone who accidently left it behind. You know how people forget things," she was stumbling for words. Lying was tearing her apart. It was only a matter of time until she folded.

"You're keeping something from me. You'll eventually tell me," he said with confidence, and Ellie knew he may just be right.

***

Ellie woke up, gasping for air. Her heart thumped wildly. Drenched in sweat, her hair was damp, and her pajamas were wrinkled and clung to her soggy skin. She checked the clock. It was a little after one in the morning. She tossed back on her other side, and closed her eyes trying in vain to fall asleep. There was no way she could go back to sleep after that nightmare. No way.

She couldn't remember what the dream was about, only the fear it gave her and the physical evidence of its sheer terror. The images were unclear and still fuzzy in her mind. She got out of bed and shuffled to her bedroom door. It was partially open and creaked as she pushed it further open. The darkness inhibited her sight and made it a challenge to navigate. Her fingers slid against the walls as she guided her way toward the kitchen.

The moonlight shined through the open blinds in the living room windows. She didn't notice him at first and had forgotten it had become his second bedroom. Her eyesight wasn't the best at night, and she was still a little groggy.

"Ellie," he said, startling her. She screeched. "Sorry." He chuckled.

"Papi," she breathed and moved closer to him. He was sitting on the couch, alone and in the dark. This concerned her.

He patted the couch, inviting her to sit next to him. Bosco slept on the floor. "I wondered where he was," she said, gesturing to her half asleep dog.

"He heard me open the refrigerator."

"Figures." She laughed. "You're up late."

"So are you."

"I had a bad dream." Her brows furrowed.

"It's probably a result of everything that happened to you in the last two days." He sounded worried.

She shrugged it off. "I don't know. I can't remember it—the dream I mean. It woke me up though." She ran her fingers through her hair and sat back against the couch cushion and sighed.

He leaned back in similar fashion.

"Dad, why are you up? This isn't the first time I've heard you out here this late at night." A part of her wanted him to admit it out loud, so that she could share in his pain and tell him she felt the same.

"I couldn't sleep," he answered vaguely. "Sometimes it's easier to sit and think about nothing."

Instead of tossing and turning and laying in bed thinking about everything.

"But you need your sleep," she pressed.

He stretched and yawned. "And so do you." He stood up and offered her his hand. "Get some rest. We'll talk more tomorrow."

Ellie knew he was sweeping it all under the rug, avoiding what was blatantly obvious to her, to him, and to Jonah, but she'd be a hypocrite if she forced him to discuss it. She could guard her feelings about her mom as well as he could. After all, they were just alike.

CHAPTER 11

A few days had passed and things were still gnawing at Ellie. *What was Sam's family hiding from? Why did they steer away from twenty-first century inventions? And what was the deal with his inability to tell time?* Ellie was never one to settle, to accept things as they were. And even though she tried to shove these questions to the back of her mind, they loomed to the forefront of her thoughts. She wanted answers.

Ellie hadn't run in three days. Three entire days. This was a record for her. It was a strange phenomenon to roll out of bed whenever she felt like, to traipse around the house in her pj's and to have no plans for the day, like most kids her age on summer break. She never understood the appeal of sleeping in and lounging around the house for hours like most of her friends did. Running had always taken priority. And now it was on the back burner.

Her leg was healing fast but still throbbed an intense and unbearable phantom pain every so often. Sometimes it'd burn, and she swore she could feel the snake's fangs sucking into her. The antibiotics lessened the swelling and had kept her from getting an infection, but they did not stop the pain.

The day after Ellie came home, she followed her daily ritual by getting up and out of bed at the break of dawn ready to run, but the moment her legs hit the pavement, she shrieked in agony. It wasn't what she had expected. Sure, she thought there'd be some issues, but not like that. Not that much pain.

"It'll be a while. Be patient," her dad told her. "You need to give it time to heal."

"How long?" she said, wondering if she'd have to wait more than a few days. One day was bad enough, three was miserable, and a week would be absolutely brutal.

"I don't know, maybe three to four days. Give your body some rest, Ellie." His fingers touched the tip of her chin and he smiled.

She pouted and replied, "I'll lose my stamina. You know if I don't run for a few days, I'll lose my time." Her time. She was obsessed with it. If she was going to run on the cross country team for the University of Miami, the last thing she needed was to start off with crappy time.

"You'll get it back. Get. Some. Rest," he ordered.

"Fine," she grumbled and stomped toward her room.

Ellie wasn't the complacent type, and not running was out of the question. Pain or no pain, she was going to do it no matter how much her father protested. She had to at least jog. She couldn't stand sitting around the house doing nothing. It made her feel like she was withering away. Running was her everything.

Tomorrow, I've got a date with my IPOD and my Nikes.

***

Back into her old routine, she woke up as soon as the the sun shined into her room. She shot out of bed, exhilarated by the idea of running again. She could do this. She would do this.

She threw on a pair of baggy running shorts and pulled a sports bra and t-shirt over her head. The room felt chilly, and she wanted to make sure she was dressed just right for the elements. She put on a headband, pulling the long bangs out of her face, and then grabbed the bulk of her remaining hair and pulled it up into a pony tail, grumbling in irritation the entire time. Enough was enough. She was going to cut it off later that night.

Exiting her room, she tiptoed her way to the kitchen. Her father was fast asleep on the couch—snoring loudly. Every now and again, he'd stop, and the room would be absolutely quiet, but then he'd start up again, snoring louder than before.

Ellie opened the refrigerator and grabbed an ice cold bottle of water. She closed the door and spun around, seeing the cookies she had baked with Jonah the night before. They were on a plate and wrapped securely in Saran Wrap. She peeled back the Saran Wrap and grabbed a handful, placing them in a plastic sealed bag.

She tore a sheet of paper off of a nearby notepad and jotted down a quick, nondescript note to her dad. He'd be angry when he awoke and saw it, but that didn't deter Ellie in any way. She was going to run despite how her father would react.

"Went for a run. Be back in a few hours."

She checked the time on the microwave oven and checked her watch to make sure the time matched. She wanted to ensure she knew how long she was gone this time. No guessing for her.

After moving to the door quietly and gently closing it behind her, she placed the small bottle of water in her left pocket, the bag of cookies in the other, and began to move.

Moving slowly at first, and running at the speed of a middle-aged woman, Ellie persevered, having faith that in no time her pace would increase and she'd be back to where she was: fast as lightning. She chose a simple tune to play on her IPOD, one that wasn't too fast or too slow but just right for her cadence. Bosco ran beside her, easily keeping up with her. Ellie could feel a throng of pain every now and again but ignored it.

She continued to run, deciding not to stop to rest like she normally did. She had taken enough time off from running. She didn't need to waste any more time lollygagging around, waiting for the pain to cease. She charged ahead, knowing exactly what she was doing—running down the same path, hoping she'd see Sam again. Anyone with an ounce of authority or common sense would give her a stern lecture. They'd tell her she had lost her mind and should turn back around. She didn't care. The moment she shot out of bed, seeing him again was the only thing she had on her mind.

She reached her cross road. Ellie second-guessed herself for one split second, wondering if she was making a mistake, but her heart ruled over her head. She trudged on, pushed the bush aside and crawled into that dark cave.

***

He stood mid-calf in the shallow water. His pants were rolled up to his knees, and he wasn't wearing a shirt. The sun was shining down on him, and the temperature had risen to eighty degrees. He held on steadily to a bow and arrow. His eyes squinted, focusing fifteen feet ahead of him. He aimed and pulled back on the string, releasing the arrow. The water splashed, scaring off all of the fish.

He hit his target and slogged through the water, sticking his hand down, and pulling out the arrow. A fish wiggled as the sharp pointed blade pierced through its insides. He carried the arrow with the fish in tow, returning to where he started. He yanked the fish from the blade's entrapment and threw it on top of a small pile of fish that laid on the sandy shore taking their last breaths. He held the bow back in place, with the arrow lodged and ready to go.

Ellie's mouth gaped wide open. She hated to be *that girl*. The one who drools over a shirtless guy and gets all starry eyed just because he has pecs and abs. Those girls annoyed her. He was shirtless and attractive. Big deal. She had seen plenty of bare-chested guys on the cross country team who were just as buff if not more than him. But man-oh-man, killing a fish with a bow and arrow was beyond cool in her book.

Something about him was different. That was obvious from their conversation, the way he dressed and acted, the way he talked, and the way he presented himself. But there was more to it. Ellie wanted to know Sam, to find out who *he* was.

He looked up, holding the bow and arrow in his hand, ready to strike whatever noise he just heard. Ellie flinched, fearing the worst. He lowered the bow and arrow and smiled as soon as he realized it was her. Ellie waved at him and smiled back, trying to play it cool.

He grabbed his shirt and put it on, buttoning each button and rolling the sleeves up to his elbows. He leaned over to roll down his pants, and then stood upright, staring in Ellie's direction.

Talk about formal, she thought. Ellie moved his way.

He strode toward her, meeting her halfway.

"Hello," he said. "I didn't think I would see you again." He buttoned the last button on his shirt and formed a warm, crooked smile, his mouth open exposing the slight gap between his teeth. "Hello, Bosco," he said, patting him on the head. Bosco's tail vigorously wagged back and forth.

"I know," she answered. "Surprise!" she teased. She cursed herself for being such a dork.

"You shouldn't have taken the risk. It's dangerous for you," he said in a serious tone, frowning. His forehead creased with worry.

"I'm fine." She shrugged indifferently. "Anyways, I wanted to give you guys something. You know, for saving my life and all." She took the plastic bag out of her pocket. A few of the cookies were crumbled, and some were mushed together, and the chocolate had started to melt. She scrunched her face and sighed. "Some of them got messed up on the way. You can still eat them though."

"What are they?" he asked, eyeing the bag's contents.

She gave him a strange look. "You don't know what these are?" She couldn't believe it. *Who doesn't know what a chocolate chip cookie is?*

"No." He folded his arms against his chest and stood with his legs wide apart. She could see he was agitated. Her tone had been accusatory, and it had come across as rude even though Ellie didn't mean for it to.

"Sorry. They're chocolate chip cookies. Have one." She took out one that hadn't crumbled and offered it to him.

He took it from her and studied it, looking at it as if it were an intricate puzzle he was trying to solve. He touched the top of it with the tip of his index finger and then held it up to his nose, smelling the chocolate. "This smells good," he said.

"It is. Go on. Try it," she urged.

He tore off a small piece and placed it in his mouth. He chewed and swallowed, grinning broadly at her. "Delicious."

"What'd I tell you." She wiggled her eyebrows and smiled. "They're my all time favorite dessert."

"Thank you. This must have taken you a long time to make."

"Nah. Not really." She waved her hand up in the air. "Thirty minutes at the most. I baked them last night." She paused for a moment. "They're bake and break," she whispered.

"Last night?" he said. His face formed that same familiar look of confusion she had grown accustomed to.

"Yeah," she hesitated.

"You were bit by a copperhead two days ago, and you were able to cook these last night?"

"Two days? I was here four days ago," she corrected.

He shook his head. "No. I remember you quite well, and it was two days ago," he said with certainty. His stance was firm.

She folded her arms against her chest, looking directly into his gray eyes and raised an eyebrow. She said, "Nope. It was four days ago."

He slightly shook his head. "I think that snake bite affected your sense of time."

"Ha!" she scoffed. "You're the one who can't tell time," she snapped. "I'm not sure what you've been taught, but where I come from a day is twenty-four hours."

He mumbled something to himself, pursing his lips in frustration. He took a deep breath and finally said, "You're an obstinate woman."

"I've been called worse."

"You? I don't believe it." He tried stifling his smirk, but she could see the corners of his mouth moving upward.

Ellie sensed his tone of sarcasm and said, "Touché."

"Do you let anyone win an argument even if they may be right?"

"They're never right, so I don't *let* them win."

He scratched at his beard, appearing as if he was in deep thought and then after a moment, he held his hands up mockingly. "I surrender! I'll let you have this one even though I'm right. It's not real prudent for us to be out here in the open arguing. Anyone can see us." He checked his surroundings, peering over his shoulder suspiciously. He grabbed a burlap sack and threw all of the fish into it and tossed it over his shoulder. He picked up his bow and arrow and asked, "Are you coming?"

"Yeah, but not for too long. I don't want my dad to worry," she said, following him.

***

Ellie had been admiring the red hickory bow and the pine arrows with iron blade tips since she laid her eyes on it. It was massive, almost as big as Sam. The bow itself was five feet tall, and the arrows were the size of a small toddler. It appeared sturdy and old, well-built and not cheap or cheesy like the "Made in China" bow and arrows she saw at sports stores. This was the real deal—authentic and potentially deadly.

"That's a nice bow and arrow," she said.

"Thank you. It was my papa's," he said. "He gave it to me when I was just a youngun."

"It must be difficult to fish with?"

"No. Not really." He shrugged. Ellie couldn't tell if he was trying to play it cool or not. Fishing with a bow and arrow was not a simple every day sport that any rube could just pick up and master.

"Well, it looked tough."

She thought about his precise shot. How it took skill and years of practice to do what he had done. Not too many people could shoot at a moving target and hit the bulls eye on their first attempt. She knew she'd never offer to play darts with him. She hated to lose.

"I can teach you," he offered.

"I'd like that," Ellie blurted. She imagined herself standing in the water holding the bow and arrow killing the first fish on contact, and then running home to her dad and Jonah showing them what she did. She wondered if it was strange for a girl to fantasize in such a way.

He smiled at her, and then his eyes wandered, from Ellie's face down to her chest and then to her long, tanned legs.

She could see him staring at her out of the corner of her eye, how his gaze lingered. She turned her head, staring directly at him in a deliberate, bold move. She wanted to see his reaction, to see if he was like the guys she knew at school who drooled over any girl and whistled, hooted or hollered at them like gruff construction workers at a job site.

His face became flushed, and he quickly looked in the other direction. She was surprised by his shyness, by his embarrassment. She expected unbridled arrogance, like all the other guys she knew who reacted when she caught them as if they were saying to her that they had the right to gawk at her like a piece of meat. Not that she was the object of their attention on a consistent basis anyway, because she wasn't.

Ellie wasn't on the "it list." She wasn't the head cheerleader, or the buxom blonde, or the girl that had a circle of boys around her, vying for her attention. She was who she was, take it or leave it. And that wasn't every guy's cup of tea, especially young teenaged boys with raging hormones who cared more about physicality than any other attribute. Gauging by Sam's reaction, he wasn't remotely like those boys. He was seriously old school, like the type of guys who opened car doors and didn't curse around a girl because it was rude.

Sam's face was less rosy, and his eyes slowly met hers. "Is that how they dress in Florida?"

Ellie peered down at her t-shirt and shorts. She shrugged. "I don't know. It's how I dress when I run. Well, minus the shirt."

His forehead wrinkled in confusion.

She laughed nervously, realizing her blunder. "I mean, I usually wear my sports bra. It's too hot for t-shirts." She could sense he was uncomfortable with the subject. It was written all over his face. His posture was stiff, and he purposely looked anywhere else but at her.

She changed the subject and asked, "Can I hold the bow and arrow?"

"Yes." They stopped walking, and he handed it to her.

It was heavier than she thought it would be. "Holy wow, this is huge!" She ran her fingers over the surface, feeling each and every groove in the hardy wooden bow. She gently touched the tip of the blade, pricking her finger. "Ouch. This is sharp."

"You're not supposed to touch it," he teased. "You want to try it?"

"Really?" She beamed.

"Sure. But don't point this way," he joked, pointing down toward his foot. "I'd like to keep all ten of my toes."

She rolled her eyes at him and fully extended her left arm, holding the front of the bow.

He stood behind her, appraising her form. "May I?"

"Okay."

Seriously old school.

He touched her arms gently, trying to be careful. "You need to bend this arm more." He moved her right arm in a bent formation. "And your fingers need to be here." He brought them to the tip of the arrow sending the slightest shiver down Ellie's spine. Ellie fought it off and focused on potential targets ahead of her. "Find your target and when you're ready, pull back."

Ellie squinted her eyes, finding the perfect place to aim: the trunk of a large oak tree. She pulled the string backward and released, feeling an instant thrill, and the arrow flew several feet and then plummeted to the ground. It was simultaneously exhilarating and disappointing. She wanted to do it again but hated that she was so awful at it. There was nothing more that Ellie Morales loathed than appearing inept.

"That was good," Sam said.

She pouted. "It sucked. Go on and say it. No need to be polite."

He laughed. "All you need is practice. Try it again," he urged.

"Okay," she relented, holding the bow and releasing the arrow within seconds. The arrow flew further but still hit the ground. "It'd take years and I'd still suck." She handed him back the bow and arrow. "Thanks, though," she added. "Guess I can't be good at everything."

"Most people aren't proficient the first time they do this," he said. "It took me a while to get good."

"Why do you fish this way? I mean a fishing pole with a reel would be a heck of a lot easier. You're a glutton for punishment, aren't you?" She nodded her head up and down confidently. "What am I saying? You could go to the grocery store and buy a fish. That's what most people do."

He tilted his head to the side and squinted his eyes. "Grocery store?"

"You know, the place you buy food."

"Like a general store?"

"I guess." She formed a strange look. "No one calls a grocery store a 'general store' unless they're living in Walnut Grove with Ma and Pa Ingalls."

"Where's Walnut Grove?"

"Minnesota I think, but that wasn't my point," she started.

He cut in, "I wouldn't have thought Floridians would talk so differently than the rest of the south."

"We don't," she said. "Okay, I don't say 'y'all or fixin' but I'm not saying anything unique. A grocery store is common terminology throughout the country."

"You don't talk like anyone I've ever met," he said, standing with his arms folded against his chest, staring at her in the most peculiar way.

"Same here," she said and then asked, "*Where are you from?*"

"The south," he answered.

"I know that. Anyone within an ear shot can hear your drawl. I meant, where in the south are you from?"

"Why do you need to know?"

"That's what people do when they're becoming friends. You know, ask questions to learn about each other," she said. "Anyways, what's with all the mystery? You can ask me a million questions, but I can't ask you one simple question. All I want to know is where you're from," she said with irritation, annoyed by his evasiveness.

"I answered your question," he snapped.

"No you didn't. I asked where you were from and you gave me a vague answer. That's like if you asked what I ate for breakfast and I answered food."

He ran his hand through his hair and muttered something under his breath. He breathed heavy, and his lips were pursed. He didn't respond for almost a minute. Finally, he said through clenched teeth, "I'm trying to protect you." His eyes pierced into hers. "It's unsafe for you to be out here with me, let alone knowing information about me could put you in serious danger."

Ellie swallowed hard and wondered, *What have I gotten myself into?*

CHAPTER 12

"Maybe I should go?" Her voice was shaky and unsteady.

Reality set in. Maybe he wasn't all he was cracked up to be? Maybe it was time she thought first and then leapt, instead of the other way around? What if her life was in danger? This was the type of situation her father told her to avoid. Now she was in hot water and she had no idea how to back peddle her way out of there.

"It wasn't my intention to make you uncomfortable." Concern showed in his gray eyes. "I apologize."

"Well, you did," she said, still reeling from his tone, from his secrecy.

"Again, I apologize. It was not my intention..."

One look into his sincere eyes, and she was a goner. Dangerous or not, he just didn't appear to be a threat. She hoped that her instincts weren't wrong.

"I know," she interrupted with frustration, a wrinkle formed at the bridge of her nose. "Look, if you're in some kind of trouble with the mob, there's no way they're going to come out here in the middle of frickin' BFE."

"What?" he said. "Oh forget it." He stared at her for a moment and said, "I don't know if it's best for me to be telling you too much about me. I enjoy your company, but I sure don't want you to get hurt, either."

"You're a bit dramatic aren't you?" she kidded, trying to lighten the gloomy mood. She grew serious once she saw he wasn't laughing with her. "I just wanna give these cookies to your family to thank them for being so kind to me. Well, everyone except your uncle Caleb," she said and his lips curved upward, forming a hint of a smile. "Let me do this, and I'll be on my way."

"All right. If you insist."

"I can take care of myself anyway," she made sure to add.

"I believe you can Miss Ellie." He chuckled, looking at her in wonder.

"And what's with all the 'Miss' stuff? Could you just call me Ellie like most people do?"

"If you insist." He smirked.

"Is something funny?"

"I've never met a woman like you," he said.

"Well, I've never met a man like you either, Sam," she said, and they trekked on.

***

Virginia's hands were deep into a bucket full of water. It sloshed as she moved them up and down. A washboard leaned upright in the bucket. She took a piece of clothing that resembled a shirt and rubbed the two together, the fabric going against the grooves of the board. She scrubbed vigorously for a few minutes and then rested for a moment, wiping the sweat from her brow with her arm, and then returned to work. Caleb and Granny were pulling weeds in their garden. Caleb was bent over using a short stick to balance while pulling a weed with his other hand. It looked difficult and even though Ellie didn't care for him, she had to admit he was a strong old ox with an incredible sense of balance. Moses hacked at a long piece of wood with an axe, chopping it into smaller logs perfect for a fire. Everyone was working, going about their daily lives. This was their routine.

"Geez. When do you guys rest?" Ellie said, noticing that no one sat idling. She was willing to bet Jonah was just rolling out of bed and eating a bowl of cereal while lounging on the couch.

"There's too much to do."

They headed toward the garden. Granny pulled stubbornly on a weed that was far too lodged in the ground. "Dern thing won't come out," she fussed. She used both hands and tugged on it with all of her might. A smile of satisfaction came across her wrinkled face as the weed came out of the ground.

"Granny," Sam said. "Ellie brought us a gift."

Granny stood up straight. She cupped her hand over her eyes, shading them from the bright sunlight. Caleb stood up, grabbed onto his crutch, and glared at Ellie. She stared him down for a second and pointed her attention toward Granny.

Granny offered her a slight smile, exposing a multitude of missing teeth. Those that remained were stained a brownish tint. "You come alone again?"

"Yes," Ellie answered.

She shook her head and made a "tisk, tisk" sound. "Girl like you shouldn't be out on her own."

"I wanted to thank you all for helping me," Ellie said, ignoring Granny's snide remark.

Moses and Virginia stopped what they what they were doing and wandered over to Ellie and Sam.

"Hello, Ellie," Virginia said and hugged her. Virginia was super touchy, and although Ellie was an affectionate person, it threw her off guard.

Ellie felt sorry for her. She suspected that beyond her pleasantries and sweet disposition was hidden sorrow that was slowly consuming her like a virus. Ellie knew the feeling. The first few months after her mother passed away, she made sure to put on the pretense that everything was okay, that she could handle it all. But beneath her tough exterior was a girl who still needed her mother. Sorrow attracts sorrow, and Ellie could smell it a mile away.

Moses slightly smiled at Ellie, and she gave him a warm, broad smile in return.

"Hi, Virginia, Moses," Ellie said. "I brought you guys some cookies."

Sam showed them the bag full of cookies. Granny inspected it, running her finger across the plastic surface. "Queer poke you got 'em in," she said.

"Ziploc," Ellie answered. "They're a staple in our household."

Granny opened it and took a cookie out. She held it up to her nose and inhaled. "Smells real good," she said, licking her lips.

"Chocolate always smells good," Ellie said.

"I've had the pleasure of eating one. It was delicious," Sam added.

Granny tore half of the cookie and placed it in her mouth. She chewed and swallowed. "That's down right good," she said. "This here cookie as you call it. It's like a macaroon?" She tore the other half and popped it in her mouth.

"I guess so. I've never had a macaroon."

"I wouldn't eat those," Caleb interrupted. "Could be somethin' bad in 'em." He glowered at Ellie.

Ellie rolled her eyes at him. "What's your problem?" she asked, brewing with anger. "You're really paranoid. There's a diagnosis for that you know!"

"Calm down girl." Granny touched Ellie's arm and patted her hand. "Caleb don't mean no harm. He takes longer to warm to people."

"I don't mean to be rude," Ellie said to her.

"I know. Let's get out of this here heat and sit down for a spell." Granny headed inside to the cabin. "This here heat makes us meaner than a poke of rattlesnakes."

Ellie followed closely behind, checking the time on her watch. It was eight o'clock in the morning. She was a fast runner, but not that fast. The run had to have taken well over an hour and a half, and stopping to talk with Sam took up more time. She shook her wrist, wondering if the battery was dying, but the hands continued to wind away, moving second by second.

She followed Granny inside of the cabin. It was less sparse, full of more furniture, and was much more lived in and full of life than the other cabin where they had taken care of her.

"This here's me and Virginia's cabin," Granny said, which explained the plain décor that the other cabin displayed. The other cabin was for the men who didn't care about curtains, rugs, and other things that might make a place feel more like a home instead of a bare room.

"It's pretty," Ellie said, taking it all in, from the red gingham curtains hanging in the windows to the cherry wood chest-of-drawers.

A small round table with five chairs sat near the entrance. There were two twin-sized beds. They, like the beds in the other cabin, were covered in quilt bedspreads. Between the two beds was a small oak table with a lantern on top. A fireplace centered the room, and two wooden chairs circled around it. A patchwork quilted rug accented the area. The cherry wood chest of drawers captured Ellie's attention. A grand piece, it looked more pristine than the rest of the furniture, like something from the turn of the eighteenth century.

Granny sat down on one of the chairs and motioned for Ellie to do the same. The rest of the group followed suit, with the exception of Caleb who chose to stand near the doorway, his lips pursed, and a constant scowl glued to his weathered face. Anytime Ellie glanced in his direction, he made sure to give her a dirty look, sealing his disdain for her. Their feelings for each other were mutual. He didn't trust her; she didn't like him.

Granny squinted her beady blue eyes at Ellie. "Them cookies were good. That was real nice of you to bring 'em to us."

"Thank you," Ellie said.

Sam opened the bag and offered a cookie to Virginia and Moses who eagerly accepted. If Granny ate one, then they would too, despite Caleb's protests. Granny took another cookie, bit into it and chewed

Food still in her mouth, she said to Ellie, "You shouldn't be out by yourself. What's your pa think about you goin' out alone?"

"He doesn't care," she lied. He *did* care and that was the problem. A part of her felt a pang of guilt for leaving the house the way she did. She knew it'd be a matter of minutes before he woke up and saw her note. He told her not to go out, and the first thing she did was disobey him. She berated herself. Why couldn't she be like other daughters and do as her father asked?

Granny's lips puckered, and she crossed one leg over her other, exposing a pair of worn, scruffy boots and filthy, tattered stockings. Ellie couldn't believe she wore that in this heat. Religious sect or not, it was ludicrous to dress the way they did during the dreadfully hot days of summer.

"I 'spect you're tellin' me a fib," she probed.

"No. He's fine," Ellie said, a slight lilt in her voice was a dead giveaway that she was, in fact, fibbing. Ellie was amazed by Granny's acute perception. Sure Ellie was an open book, but Granny's judgement had been quick and to the point, and she didn't even blink an eye accusing Ellie of lying.

Granny smacked her lips and gave her a skeptical look and then said, changing the subject, "Are you thirsty?"

"I'm good. I have water." She tapped her pocket, feeling the small plastic bottle against the thin mesh fabric of her running shorts. The bottle had warmed to room temperature, acclimating to the summer heat. She pulled the bottle out of her pocket and twisted off the lid. They all watched her in amazement as if she were performing a unique circus act. She held the bottle to her lips and took three hard gulps, nearly finishing off the contents. She twisted the lid back on and placed the bottle back safely in her pocket.

"That's a queer cup you're drinkin' from," Granny said. Virginia and Moses' mouths gaped open, their eyes wide. Sam placed his fingers to his temples and let out a heavy sigh in frustration.

"It's just a water bottle." Ellie tried to brush it off but realized that Sam's family was sheltered beyond reason. Everything she took for granted, they knew nothing about.

Granny leaned forward; her hand rubbed her sagging chin. A few long hairs that needed to be plucked were now evident by the sun shining into the room. "I've never seen one like it," she said. "You seem to be 'sposing us to lots of queer things."

Ellie shrugged her shoulders.

Granny shifted her legs and a few bones cracked. "Can you tell us any news about the war?"

Sam moved forward, his hands held up as if to stop Granny from asking her question. "Granny, I don't think..." he started.

"Let her answer me," she said, shushing him and looked back at

Ellie.

"Okay," Ellie said, unsure of where Granny was headed. Asking about the war seemed like a random, out-of-left field type of question.

"They still fightin'?" Granny asked.

"In Iraq or Afghanistan?" Ellie asked.

Granny's wrinkled face scrunched, forming more lines and creases. "Whatcha mean, 'Iraq or Afghanistan'?"

Ellie gave her a peculiar look. "You asked about the war. I assumed you meant..."

Granny huffed. "I'm talking about the war between the North and the South."

"The North and South of what?" she asked.

"In this country," Granny answered her with a tone of irritation, as if Ellie just asked the most ridiculous question.

Ellie raised an eyebrow and checked all of their expressions—serious and yearning for an answer. This wasn't a joke.

"You aren't joking are you?" she said, seeing their expressions remained the same. "How long has your family been here?" *Generation after generation had to have lived cooped up in their little world of oblivion*, she thought. There was no other explanation. It just didn't add up. None of it did.

Granny stayed silent, gauging Sam's reaction, which Ellie noticed was a first. From what she had witnessed, Granny was the one who ran the household, but in this instance she was looking to him to guide her.

"Two years," he answered with a strained expression, looking directly at Ellie. She could tell he didn't want to divulge that information.

"Two years," Ellie repeated in disbelief. "Have you all been under a rock? 'Cause I don't know why you would think we're in the middle of the Civil War!"

"Girl, what are you gettin' at?" Granny asked, a hint of frustration harboring under her raspy voice.

"I'm saying the Civil War ended a long time ago. Like way before you all were even born."

"That ain't possible," Sam chimed in.

Ellie folded her arms against her chest defensively and leaned back into her chair. Her eyebrow raised, and she said in a challenging tone, "Yeah, Sam, it is."

If he was going to argue with her about facts, she'd bicker with him until the sun set and prove her point.

Sam sighed heavily and pressed his fingers against his temples one more time. A look of bewilderment and irritation crossed his face. Ellie was too wound up to think about all of the implications, about the fact that they believed they were sitting in the middle of a war that had been over for over one hundred and fifty years.

The room fell silent.

Virginia quietly got up and walked over to the chest of drawers that Ellie had admired when she first entered the room. She pulled on the top drawer and took out a small photograph—no bigger than the size of her hand. She held onto it carefully for fear of fraying the delicate edges and headed over to Ellie. She clutched onto it and held it front of her.

"Virginia," Caleb hurriedly hobbled over to her and grabbed her arm, "what are you thinking?" His voice was threatening. A few of the hairs on Ellie's neck stood up. She could feel him breathing behind her. "She ain't to be trusted."

Virginia shrugged his arm off of hers. "Leave me be," she said in a stern voice, surprising Ellie. Virginia's soft, high-pitched voice and sweet face had made her seem docile.

She then directed her attention toward Ellie. "This here is Sam and my fiancé, Ernest, right before they left to fight in the war. Granny and me made their uniforms." She pointed to their jackets. Belts cinched their waists. Sam's Bowie knife was secure in his leather sheath. A strap crossed his chest with a canteen hitting him at the hip. "Ernest's got his mama's spoon that she had when she was a youngun." Ellie noticed the spoon, standing upright, snug tight against his stomach. "Said he'd need it to eat with," she said, her finger ran across his youthful face.

Ellie studied the picture closely, noticing Sam was a few years younger. The photograph was more yellow and brown than black and white. The outside edge was a rectangular white line that formed the shape of the picture. Neither Sam nor Ernest was smiling in the photo; both looked intimidating even though they couldn't have been much older than she was.

"I think he knew he would miss home and needed a keepsake." Her eyes began to water. She was on the brink of tears. "He took a locket of my hair with him, too." She touched a long strand of her blond hair. Sam moved over to her and took the photo from her hand.

"You've said enough," Sam said, his hand firm on Virginia's shoulder. Ellie's eyes followed him as he took the picture from her sight.

"But she may know where he is," she pleaded, looking up at him desperately. "Ellie," she said, getting her attention, "if the war is over, can you tell help find my Ernest?"

Ellie swallowed, feeling a conflicting mixture of emotions. A part of her felt sympathy for Virginia. She could see she was in love and missed her fiancé. The other half of her was full of fear because what they had just shown her didn't make any sense. And the things that they were saying made them all seem insane.

"I can't," Ellie said. Her head was beginning to throb.

"His name is Ernest Gosset Price," she began. Sam squeezed her shoulder and interrupted her.

"It's time you left," he instructed Ellie.

"No!" Virginia screamed, slamming her fists against the table. "Ernest is gone, and she may be able to tell us something. Anything," Virginia said, searching Ellie's brown eyes.

Ellie got up, her legs wobbling and her voice shaky. "I, I can't." She shook her head. "I told you. The war is over. It has been for a long time. Either you all are delusional or you're playing one sick twisted joke on me. Either way, I'm outta here." She bolted toward the door, brushing past Sam and Caleb with Bosco in tow. She stood at the doorway and said, "By the way, you can get those kind of photographs made at Six Flags. I know 'cause my brother and I had ours done a few years ago."

"I'm telling you the truth," Virginia cried, and Ellie could tell that she really believed the things that she was saying to her. Granny reached over to comfort her. Caleb frowned at Ellie; his normal look of mistrust had turned into sadness.

"If the war is over, then tell us who won," Sam said, staring directly into her eyes.

"What does it matter? You all will continue to stay cooped up in your land of oblivion anyways," Ellie scoffed.

"It matters. Tell us who won." They all looked to her with

desperation.

Guilt consumed her. She didn't understand how could she feel any remorse when she barely knew these people— they were either master manipulators or certifiable. They had saved her life, and she had paid her debt. She didn't owe them anything else. And even though Ellie swore she'd never ever say things without thinking ever again, that the last time was when she lost her mom, she forgot all of those sentiments and blurted, "You wanna know so bad, go to the library and look it up!"

She jetted out of the doorway and ran as fast as she could in the opposite direction, trying to forget she had ever met them.

CHAPTER 13

She ran and ran until it hurt, until she couldn't catch her breath and her chest felt caved in and her legs throbbed in pain. She stopped to take a deep breath and slumped against a lone tree. There she began to cry, sobbing uncontrollably, the ugly kind of tears. The miserable kind—the type that continued to flow despite her efforts in fighting them. She sniffled and moaned, slowly finding her way onto the ground: her legs pressed against her chest, and her arms bound tightly around them. She wiped her wet face with the back of her hand and dug her nails into her legs. She winced from the point of contact and quickly retracted her fingers. That was proof that this was not a dream.

Bosco licked her wet face, his tongue full of saliva and his breath an odor of dog food and other scraps of food that had probably fallen to the kitchen floor by accident or on purpose. Everyone in the Morales house was guilty of feeding him their table scraps.

"No," she said, pushing him away, but he continued to persist. "Bosco, don't." The more she protested, the more he slathered her face with wet, sloppy kisses. "I can't explain it, Bosco. I can't understand any of it," she said. "None of this makes any sense. I really think they believe what they're saying. Why do I like the crazy ones?" She sucked in air and looked up into the sky. "Who's crazy? I'm talking to a dog." She laughed at herself. "What if they're telling the truth?" She sat for a few more minutes thinking of all of the possibilities and every single scenario wasn't good. She patted Bosco on the top of his furry head and stood up. "Come on." She gestured. "It's time we got home."

***

She trudged up the driveway, utterly beat. It had been a trying morning to say the least. Jonah was outside attempting to make shots into the basketball hoop.

"Where the hell have you been?" he asked Ellie.

She continued to walk with slumped shoulders ignoring his question.

"Hey. I was talking to you." He threw the ball at her, missing her by an inch.

She didn't even flinch.

"Okay Zombie. Dad's frickin' pissed at you by the way." He started to dribble the ball again.

Ellie stopped and turned to look at Jonah. "What the hell for?"

"There's the sister I know." He smiled. "For being gone all day. What else?"

"What?" she asked petulantly. She had forgotten to check the time on her watch when she left in a hurry.

"Dad. I'll be back in a few hours," he raised his voice mockingly and placed his hands on his hips. "Oops, I can't tell time." He batted his eyelashes and then rolled his eyes at her. His voice back to normal, he said, "You almost gave him a heart attack earlier this week. You almost did it again. Smooth move Ex Lax."

"Just piss off." She pursed her lips, glowering at him.

"No need to get your panties in a twist. I'm just sayin', quit being gone so long because Dad doesn't like it, and I get stuck hearing about it or dealing with him slamming cabinet doors and beating every inanimate object in the house. Why do you think I'm out here?" He patted her on the arm condescendingly. She jerked it away from him. "Touchy aren't we?" he teased.

"I wasn't gone that long. Three hours at the most. If Dad can't handle that, how's he gonna deal with it when I'm in college?

Anyways, it's 11:30," she said, holding up her watch.

"Either your watch doesn't work or you can't tell time worth a crap. And you're sadly mistaken if you think Dad is going to give you more freedom when you're at school. Quit dreaming. He's kept a closer eye on us since Mom..." He bounced the ball and shot a basket. "Bam, in your face!" he shouted.

Ellie rolled her eyes. "I'm going inside."

"Good." He fanned his hand in front of his nose. "It was starting to smell out here."

She examined her watch, seeing that it clearly showed 11:30 in the morning. She shook the watch to make sure the hands were operating. Both hands continued to move around in a circle, second by second.

She turned the knob and pushed the door open. The TV was blaring. Her dad was in the kitchen, cleaning the counters. His hands vigorously moved back and forth over and over again in the same spot.

"I think I could lick that and be okay, Dad," Ellie said, coming from behind him.

He dropped the cloth and spun to face her. "Where have you been?"

"I left a note," she said, knowing that wasn't much of a defense.

"Your note said you'd be back hours ago! Where have you been?" He tapped his foot impatiently, waiting for her to answer.

She messed with her hair and then opened the refrigerator, pulling out a carton of apple juice. She opened it and took a long swig. "I was in the woods running and lost track of time," she said, feeling guilt for telling a white lie. She never could look at him when she lied, and he knew it. He just didn't want to face it. Like any parent, he over-looked it even though it was right in his face begging for him to notice.

"This whole time?" he asked with an incredulous expression.

"Yeah," she lied.

"Not again. You hear me. I mean it," he said with authority. "I told you I didn't want you going back. You don't listen, Ellie." His forehead wrinkled, and he let out a long sigh.

"I won't, okay." She held up her hands surrendering.

He pulled her toward him and gave her a hug. "You and Jonah mean everything to me," he whispered to her.

"I know," Ellie said; that familiar feeling of pain in her chest resurfaced.

"Then don't do it again." He let go of her and placed the tip of his thumb under her chin, giving her that look. She hated that look.

"I won't," she whined. She placed the carton back in the refrigerator and closed it. "I'm gonna take a shower."

He gave her a weary, forced smile. He looked exhausted, more tired than she had ever seen him.

"Sorry I worried you, Dad," she said as she left the room.

She entered her bedroom and closed the door behind her, collapsing onto her bed. Thoughts raced through her mind. She worried about her dad because she knew things couldn't continue as they were. But for the time being, he'd have to wait because something else was in front of the line, taking precedence over everything else.

She glanced at the clock on her bedside table. *How is it three o'frickin' clock in the afternoon? I know I wasn't gone that long, maybe two to three hours at the most.*

She rolled over onto her side and patted the bed for Bosco to jump up. He lay down next to her.

"We weren't gone that long were we, boy?" she said, running her hands up and down his belly. "A few hours at the most. Something is seriously off."

***

Despite her dad's warnings, Ellie woke up early as usual for her morning run. She stayed on the trail, and avoided the cave and Sam all together. She wasn't going back until she had more answers. Until things made more sense, and she wondered if they ever would, and if she'd ever see him again. Was she crazy, she wondered? To want to see him again even though he seemed locked in another era, living in his own reality.

She returned home, took a shower, got dressed, and planned to drive into town later that morning to use the internet at the library. When her parents had purchased the home, her dad refused to spend money frivolously on things that he thought weren't needed. Things like the internet.

"You don't need the internet. It's bad enough I'm spending money on satellite TV. All you and Jonah will use it for is to get on that stupid Facechat site."

"It's Facebook, Dad," Ellie had corrected. "And that's not why Jonah and I need it. Being without the internet is like living in the dark ages. It's as bad as not having a phone," she argued.

"Until you earn your own money, you'll have to suffer through it, Ellie."

***

She entered the kitchen and made herself a breakfast sandwich: sausage and cheese on an English muffin. She poured a tall glass of water and drank it all within a minute. Jonah came into the kitchen, still half asleep, his hair a ratty mess and his eyes puffy from too much sleep. He rubbed his eyes and yawned.

"Where are you going?" he asked.

"The library," she said, chewing on her sandwich.

"Like you read." He opened a bag of bagels and laid two slices out on a paper towel.

"I read, Shrimp." She wiped the crumbs from her mouth.

Her dad came into the kitchen and took one look at Ellie. He noticed she was dressed to go out and not to run, and asked, "Where are you off to?"

"Geez. It's like the Spanish Inquisition around here," she said to both of them. "I just told Jonah I'm going to the library."

"To get a book?" He placed his hand to her forehead. "No fever."

"Very funny, Dad," she said. "I do read you know."

"Bullshit," Jonah coughed, spreading cream cheese on his bagel.

Her dad swatted him on the arm and gave him a stern look. "Watch the language," he warned. "I don't like you cursing."

"Sorry," Jonah cowered.

"I'm going so I can use the internet," she explained. "Can I borrow your car, Dad?"

"You're driving all the way into town so you can chat with your friends on that stupid face site or twit with your friends on that tweet site," he huffed.

"It's tweeting," Jonah said, laughing.

"Tweet, twit, doesn't matter. That's a major waste of gas, Ellie."

"I've gotta take care of some things for school," she lied.

"Oh," he said. "Well in that case, it's okay."

"Like what, Ellie?" Jonah asked, baiting her. He was onto her. He took a bite of his bagel and chewed his food with a smug look.

"There's a survey I have to fill out for housing. You know stuff like that," she said, the lilt in her voice resurfaced, and she couldn't make eye contact with either one of them. Her dad was too distracted searching for his car keys to notice.

Jonah gave her a disbelieving look, raising an eyebrow.

"Just drive careful. These roads can be dangerous. Some of the locals drive too fast on them," he said, handing her his car keys.

"I will. Promise." She smiled and then stuck her tongue out at Jonah when their dad wasn't looking.

Ellie grabbed her purse and headed to the door that opened to the garage.

"Do you need cash?" he called after her.

"I'm good, Dad," she yelled and pushed the door open. The last thing she wanted to do was take money from him when all she had been doing lately was lie to him. That would be the final blow. It'd make her sink lower than she ever had.

She clicked the button on the keys, and the door to her dad's blue Honda CRV unlocked. She opened the car door and sat down in the driver's seat. Just as she was about to close the car door, Jonah entered the garage from the inside door.

"What do you want, Shrimp?"

"I'm going with you," he said.

"No you're not." She closed the door and started the car.

He opened the back door before she had time push down on the lock button.

"Great," she muttered. "I told you, I'm going alone."

"Nope. Dad said I could come with. He felt better about me going with you."

"Like I need a chaperone." She rolled her eyes.

"That's not all you need," he retorted.

She looked at him in the rear view mirror. "Get in the front. I'm not your frickin' chauffeur."

He climbed toward the front and plopped down in the passenger seat. Giving her a smug look and rubbing his hands together, he said, "Let's go."

"Why are you so intent on going?"

"Why do you think?"

"I don't know. Maybe 'cause you're bored and you have nothing better to do than follow me around," she replied. "Get a life."

"Think again," he said. "I'm so onto you, Ellie. You're hiding something."

"Whatever." She let out one heavy breath of exasperation and backed the car.

He placed his hands behind his head, giving her an arrogant smirk. "Just one more hour until you confess."

Ellie turned up the volume on the radio, muffling out any other things Jonah was going to say. He was right. She would crack and crack soon. She just wondered if he would think she was headed for the looney bin once she told him the entire story.

***

The library was in the center of the town of Mayfield, North Carolina. Mayfield was one long strip of road with brick storefront businesses and cobble-stone sidewalks. It was like any other small town, complete with a post office, pizza parlor, a few other restaurants, clothing stores, an old white church with a steeple, and a couple of odds and ends. It was the type of place that had Mother Nature on its side. Surrounded by scenic waterfalls and gorgeous mountain views, Mayfield was popular with tourists, and the town reaped the benefits.

The library, a stone covered building erected in the early 1920s, stood on top of a hill in the middle of town. It and the white church were the most noticeable and most picturesque structures.

Ellie pulled the CRV into the parking lot and turned off the car. She jumped out, closing the door behind her. Jonah did the same and walked with her inside the antiquated building. An elderly lady with tortoise-shell pointy glasses and white curly hair greeted them as they entered.

"Can I help y'all?" she asked.

"I need to use the internet," Ellie replied.

"Down that way and to your left." She gave them a pleasant smile.

"Thank you," Ellie said, marching toward the computer-filled room. For a library in the middle of a small town, the amount of technology was impressive, and all of the computers were new—like a college or university library.

Row after row of computers sat on narrow tables. There was only a foot of room between each table, which left each person almost sitting on top of each other. The room was full of people—mostly elderly—surfing the web for free, trying to stay in touch with the twenty-first century. Ellie found an empty chair in the far corner of the room. Jonah pulled up a chair next to her and sat back, watching her click away.

"Go away," she shooed him.

"No. I'm fine here," he said, moving closer to her and looking over her shoulder.

"You're annoying." She tightened her jaw and let out a heavy sigh.

"Quit stalling, and do what you came here to do, Ellie."

She took a whiff and said, "You stink, Shrimp. What'd you eat today, an entire bowl of garlic?"

He cupped his hand in front of his mouth and nose and breathed. "It's not that bad."

She gave him a look.

"Fine. It stinks a little," he admitted. "I didn't think the garlic cream cheese would be so strong."

"Well, it is. You could ward off a vampire with that stench. Did you brush your teeth? And your hair, it's a crazy mess."

He touched the top of his head, trying to pat down a few strands that were sticking up. "You're just trying to distract me," he said.

He could read her so well. She clicked on the keys typing in "Ernest Gosset Price," seeing what results she got.

"Who is that?" Jonah asked.

"Shh," she said. "We're in a library."

He poked her in her ribs. "Tell me who it is. Is it a boyfriend?"

"Ow," she moaned. "No. Just shut up," she said, becoming annoyed.

"It is. I knew it. You have a boyfriend, and you don't want Dad to know," he said confidently.

"Yeah. That's it. You've caught me," she said, her voice flat.

A librarian stormed over to them, barging in on their spat. "Please keep your voices down," she ordered.

"Sorry," Ellie said.

"Yeah, sorry," Jonah added.

The librarian walked away, and Ellie turned to face the computer screen. She scrolled down the screen with her mouse, searching for any mention of Ernest Gosset Price.

"Are you gonna tell me what's going on?" Jonah asked, peering over her shoulder. "Why are you stalking some old dude?"

"How do you know he's old?" Ellie asked, clicking on the mouse.

"It's an old guy's name. No one below the age of seventy is named Ernest or Gosset."

"Shh," someone across from them whispered.

Ellie lowered her voice to a near whisper, "I'll tell you once I'm done. Go find something to do," she said. "You're like a gnat in the woods." She waved her hand in front of her face.

"Whatever. I'll hold you to it. I'll be back." He got up to leave.

Ellie looked back at the computer screen. She wasn't sure what she was looking for—maybe a sign, something to tell her that he didn't exist, but the search results contradicted that theory. The first and only link that popped up with his name in it was in reference to the town of Mayfield from the 1970s. Ellie clicked on it, and scanned the article. The old white church had been restored by the town residents, and a group picture had been taken. In caption below the picture: *Far left, Ernest G. Price.* The quality of the image was poor, and Ellie couldn't see his face clearly, but he looked young, maybe Sam's age or a little older. She searched the other results and found no other image or mention of an Ernest G. Price.

She didn't know if it was him; if the Ernest pictured in the Mayfield town photo was the one Virginia spoke of. All she knew was she had proof that someone with that same name had existed in Mayfield, the closest town to the hiking trail. She didn't know if it was a coincidence, that a man with the same name appeared in town over thirty years ago. The time frame didn't add up. None of it did.

How could it be the same man, she wondered?

She stopped her search for Ernest and typed in "American Civil War," finding an article that gave basic facts of when it began and ended and who won. This was her solid proof to them that the war was over, and had been for a long, long time. She clicked "print" and then got up, taking her purse and her jingling keys. She received a few glares from library patrons and headed over to the printer. She grabbed the papers and folded them neatly in her purse.

Jonah stood in the library lobby watching people as they came and went.

He turned to face her before she said anything. "I could hear you coming, Thunder Foot. You done?"

"Yep. Let's go." He followed her outside to the CRV. Ellie turned the ignition. Facing him, she said, "Let's get something to eat. I'll tell you about it all over lunch."

"Good. 'Cause I'm hungry again."

She touched his arm and said, "You can't tell anyone. And you have to promise to believe me no matter what."

"I can tell when you're lying, Ellie."

"I know," she breathed. "Just promise me you won't call me crazy because what I'm going to tell you is going to sound like I'm cuckoo for Cocoa Puffs. K?" she said, gauging his reaction.

"You've been on the crazy train for a while," he joked. She hit him on the arm. "Ow. That hurt," he complained, touching the red spot on his arm. "How do you do that?"

"I mean it. Promise," she said.

"Okay," he relented.

***

Ellie told Jonah the entire story—including every detail—from the beginning to the end. He stayed quiet, allowing her to spill her guts, to confess what had been on her chest for some time. She wanted to tell someone; she needed to.

She let out a deep breath. "I feel better," she said and then tried reading his blank expression.

Jonah wiped the corners of his mouth with his napkin and took a sip of water. He clasped his hands together and placed them on the table. He was remarkably calm. Ellie expected him to be speechless, to be rattled by what she had told him.

"I don't think going back is such a good idea," he said.

"I have to."

"They could be some weird Deliverance type of cult and force you to be their mountain wife. It's been done before," he said. "You've heard those stories about hillbillies kidnapping women."

"They're not like that," Ellie defended. "And they're not hillbillies. Quit stereotyping."

"Oh yeah. Well, from what you've told me, they think it's the Civil War and don't have electricity or running water. Plus, they're hiding from the cops."

"You don't know them. They saved my life, and they seem harmless. Sam, he's a good guy," she started, a shade of red tinted her tanned cheeks. She couldn't believe she was having that type of reaction. *How lame*, she thought.

"You like him." He sighed. "Really? This is about a guy?"

"No," Ellie said, telling a half-truth. Some of it was about a guy, and that guy was Sam.

"Sure, Ellie. Whatever," he scoffed. "Be smart, and don't go back there."

"I'm going back," Ellie argued.

"Figures." He rolled his eyes in exasperation. "When you do, I'm going with you. I gotta see Pa and Ma Kettle for myself."

"What if they're telling me the truth?"

"It's not probable."

"But what if, Jonah? What if?" Ellie said, getting lost in deep thought, thinking that there may be some truth to what Sam's family had told her.

He snapped his fingers in front of her face. "Wake up, Ellie. It *can't* happen."

She leaned forward and looked around the room before whispering, "But how can you explain that you and Dad said I was gone for over a day, and they said it was five hours? And what about the other day? I swore I was gone for only a few hours. I showed you my watch. It read 11:30."

"This isn't Star Trek, Ellie. You can't have two different time portals. It's called they lied to you, or you were so out of it by the snake bite that you didn't know what time of day it was. And the other day? Well, that doesn't surprise me. You can be totally oblivious when you run sometimes. Several hours could pass, and you would hardly notice. Obviously your watch is a piece of crap."

"Go ahead and stare at me like I'm a moron. I know there's more to the story, and I'm going to find out."

CHAPTER 14

Ellie's dad stood over his bed, folding his clothes and meticulously placing them in his suitcase. Although he and Ellie were just alike in so many ways, they differed where neatness was concerned. Ellie relied on him when it came to packing. She usually wadded her clothes and threw them haphazardly into her suitcase, hoping everything would fit. He would always come behind her and refold everything. He even ironed her clothes— complete with military creases and starched, stiff collared shirts.

"Dad!" she called, searching the house.

"In here," he answered.

Ellie had a hard time going in that room—it reminded her too much of her mother. She stood at the threshold of the door, refusing to budge any further. Jonah plopped down on the bed next to his dad's weathered suitcase—one he had since he met Ellie's mom.

"What are you doing, Dad?" Ellie asked, worried that they were leaving. The last thing she wanted to do was go back to Florida. Not now. Not when things were starting to unfold. Not when she was close to getting answers.

"I have to go back to Florida for a triple bypass surgery. I should be back in five days."

"They couldn't get anyone else to do it?" Jonah asked.

He zipped up his suitcase and looked at his children. "No. The patient is a good friend of mine. He asked that I perform the surgery."

"Who is it?" Ellie asked.

"Dr. Howard. You've met him a few times," he said nonchalantly and grabbed the suitcase, holding onto the handle and lugging it with him toward the front of the house as Ellie and Jonah followed. "I don't want to leave you two here alone, but it doesn't make sense to drag you back and forth with me."

"And it costs more in plane tickets," Jonah pointed out.

He laughed, and said, "That too. No sense in throwing money away."

"We'll be okay," Ellie said.

"That's my hope," he said, giving her a look. "My flight leaves tomorrow morning. So, you'll have to drive me to the airport."

"Okay," she agreed.

"I won't be gone that long," he said. "Ellie?"

"Yeah."

"I don't know what's gotten into you lately, why you don't listen to me, and why you're out all hours of the day without a word, but it's going to stop," he said in an authoritative tone. He placed his hand under her chin. "Got it?"

"Yes sir," she said, adding the "sir" because she knew he meant business.

"I mean it. No more. I don't like leaving you two here alone when you've been acting this way. I'm trusting that you'll take care of your brother while I'm gone," he said, raising an eyebrow and tilting his head to the side. "And you won't be disappearing on him?"

"You can count on me," she said.

"I hope so, because you're treading on thin ice, Ellie. Very thin ice."

***

Jonah tagged along with Ellie to drop their dad off at the airport. The drive was a long one—a little over two hours—longer than Ellie thought it would take. Two-lane, curvy mountain roads extended any trip. A quick ten mile excursion could turn into a forty-five minute drive.

Ellie had one thing on her mind and one thing only: Sam. She was going back on that trail as soon as they got home. Nothing was going to stop her. She'd miss her dad, but his absence for the next five days was perfect timing. This gave her time to go back and get the answers that she needed without her dad standing in her way.

Cars zipped past her as she drove home. A few cars beeped their horns, one driver slowed down to give Ellie the finger, and then passed her in a huff.

"You drive like an old lady," Jonah said.

"So," she said, both hands gripping onto the steering wheel. "I'm not about to drive like a maniac on this road."

"You could apply some pressure to the accelerator. The car won't drive on its own," he said.

"You didn't have to come along."

"He's my dad too."

She sideways glanced at him, making a skeptical expression, and then focused back on the winding road. "That's not the only reason why you came."

"What else was I going to do? Hanging with you seemed like a better choice than sitting around in that realm of depression. Anyways, I'm going with you to Ma and Pa Kettle's home in the woods too," he said.

"No you're not," she raised her voice.

"The hell I'm not. I told you yesterday I was. If you don't let me go, I'll call Dad and tell him what you're doing," he threatened.

"What happened to my sweet fifteen-year-old brother? The one I could boss around?"

"He grew up and found out his sister liked hanging out with people who are bat shit crazy," he replied.

"Seriously, Jonah. You're ticked off all the time. What gives?" she said, turning down the radio.

"Are we really going to go there, Ellie? I don't think you want to."

"What does that mean?"

"I think you know."

She tightened her lips and turned the knob on the radio, allowing music to fill the car their entire ride home.

***

As soon as they were home, Ellie hurried into her bedroom and changed into a pair of jeans and a pale blue t-shirt. She pulled her hair up into a pony tail and put an old baseball cap on top of her head. She grabbed a navy blue zip-up hoodie and packed it into her backpack in case she needed it later. The temperature had dropped and it no longer felt like a warm summer's day. The air was cool, and the sun was hiding behind the clouds. It would get colder the later it got in the day.

Jonah met her at the door with a backpack slung across his shoulder.

"What's in the backpack?" she asked him.

"Water. Food. Enough sustenance to keep my sister from turning into a major grump," he said. "So you don't get hangry."

"Ha. Ha," she said sarcastically. "Good thinking, though, Shrimp."

"Like usual."

"Don't get cocky," she said and spun in the other direction.

"Bosco!"

Bosco ran into the room upon her call, his tail wagging and his tongue out.

"Okay, we're ready to roll," she said.

***

"How much longer?" Jonah griped as they winded their way through the woods.

"Quit being such a baby," Ellie ordered, leading the way. She liked that she was back in charge again. This was her territory. It's where she ruled. He couldn't boss her around here.

"We've been walking forever." He slumped his shoulders and frowned.

"Only an hour. I checked my watch when we left," Ellie said. "We probably have another hour to go. Can you handle it?"

"Is this the same crappy watch that lost 3 and a half hours the other day?"

"Whatever," she mumbled.

They continued to walk on the well worn trail, passing tree after tree. A strong breeze from the west swayed their branches back and forth. Animals rushed to shelter, tuned in to the inclement weather.

"It smells like rain," Ellie said, noticing the drop in temperature. It was cool yet humid, and the air had a mossy scent.

"It can't smell like rain, Ellie," Jonah argued.

"Wanna bet?" she challenged, continuing to trudge along the trail, knowing that the cave was almost upon them. She looked up, seeing the sky was no longer gray and cloudy but dark and ominous. A storm was brewing. They continued on the trail in silence, hearing the ruffling of trees and the whisper of the wind.

Ellie knelt to the ground, pushing the rhododendron bush

out of the way. She indicated for Jonah to follow suit. He made a strange face, and she nodded encouragingly, waving for him to crawl behind her.

He dropped to all fours and followed her closely. Ellie took the flashlight out of her backpack and turned it on. The bright light shined in the pitch black cave. Ellie stood up and told Jonah to do the same. She walked toward the exit, following the flashlight's beam of light.

"This way," she said to Jonah.

They continued to head toward the exit as Ellie steadily held the flashlight in her hand.

For some reason she expected Sam to be on the other side of the lake, gathering firewood or fishing with a bow and arrow. But he wasn't.

She looked in every direction, a small part of her hoping he'd show up, but the search was in vain, and he was nowhere to be found. She watched as Jonah looked up, staring at the massive granite and tilting his head down to see the jade colored lake that separated the two rock walls. She could tell by his expression that he was in awe, truly impressed by the site in front of him.

"Beautiful, isn't it?"

"Unreal," he said, still taking it all in.

"Come on. We've still got a ways to walk and that rain cloud is getting closer." She gestured for him to follow.

They continued to move through the dense forest, pushing thorny bushes out of their way and pressing forward. The smell of burning wood permeated the air. A soft, low voice could be heard far off in the distance. Bosco was the first to hear it, and then Ellie noticed. Bosco charged ahead, leaving Ellie and Jonah behind.

"Where's he going?" Jonah asked.

"To Sam," Ellie said. "He hears him singing."

They continued their way toward Sam's voice. Bosco barked, and Ellie heard Sam stop singing and speak to him in a soft, friendly voice. Her heart skipped a few beats, and her palms became clammy.

Sam sat on one of the tree stumps, Bosco rested next to him, his head on Sam's lap. He patted him on the head and hummed quietly. It was just him out there; no one else was outside.

"Sam," Ellie said in a quiet voice. He turned to face her, his smile weak.

"I didn't know if I'd ever see you again," he said, slowly standing up. "Then Bosco showed up, and I hoped you weren't far behind him."

"I know," she answered. "I brought my brother Jonah with me." She pointed to Jonah who offered Sam a smile as he glanced around, noticing the rustic cabins and all that surrounded it.

"Hey." Jonah waved, studying Sam's odd sense of fashion.

"Hello," he said.

"Where is everyone?" Ellie asked.

"Inside," he said and grew quiet for a moment. "They ain't in right spirits."

"You mean they're sad?" Ellie asked, plopping down on one of the stumps.

He sat down next to her. "No. They ain't sad."

"What's wrong?" she asked with concern. Her heart ached. She didn't want anything to happen to these people. Crazy or not, they had big hearts and didn't hesitate to save her life.

"They have been feeling ill," he explained. "We all have.

Sometimes when we get up after sitting, the ground seems to be moving fast, and all of us feel so spent," he said with a sad expression. "We're plumb tired. All of us." His hair was more unkempt than usual, and his facial hair was longer.

"I'm sorry," Ellie said consolingly. "Maybe you all have the flu?"

"No. We ain't that kind of sick. It's difficult to explain."

"Try me. My dad is a surgeon, and I used to read his medical books for fun."

"You'd look at them for nudey pictures, Ellie, not to enlighten yourself," Jonah added.

She shot him a dirty look and continued, "Maybe I can help."

"That's real nice of you, but I don't know that you can. What we're feeling ain't a sickness. I don't right know what it is," he said, frowning. He stood up and offered his hand to her. Ellie took it and got up from the tree stump. "I'll take you'uns inside. Looks like rain." He looked up at the dark clouded sky.

The roar of thunder startled Bosco. He nuzzled closely to Ellie, whimpering at the rumbling from above. "It's okay," she said in a soothing, hushed tone. "He's scared of lightening," she explained to Sam.

He quickly nodded and motioned for her and Jonah to follow him inside his cabin. Droplets of water began to fall from the sky, faint at first, and then in buckets within a matter of seconds. They stepped up their pace, running into the cabin.

Their clothes were damp. Ellie and Jonah stood at the cabin's entrance, and Sam motioned for them to sit down at the table.

"Where is everyone else?" Ellie asked, her voice echoing in the empty room.

"They're over there." He pointed to the other cabin. "I figured we could talk for a spell before we see them."

Sam waited for Ellie to sit down before he sat on one of the chairs.

"This table is nice," Jonah said, feeling the grain of wood with the tip of his fingers.

"Thank you," Sam said. "Me and Moses made it."

"I'm impressed," he said. "I can't build jack squat."

"That's not all you can't do," Ellie quipped.

Sam interrupted their squabble and said to Ellie, "I'm real glad I got to see you again."

"I'm sorry I left the way I did. Me and my mouth." She exhaled. "I found something I thought you needed to see."

"What is it?" he asked.

She took the back pack off of her shoulders and unzipped it, pulling out the neatly folded papers from the library. "This," she pointed, "is proof that I wasn't lying to you. That the war is over."

She pushed the paper further in his direction and allowed him to let it sink in. She wondered how he would take it. Would he be in shock? Would he be just as confused as she was about the whole thing?

He read the entire sheet of paper, word for word, not missing one single detail. She could see he was distraught, his forehead was wrinkled, the lines around his gray eyes creased. His lips twisted to the side into a crooked frown. "I don't understand," he said almost with desperation. "How is this possible?"

"I don't know, Sam, but I felt you needed to know. The war is over and has been for a very long time."

"We've been here for two years. I was fighting in the war a little over two years ago, and you're telling me it's been over for how long?" he asked, searching her face.

"Almost one hundred and fifty years," she whispered, realizing the epic proportions of the words she just uttered to him. "It's 2013, Sam."

He cupped his hands on both sides of his cheeks. "That don't seem right. It's only been two years," he stated emphatically.

She touched Sam's arm. Jonah noticed and raised his eyebrows. She shot him a stern look and continued to keep a firm hold onto Sam's arm. "I'm telling you the truth, Sam. You have to believe me. I don't know how this happened, but for some reason time has slowed down for you and your family."

He scanned the paper over more than once and sat silently, taking it all in. He pressed his fingers against his temples and let out a long winded sigh. Silence pervaded the room.

"I reckoned you were telling the truth," Sam finally said. "None of us want to accept it, but you talk so queer and that device you had on you wasn't like anything we had ever seen."

"I wish I had an explanation for you, but I don't," Ellie said.

"It don't add up. None of it does, but if you say it's over and this paper does too, I have to accept it on a leap of faith. I know you ain't lying to me."

"I'm not, Sam."

His eyes began to water. "Everyone I knew is gone now," he said in a whispered tone. "They're all gone." He looked down and slightly shook his head.

Ellie placed her hand on his, trying to offer him comfort.

He looked up at her with sad eyes. "Everything I knew ain't ever going to be the same. If I went back to Sawyer, it'd be different. Can you imagine waking up one day and discovering everything and everyone you knew was gone?"

"No, Sam, I can't. I'm so sorry," she said, struggling to find the right words to say.

He took a deep breath and blinked his watery eyes. "It ain't your fault, and there's nothing you can do. It is what it is," he said and sighed.

Sam stared out the window, watching the rain fall. Ellie looked at Jonah, who was just as much at a loss for words as Ellie was.

After several minutes of silence, Sam finally spoke and asked, "What else were you going to show me?" He looked down at the other paper.

She slid the paper in front of him. "Is this the Ernest Price you knew?"

He picked it up, studying it carefully. He peered at it closer, his face a few inches from the paper, "It could be him," he said, looking at her and then at it again. "I can't right tell."

"Is it Virginia's fiancé?" she pressed.

"I can't see his face clear enough. Don't right know how it could be him. When did you say this was from?"

"The 1970s. Almost forty years ago," Ellie said, her voice at a near whisper.

He got up and stalked toward the front door. He wobbled a bit and tried to catch his balance. Ellie stood up and moved close to him.

"Are you okay?" she asked.

"How can it be him?" he said more to himself than to her. He opened the door, sticking his hand outside, allowing the pellets of water to hit the surface. And he stood there motionless—staring at nothing, allowing the rain to soak his hand. The strong force of winds blew rain toward him, dampening his clothes and the cabin. Yet there he stood. Ellie watched him, wondering if he was going mad. She would if she were in his shoes. With the little bit of information she uncovered, she felt unsettled.

He pulled his hand toward his chest and gently closed the door. He scanned down and inspected his clothes, seeing they were moist. "I wanted to see if I was dreaming," he said to Ellie. "To see if you're really here, if any of this is real. But if this isn't a dream, how come it feels like one?"

"It's all real, Sam. I'm not making this up. I'm really here, and what I'm telling you is the truth," she said, looking up into his eyes. "We're not in the middle of a Civil War. And Ernest? I don't know if it's him, but we need to find out. For your sake and for Virginia's."

He ran his hand across his neck and squeezed. "We can't tell her anything until we know for sure. She's been heartbroken since he left. I don't want her disappointed. It will kill her."

"If it is Ernest, why did he leave?" Ellie asked.

Sam shrugged his shoulders and took a deep resounding breath. "He went to see if the war was over."

"But how come he never came back?" The clap of thunder rattled one of the chairs. Bosco whined and cowered behind Ellie. "It's okay," she said to him.

"I don't know, Ellie. I don't understand any of this," he answered and then asked, "The Yankees won?"

"Yes."

"And slavery, is it abolished?"

"Since the war ended," she said.

He breathed a sigh of relief. "Good." He smiled. "That is the best piece of information I have received in a very long time."

"You're against slavery?" she asked.

"Just because I fought for the Confederacy don't mean I'm for slavery," he said defensively and then realized his abrasiveness. "I apologize," he said.

"It's okay." She folded her arms tight against her chest and slightly shivered.

"I'll start a fire," Sam said, walking to the fireplace. "There's always a draft in this room. Today more than others."

Jonah whispered to Ellie as soon as Sam was out of earshot, "I thought you were full of it, but Johnny Reb is the real deal."

"I told you I was telling the truth," Ellie shot back.

A stack of logs sat inside of the fireplace set for a fire. The logs sat on a a pile of dry pine needles. Sam picked up a piece of flint rock and a small piece of steel from the mantle. He bent down close to the stack of logs and pine needles, placing the flint on top of it. With one hand, he held onto the steel and struck it against the flint. A spark was sent down to a thinner strand of pine needles. The flame ignited the rest, and a fire was started. He blew on the flames, causing the fire to dance its way up to the chimney. The smell of burning wood soon filled the room, and immediately Ellie was comforted.

Ellie sat down on the floor, hovering close to the fire. She rubbed her hands together. Sam pulled a quilt off one of the twin beds and wrapped it around Ellie's shoulders. "Here."

She smiled at him as he sat on the floor across from her. Bosco rested between them, hogging most of the space and reaping most of the benefits of the warmth.

"Come over by the fire," Ellie said to Jonah.

He picked up a chair and took it with him over to the fireplace.

He sat down, his legs stretched out and crossed at the ankles and leaned back, allowing his hands rest in his lap.

"You can come closer," she said. She mouthed, "what's up" to him.

He mouthed, "nothing," and then said out loud, "I'm not that cold. You're the sissy who can't handle temperatures below eighty degrees." The rain continued to fall as the droplets of water pounded the cabin's roof. "It's not going to let up," Jonah said, looking outside. His brows furrowed, and he gave Ellie a look of concern.

"I told you it smelled like rain." Ellie gave a cocky smile.

"You can't smell rain," Jonah insisted.

"Yes you can," Sam said. "The smell of the Earth fills the air— the trees, the dirt, animals—their scent becomes more prevalent. When I can smell it all, I know a storm is a coming."

"Or you can look up in the sky," Jonah said.

"I won't argue that." Sam let out a soft chuckle, and Ellie was glad to see a glimmer of happiness in his sad gray eyes. What she had just shared with him didn't make any sense, and she knew he was still in shock from what she had told him. "Like Miss Ellie, I mean Ellie," he corrected, "was saying, the rain lets you know she's coming. She's a prima donna that way. Sometimes she puts on a big show for you—like today. Other times, she just teases you, giving you a brief taste and making you want her even more. On rare occasions, she feels like sharing and allows the sun to shine his rays while she gives you the best of her." He bent one knee against his chest and folded his arm over it, his other leg stretched out, and his shoe touched Ellie's. "And when that happens, I try to savor it as much as I can."

"What's with the philosophical discussion about rain?" Jonah said and sighed.

"It's true," Ellie said. "There's nothing better than dancing in the rain while the sun shines down on you."

"Oh, brother," Jonah mumbled and rolled his eyes. He opened his back pack and took out two bottles of water and two granola bars. He kept one of each for himself and handed Ellie the others. "I'm in the land of Bizarro," he added.

Ellie shot him a dirty look. She opened her bottle of water and sipped. She looked at Sam who was watching her. "Sorry." She swallowed. "Do you want one?" She pointed to the granola bar.

He shook his head and smiled. "No, thank you."

"Sam, why did Ernest leave to see if the war was over? Why didn't you go?"

"That's a long story, and one I'm not too positive I'm fixin' to share," he said, bending his other leg against his chest and tightly locking his arms over them in a protective stance.

"We've got time," she said, ignoring the last part of his statement. "It's not going to let up outside, and Jonah and I may have to stay the night." She was being persistent, but she had just as many questions for him as he had for her.

"We will?" Jonah said.

"Yeah, unless you want to walk in the woods at night with the coyotes," she answered.

"On second thought, that bed isn't looking so bad right now."

"Anyways, we're all ears." She looked at Sam, giving him an encouraging smile.

"I don't right know that I'm ready to share that side of my life with you," he said pensively.

"Oh." Ellie looked down and frowned.

His foot gently tapped hers, causing her to look back at him. "It ain't a pretty story, and I'd like for you to not hate me."

CHAPTER 15

"I can't imagine there'd be anything that would make me hate you Sam," she said.

"This might, Ellie." A look of worry crossed his face.

"I'm not so easy to judge," she said, trying to soften the mood.

He gave her a crooked smile. "I believe you," he said and his smile faded. "Some things are so terrible you can't help but judge."

The burning wood crackled, and the wind continued to blow violently. Jonah yawned and looked at Ellie sleepily. "What?" he said to them.

"I can't believe you're tired." Ellie said.

"Our little workout wore me out, and I didn't get my required sleep." He let out another yawn.

"You can rest on one of those beds if you'd like," Sam offered.

Jonah stood up without answering and ambled to the closest bed. He plopped down on it and curled himself into a fetal position. Within minutes he was fast asleep.

"Sorry." Ellie felt compelled to apologize, afraid that he appeared rude to Sam.

"Don't be. That bed hasn't gotten much use anyway. Your brother seems to care a lot for you."

"Yeah. He just has a funny way of showing it sometimes."

"I still don't understand any of this," he said.

"I know, Sam, and I wish I could explain it to you. All I know is what I told you." She formed a reassuring smile, but deep down, she was just as confused as he was.

"It's a lot to take in," he admitted.

"If I were you, I'd be a wreck. Considering what you've just learned, you're really calm," she said.

"I ain't that calm. I'm just trying to get my thoughts together. I just need time is all." He realized what he just said and laughed. "Time?" He laughed again. "I guess I don't need more of *that*."

Ellie got onto her knees and spread the quilt out onto the floor. She lay down on it, her elbow resting against the hard floor and her hand propped up behind her head. She looked up at Sam and thought that if slow music was playing, candles were lit, and her brother was gone, it'd be very romantic.

"Would it be impolite if I asked you how old you were?" his voice was at a near whisper.

"No." Ellie smiled. "That's one of the first things you usually find out about someone when you're becoming friends with them."

"I feel like I'm being improper," he said, explaining himself.

"Nope. Not at all," she answered assuredly. "I'm eighteen. How old are you?"

"Older than you."

"That's not an answer. How old?"

He shifted his weight and crossed his legs. His elbows rested in his lap and his finger tips pointed under his stubbly chin. "Twenty-one."

"Oldie," Ellie teased.

"If I'm old, then you must think Granny is ancient," he said.

"Granny is ancient, but don't tell her I said that. I'm afraid of her reaction."

There was little light left in the room. It was dusk, and the sun had long been hidden behind the rain clouds. The lit fire gave a hint of illumination, just enough for Ellie and Sam to see each other.

"What is your full name?" he asked.

"I give you free reign to ask me any questions you want and this is what you want to know?" She laughed and said, "Elisabeth Sofia Morales."

"I like it. I've never heard a last name like yours."

"My dad is Cuban. You probably don't know too many Cubans wherever it is you're from," she said, putting emphasis on the last part of her sentence. She stared him in the eyes, waiting for a response.

"Georgia." He blinked without an expression.

"I figured." She lay down on the quilt and stared up.

"That ain't true and you know it," he said, cocking an eyebrow.

She rolled back over on her side, blowing air out of her lips in a frustrated manner. "Fine. You win."

"This is a first," he kidded.

"Very funny." She stuck her tongue out at him and then quickly retracted it, feeling foolish for flirting so ineptly.

"How many people do you have in your family?" he asked, trying to quell the weirdness that they both felt.

"It's me, Jonah, and my dad," Ellie answered, purposely being evasive.

"And your momma, she's gone?"

"Yes." Answering made it too real. "How did you know?"

"You talked about her in the past," Sam said, noticing her sudden change in demeanor. "I'm sorry," he added. "Mine is too. I don't remember her. She passed when I was a little boy."

"I'm sorry." She felt an instant connection. This was one thing they shared—the loss of their mother. "What about your dad? Where's he?"

"He passed ten years ago. Granny's been taking care of me since that time."

"Is it just you and Virginia?"

He nodded and then asked, "What does a girl your age do in these times?"

"This is your last question and then I get to ask them," she said in a demanding voice, and then smiled. "Let's see," she tapped her fingers against her chin, "go to school, hang out with friends, the usual."

"Do you go courting?"

"Only if you're in a period piece movie." He titled his head to the side and gave her a confused look. "We date. It's called dating, not courting," she explained.

"And do you date?" he asked.

"Sometimes," she said, forcing a straight face. She really wanted to smile and tell him he was a cutie for asking. "What about you?"

He pointed to himself.

"Yeah. You. Do you date?" she asked again.

"I courted a girl before the war, but I haven't seen her since then." His eyes evoked a look of sorrow.

"Sorry," she said, but really, she wasn't.

"It's all right. If the war hadn't started, I don't right know if I would have continued to court, I mean, date her."

"Why's that?" Ellie pushed herself up off the floor and sat upright with her legs crossed, one over the other.

"She had her ideas; I had mine. The two didn't mesh," he said indifferently, but Ellie could tell there was more to the story, and she was desperate to know.

"Like what?"

He guffawed and said, "Look who is asking all of the questions now."

Ellie looked down feeling embarrassed. "I'm so nosy sometimes," she berated herself.

"You mentioned going to school. What type of school do you attend?"

"I just finished high school and will start The University of Miami in the fall. Who knows what I'll major in?" She let out a nervous laugh. "My dad, well, he'd like me to go pre-med like him, but I'm thinking law school. I love to argue, if you couldn't tell."

"I could not tell. You like to argue?" he teased and then asked, "Women can attend the university to study?"

"Oh yeah. Like since forever ago. More women go to college now than men do," she said. "Did you go to college before the war?"

"No." He shook his head and looked down reflectively. "Only rich people go to college and we ain't rich. I wanted to. Went to school as long as I was able. They all call me 'the thinker' 'cause I'm always reading. Used to get fearful teased for liking school as much as I did."

"I hardly ever read. Wish I did, but running comes first." She bit on her lip and scratched the back of her head, staring at Sam pensively. "Why'd you all end up here, Sam?" she asked, throwing his rules out the window. Who cares that he was purposely being vague—that he wasn't sharing a large part of himself with her. She was a master at putting puzzles together; his just might take longer.

He leaned forward and touched the top of her hand. Ellie looked up at him earnestly and their eyes met. "I don't mind you asking me questions. It's just…" he hesitated "some things I just figure you're better not knowing."

She realized she had been holding her breath and exhaled.

"Okay. You keep saying that, and I keep telling you that I don't judge. But whatever. How about you tell me what you want me to know then? I won't ask; you just tell."

***

"I was born in Sawyer, Georgia. It's a farming town in the Appalachian mountains," he explained. "My parents and grandparents were also from there. We're Scotch-Irish, and my ancestors came to America from the big island. They settled first in Pennsylvania and then found their way to Sawyer." He paused for a moment. "Our lives were right quiet. We mainly focused on farming and nothing else. Work came first, and then when some time allowed, we'd let some of life's pleasures slip into our day." He smiled and said, "Playing the fiddle and singing a tune while dancing a jig was one my family's favorite things to do. We come from a long line of musicians. My daddy and his daddy before him were able to sing a tune in perfect pitch."

"Is that who taught you how to sing?"

Sam nodded and then said, "I learned to love music at a young age. Singing brought me joy. It became my favorite past time and filled some life into my days when they felt empty. There were others in Sawyer who enjoyed hearing me sing, but thought I was plumb crazy for being so studious and humming all the time. They said I wasn't like everyone else." He shrugged. "I guess it's 'cause I wanted more out of life." He frowned. "Sometimes it ain't easy being different. You try so hard to be normal but it don't feel right. I just wanted to soak up as much knowledge I could," he said.

"There is no such thing as normal, Sam."

He blinked in recognition to what she said. "I ain't never been anywhere outside Sawyer till I fought in the war," he told Ellie, the fire reflected into his gray eyes, and Ellie could see they were lost in thought.

"Sure I'd been on adventures to London and Monte Cristo through the written words from my favorites, Dickens and Dumas. These were places I'd smelled, tasted, and touched—places that felt real to me as if I was a part of the adventure. But it was all fantasy, in my imagination." He pointed to his head and tapped. "I wanted to travel—to meet people different than me—to talk with strangers and use my five senses in unknown places. But there weren't no money, and the country was at war. The idea of packing up and traveling around the country wasn't a realistic one."

"Where'd you go when you fought in the war?" she asked, and he held up his finger and gently skimmed it against her lips shushing her. His finger lingered longer than needed on Ellie's parted lips, and she could feel a few goosebumps forming on her arms. She was thankful she had on her hoodie so he couldn't see them.

"Let me finish," he said playfully and formed a crooked grin. "I was in Savannah for a while. It was different than Sawyer—bigger, bustling with people, and hot. The air was thick with heat. I've never been so miserable in my life. 'Course the weather wasn't the only reason I was miserable. It was a terrible time to be there— everyone was full of fear. You could see it in their eyes, in the way they moved. And I never thought I would feel this way, but I missed home. Ain't that how it always is? You don't yearn for something until you don't have it with you anymore."

Ellie knew that was the truth. She nodded in understanding, giving Sam the signal to continue.

"There's this thing about home. Nothing ever smells as good, tastes as good, feels as good, 'cause it ain't home, it's a replacement, and it'll never compare 'cause you're constantly looking back, thinking about how great home was. I'm at a place in my life now where I don't compare, because looking back causes me too much pain."

"Would you go back?"

"No." He shook his head slightly. "I want to explore and see the country, and I can't do much of that in Sawyer. It'll always be home to me though." He cleared his throat and asked, "I'm thirsty. Do you want a drink?"

"Sure," Ellie said, looking at her empty water bottle and feeling a scratch in the back of her throat from the granola bar.

He stood up, strolled over to the table for the jug of water, and carried it back with him. Ellie watched as he glanced at Jonah and then back at her.

"He's not going to wake up anytime soon," Sam said, handing her the jug and allowing her to take a sip first. He leaned next to the fireplace, his ankles crossed, and his arms propped up on the mantle. Ellie reached up to hand him the jug after she took several vigorous sips. He held it with both hands and drank.

"Probably not," she answered. "Did you join the Confederate Army?"

He bent over and put the jug down on the floor and then shot back up. "I thought you said you weren't going to ask any questions," he teased. "Yes. I joined the army," he answered. "Everyone did."

"So you wanted to join?"

He inhaled a heavy breath. "It was what you did."

"What's that mean? Just because everyone else joined, you did too?"

He tugged on a few hairs on his chin thinking for a moment. "No. It wasn't like that. If you were an able bodied man from the south you joined," he said it like it should be clear as water to her, but Ellie was still struggling with the concept.

"K," she said. "I get it. It was..." she held up her fingers and made quote marks "the thing to do."

He had become so accustomed to her sarcasm, he let it slide off his shoulders. "If you didn't join, you were a scallywag, a loathsome sort. Only reason a man wouldn't join was 'cause he was too old or already injured. Ernest joined with me. We were," he started and then corrected himself, "I mean are best friends. He asked Virginia to marry him right before he left, and she eagerly accepted. She's been sweet on him since we were younguns. We all joined together: Rufus, Horace, Jeremiah, Ernest and me."

"Who were Rufus, Horace and Jeremiah?"

"Horace and Rufus Boyd are my neighbors. We grew up right next to each other since I was a youngun. Granny don't much like them, said they're trouble. They are always getting into something, I 'spose." He shrugged. "I don't mind them much. Horace saved my life in battle. I can't forget something like that."

"That's understandable," Ellie said sympathetically. "How'd he save your life?"

"A Yankee soldier had me pinned to the ground with his sword at my neck. I knew he was going to strike me dead within a matter of seconds. Horace came from behind him and stabbed him," Sam answered with a wry face.

Ellie shuddered, picturing what Sam had just shared with her.

"Granny wasn't too keen on them being here with us, but I

couldn't leave them stranded..." Sam added.

"What about Jeremiah?" Ellie asked, killing the silence.

"He's my cousin, Uncle Caleb's son. He lied about his age to get into the army. Never understood that." Sam shook his head, looked down and then peered back up at Ellie.

"Was that common?"

"Yes. There were plenty of boys in the army with us." He gave a pained expression. "Sad to see when their life is stolen right before your own eyes. We had one boy in the company with us who was fourteen years old. Never got to live," Sam said, the sound of resentment in his voice, "to see anything."

Ellie changed the subject, seeing it was a sore subject for him. "Why'd they all go to see if the war was over?"

"Safer in numbers. If they were going to be attacked, they had a fighting chance to stay alive."

"Why didn't you go with them, Sam? How come Jeremiah didn't stay behind?" Ellie knew she was prying, asking questions that he didn't want to answer for whatever secretive reason.

"I had my family to take care of," Sam said, leaving Ellie unsatisfied with his answer. "Jeremiah insisted on going, and we allowed him to. I wish he was here with us right now."

"Did you..." she started and hesitated.

"What?" Sam asked, encouraging her to continue.

"Did you own slaves?" She knew it was brazen to ask, but she had to know.

His jaw tightened, and his eyes flickered. His hands gripped onto his thighs. "I ain't never had a slave. No one in my family has. We do all our farming by ourselves."

"I thought," Ellie started, but Sam cut in.

"You just assumed 'cause I fought in the war and 'cause I'm from the south? Well, you're wrong," he snapped, his voice loud and his breath short and raspy.

She got up off the floor in a hurry and stood near him. "It was a reasonable question; no need to get bent out of shape," she shot back. Her crossed her arms defensively; she raised her eyebrows, glaring at him.

Sam continued to breathe heavy. They were inches apart, so close that they could smell each other's breaths. Still seething in anger, Sam shook his head, disgusted.

He pointed his finger at her, his eyes narrowed. "Fire in the heart sends smoke to the head."

"What?"

"It's a German proverb. It means we should stop quarreling. I see my point; you see yours."

"That's it?" Ellie said with frustration, her tone still clipped. "I get some old school mantra and all is supposed to be forgiven?"

"What more do you want?" he asked with exasperation, throwing his arms up in the air.

"I don't know," she said with a pout. Arguing was so natural and winning was always her goal.

"Your ears turn red when you are angry," he said, a hint of a grin showing.

She touched her ears, feeling their warmth. "No, they don't," she said, still cupping them.

"Yes, they do." He laughed. He took her hands off of her ears and replaced them with his. "They're red from here to here." His finger slid from the top of her ear to the bottom of her ear lobe causing Ellie to lose her breath.

"So?" she said, catching her breath, refusing to make eye contact with him.

Sam softened his tone and said, "I didn't mean to raise my voice at you. That was uncalled for."

"I accept your apology," she said in a haughty tone.

He laughed in disbelief. "I didn't apologize, but if it will provide you comfort, I am sorry. Do you have anything you want to say?" His tone sounded parental, and Ellie didn't like it.

"The rain has stopped," she said, gesturing to the window.

He raised an eyebrow.

"Okay. I'm sorry for being rude," she said in childish fashion and then changed her attitude after reading his face. "It's who I am, and I can't help it."

"I believe you can," he argued. "When you argue, try to listen to the other person's side. There is always another side to the story," he said and let out a sigh. "This is new for me."

"What is?" Ellie stared up at him, noticing the small indention in his chin, the few freckles he had on his nose, and the way the right side of his bangs curled up. She was tempted to wind the curl around her finger and twirl it.

"You're different— not like any woman I've ever met, and you're asking me all these questions."

"I just want to know you," she admitted unabashedly.

"I want to know you too, but you need to be patient with me -with all of this. I'm just as confused about all of this as you are." He placed his hand on her shoulder, and she immediately felt static electricity, like when she took her clothes out of the dryer and they clung together, creating an instant spark. The jolt ran directly from her shoulder to her beating heart.

"Okay," her voice was low.

Something about Sam stirred her up, making her insides feel like a tornado whirling round and round again. It wasn't like her—to feel this way and get all worked up over a guy—but she couldn't deny the attraction she had for him. The strange man from another time who still was a mystery to her.

"What are we going to do about this Ernest you found in that photo?" Sam asked, taking his hand off of her shoulder, and Ellie wondered if she had read him all wrong. But she felt the spark, the intense sensation the moment he had touched her.

A look of disappointment crossed her face, and she decided to quit being so swoony over him. There were more important things to contend with. "We should probably go to town, to see what someone in that church may know. Maybe they'll be able to tell us something. We can go together and see," she offered, trying not to sound too hopeful. She wanted to spend more time with him.

He nodded his head. "I agree."

"Good." She smiled and marched over to Jonah. She stood next to the bed and turned to face Sam. "I don't know how it could be Ernest—how he's older than you, or how you're here. But you're real, and you're here even though it doesn't make any sense." She shook Jonah, poking and prodding him. "Get up, Shrimp. We've got some sleuthing to do."

CHAPTER 16

Jonah moaned something unintelligible. He shooed Ellie away and rolled over on his other side, his back to her. She poked him harder this time. Jonah could sleep through a war zone. If a bomb dropped outside, he'd manage to get his seven hours of sleep and REM all without once opening his eyes.

"Shrimp. You're not at home. Get up," she said in a terse tone.

"Think you should leave him be?" Sam whispered.

"No way. He can handle it. Don't feel sorry for him," she said.

Jonah sat up, giving Ellie a nasty look. He mumbled a few curse words and eloquently flipped her off with both middle fingers.

"Right back at ya," she said and hit him on the head.

He swung his arm intending to retaliate, but Ellie's reflexes were too adept, and she blocked him. "Nice try. Now get up."

He got out of bed, and yawned heavily. "Why'd you feel the need to get me up? I was enjoying my little power nap." He looked at her sleepily, his eyes still half open.

"Power nap," she scoffed. "More like full-on snooze. You've been sleeping for hours. It stopped raining." She pointed to the window.

"So. We can't go home, Ellie. It's dark out and everyone knows you don't walk in the woods at night."

"We're gonna go talk to Sam's family—to let them know what we're doing. Then we're leaving," she said, walking with Sam toward the front door.

"What do you mean 'we,' and why are we leaving in the middle of the night? Coyotes, remember?" he said sardonically, although a tinge of fear could be heard through his sarcasm.

"Sam has a bow and arrow, a knife, and a gun. And I have a flashlight. Together we're kicking ass and taking names. Besides, he's been in the army and could probably defend us with his eyes closed and his hands tied behind his back. I think we're going to be okay," she said, patting him on the shoulder condescendingly.

Jonah shrugged her hand off of him. "Whatever. This is some crazy shit and you know it."

"Just be cool. K?" she said, widening her eyes and pleading with him.

He reluctantly followed them to the door, and they treaded through the mud to get to the other cabin.

They were seated around the fire, appearing tired and sluggish. None of them were doing anything, and what little talking they had been doing ceased when Sam opened the door. Granny was the first to say something. She greeted Ellie more warmly than she anticipated.

"Welcome," she said and gestured for Ellie to sit around the fire.

Ellie wiped her shoes on the outside wall of the cabin, attempting to get rid of the mud. Thick layers of it were still caked in between each tread of her tennis shoes. She hated to track it into their home.

Virginia stood up and reached out to hug Ellie, who patted her gently in return and immediately let go of her. Guilt consumed her. She knew she was about to tell her a lie and she didn't need her getting all touchy feely—it'd only make things worse.

"This is Jonah, Ellie's younger brother," Sam introduced him. "This is my Granny, Uncle Caleb, my sister Virginia, and our friend Moses."

Virginia offered a wide grin, Uncle Caleb nodded, Granny sized him up, looking at him skeptically, and Moses smiled.

"He's the spittin' image of you, just a boy that's all," Granny said.

"I'm also better looking." Jonah grinned.

She ignored him and said to Ellie, "You left in a mighty big hurry sayin' things that ain't made any sense to us."

Ellie inhaled; her hands gripped her sides. She nodded a distinct yes and said, "Sorry I was so rude. It scared me, and I didn't know how to react." Admitting when she was wrong was hard to do. Telling Granny she was sorry was even more of a challenge. The woman could make Ellie confess to anything, even if there wasn't anything to confess to. She had the same look as Ellie's fifth grade teacher, Mrs. Rochester. She'd look down at Ellie in class with her one good eye (the other was glass) and stare her down until she'd stop whatever it was she was doing.

"We don't right know how to 'splain this. What you said don't add up. Did Sam tell you we ain't been feelin' right since you left?"

"He did."

"Ain't never been ill a day in my life. Now I feel like the ground is movin' all the time. We all do." Her wrinkled face showed signs of worry.

"I told Sam I thought you all may have the flu," she said.

Granny shook her head. "Ain't that," she offered a tight smile and asked, "If the war is over like you say it is, then I 'spect I get to go home soon."

Ellie shook her head remorsefully, hating what she was about to tell her. "You can't."

"'Cause of Sam," Granny said.

Ellie gave her a confused look. "No," she said and looked at Sam, gauging his reaction.

He cut in, "The north won."

"Well, that's good news, 'specially for you," she said to Sam, and Ellie thought that was strange. "Us too," she added. "And slavery?"

"Abolished," Sam answered.

"That's good. That's real good," she said and peered over at Moses. His eyes lit up, and he grinned wide.

The rest of them offered Moses their happiness over the news.

Sam broke their conversation, treading carefully. "The war has been over for some time—just as we all suspected when she left the other day."

"How long?" Granny asked, the gleam in her eyes slowly disappeared.

"Over one hundred and fifty years," he said with a frown, and Granny sat back in her chair in disbelief.

"This is plumb insane," Granny said. "You're tellin' me that I've been here for that long and never aged? I would've died long ago. Ain't make any sense."

Sam shrugged. "It's all I can tell you right now. We have to have faith in Ellie, that what she is telling us is true."

"Faith is blind, and so is love, Sam. Sure it ain't the other that's causin' you to believe this?" Granny asked, her wrinkled brow raised.

Sam didn't answer.

"Did you find out about my Ernest?" Virginia asked Ellie.

Ellie stammered, hating to lie. "Well," she started and Sam saved her. What was she going to tell her, that she found one reference to him and it was from the 1970s?

"She ain't learned anything. We're going to see what we can uncover about him," he said, and Ellie gave him a sincere look of appreciation.

"What about my boy? You'un's keep discussing Ernest, but Jeremiah went with him. What happened to him?" Uncle Caleb interrupted.

"That's what we're going to hopefully find out," Sam said. "Ellie and I are going to go to town to see if we can discover anything."

"He's all that I have. He never should have gone. He should have stayed right here by my side. He was just a youngun," his tone was bitter and sadness filled his hazel eyes.

"I know, and I'm sorry," Sam said apologetically.

"You ain't sorry," Caleb fumed. "We're all here 'cause of you. 'Cause of your choices. 'Cause of your conflict," his voice raised and a look of contempt filled his eyes. "Your decision cost us our lives."

"Shush your mouth, son," Granny ordered. "It was our decision as a family. Sam didn't force it upon any of us and you know it. Don't blame him now 'cause you're a hurtin'. That don't make the pain go away. It only makes it worse."

Sam placed his hand on Granny's shoulder. "Granny. He has a right."

She turned to face him, fire in her eyes. "No he don't. This ain't your doin', Sam. It ain't his either. You did what you thought was right and we supported you 'cause that's what love is. We're in this together."

"Granny, he's right," Sam said quietly. Water filled his eyes to the brink of tears.

She touched his cheek with the palm of her hand. "He ain't. You can't control fate; it has it's own twisted sense of direction." She peered at Caleb; her eyes narrowed. "Tell him you don't mean it 'cause it'll kill him if you don't."

Caleb breathed heavily, shooting Sam an indignant look. "I'll tell him when I'm good and ready. He can live with the pain of not knowing whether or not I forgive him. For what we know Jeremiah left eight months ago, but if what she says is true," he pointed to Ellie, "who knows how long it's been? I have to live with the fact that my son may be gone 'cause of Sam."

Granny frowned. "You're more selfish than I raised you to be and that's a mighty shame," she said with disappointment.

Granny had birthed three children in her life—Thomas, Sam's father, Caleb, and Virginia, her daughter who died at the young age of six from scarlet fever. Thomas idolized his younger sister and named Virginia after her out of remembrance.

A once jovial man, Caleb had turned more bitter since the passing of his wife, the injury inflicted upon him in the war, and the void of Jeremiah. He missed his son and resented that they had to move. More bitter about the war than anyone in the family, Caleb couldn't let any of it go. He bottled it all up, while everyone waited with baited breath for the day it would all explode.

"Sam, you and Ellie go on and find out what you can. Find out if its safe for us to go back home. I 'spect there ain't no home for me to go home to," she said with sadness. "This may be my last place I call home before I go to Heaven." She let out a sigh and patted Sam on the arm.

Sam quietly said to Ellie, "Let's wait until tomorrow morning to leave. Jonah's right. It ain't safe."

***

They left early in the morning. Ellie had wanted to leave as soon as possible. Time was of the essence and not on her side. Her dad would be home within days, and she knew he'd never allow her to traipse around the country with a guy. Ellie knew her father's temperament. He nearly flipped out when Ellie had to call him after her disastrous prom date. Like it or not, she was a daddy's girl.

They arrived at their home in record time. Sam led them most of the way. A natural athlete, Sam was just as fast as Ellie but more skilled in the woods than she could ever be. Moving through the dense forest— through thick brush and shoddy terrain—wasn't a challenge for him. He had been through worse, much, much worse. Trekking up and down steep hills with sharp branches and mosquitos leaving scars was nothing compared to fighting in battle. He had watched his friends die, their blood all over him, while the whole time he hoped he'd just make it through the day.

Ellie had to admit she was impressed by Sam's abilities. She was usually the one in the front—the leader, but on this day she took a back seat and let Sam be the driver. He may not have known about twenty-first century inventions, but he could survive in the most treacherous circumstances. Sam was a survivor.

Sam abruptly stopped when they arrived at their house. He peered up in awe at their home, staring at the place in amazement, as if he were seeing one of the seven wonders of the world. "This is right big," he said, his mouth wide open and his eyes nearly bulging.

"It looks bigger than it is," she said. "Come on." She motioned for him to follow her inside of the house and flipped the light switch, turning on the living room light and brightening up the room.

"What is that?" Sam asked with confusion looking up at the light bulb.

"Electricity," she said simply. "No kerosene lamps around here."

"But how?" he asked, touching the light switch and flipping it on and off and on and off again.

"Electrical currents. Remember the story about Ben Franklin and the kite?" she said.

He nodded.

"Well, there are currents that run through wires and light everything up," she answered.

"There's more to it than that. She just gave you the most basic pre-schooler's description of how electricity works. If you really want to know..." Jonah started.

"Save it for another time, Shrimp," Ellie said.

Sam flipped the switch one more time, turning the light back on. He walked around the main rooms of her home slowly, taking it all in—scanning every intricate detail. He headed over to the fireplace and slid his hand against the stone and then ran his fingers upward across the teak wooden mantle, looking up, noticing the stone touched the high beamed ceilings.

She checked the time on her watch and compared it to the microwave clock. There was an hour and a half difference between the two. Ellie peered closely at her watch and brought it to her ear, hearing the sounds of the hands ticking. It was working which didn't explain the lag in time.

"Jonah," she said quietly. "My watch says it's 8:47 but look at the microwave clock." She pointed.

He glanced quickly and gave a half shrug. "Yeah. So. That watch of yours is a piece of crap."

Ellie remembered she had brought her cell phone along and pulled it out of her pocket. She checked the time. "If my watch is a piece of crap, is my cell phone too? Look." She indicated by showing him her cell phone showed the exact same time as her watch.

Jonah shrugged again and said, "Who knows?"

"It doesn't add up." The bridge of her nose wrinkled and she squinted her eyes.

"This home must have taken a long time to build," Sam said, interrupting them.

"I don't know," Ellie said indifferently. "It's not like *we* built it."

"It's a beautiful home. Is this what all homes look like now?" he asked.

"Nah. This is our vacation home. We live in a pretty basic ranch style house in Florida—none of the frills or anything like this place has. Just a simple three bedroom house with tile floors," she talked as she headed to her bedroom, and Sam followed.

"I've gotta take a shower," she said, spinning to face him. "You can take one after I'm finished."

"Is this your room?" he asked, looking around.

"Yeah. It's kinda a mess," she said, kicking clothes under the bed, and scooping granola bar wrappers off of her chest of drawers and into her trash can when Sam wasn't looking. He was too distracted checking the rest of the place out.

"It's nice," he said, and peered down at the bed. "This is big."

"It's a queen sized bed. You can sit on it," she offered.

"It really ain't proper for me to be in here with you." He moved away from the bed.

She waved her hand in the air. "Please," she groaned. "Like that matters. I'm here to tell you 1860's social etiquette has been gone a long, long time. Most couples live together these days, and it's not a big deal for a guy to hang out in a girl's room."

His eyes widened. "Live together? You mean as man and wife,

right?"

"Most couples try each other out first, you know to see if they're going to make it as a married couple. If they can't live together, it saves them from getting a divorce later on." She rummaged through her dresser drawer searching for items of clothing.

"Divorce? That's unheard of!"

"Not now." She turned to face him, a pair of panties, bra and t-shirt and shorts were wadded into her hands. "About half the marriages end up in divorce."

"That is terrible." He sighed and sat down on her bed. "And no one objects to these couples sharing a home even though they aren't married?"

"No, Sam. It's not taboo or anything. In fact, it's become kinda weird if you don't live together first. It is what it is. One thing I can say, my parents actually loved each other. I hope to love someone like that," she said and then closed her dresser drawer. "I'll be done in about ten minutes. You can hang out here or go ask Jonah to get you some clothes from Dad's closet. We can't go out having you look like the poster boy for the Amish," she said, peering up and down at his ensemble.

He looked down at himself.

"I'm taking my shower now." She closed the bathroom door.

***

Ellie dressed in a pair of tan shorts and a mint green t-shirt. She tied her towel up into a turban, tucking her sopping wet hair up into it. Steam filled the bathroom and the smell of rosemary and mint permeated the room. She opened the bathroom door, letting out some of the hot, humid air and saw her brother and Sam sitting on her bed.

"What's up?" she asked, staring at them both.

"I had him try on Dad's clothes, and as you can see, they don't really fit him," he said, pointing at Sam's tight fitting gray polo that seemed as if it were going to rip into shreds within minutes. She could see his ankles; the jeans were also snug and were way too short. High waters. "I've been explaining the concept of indoor plumbing to him. He's flushed the toilet more than once and likes standing in front of the refrigerator with the door open."

She looked Sam over. "What'll we do?" she fretted about his clothes, taking the turban off of her head and towel drying her hair. She picked up her bottle of perfume from her dresser and spritzed a few sprays on her neck and wrists. Lemon verbena filled the air.

"That's a nice scent," Sam remarked.

"Thanks." Ellie smiled, pleased that he had noticed.

"It's right convenient to be able to shower in your home. We have to wash in the creek, and in the winter, it ain't possible."

"I guess the only thing good about that is everyone else stank just as bad so you didn't stand out," Jonah quipped. He studied Sam again, and said to Ellie, "If you guys are traveling around, he'll need a make over. He needs clothes that fit, and his hair needs to be cut."

Sam touched his brown hair, feeling the loose scraggly hairs that fell to his eyebrows. "There ain't nothing wrong with my hair."

"If you're going for the whole bowl look, then yeah, there's nothing wrong with it," Jonah said. "Trust me, Dude, I'm trying to help you."

"Fine. If we discover we have to go further than Mayfield, we'll get him a hair cut and buy him a new outfit," Ellie said. "We'll stop at Sears."

"Sears?" Jonah said. "Really? Do you *want* him to look his age?"

"Sears is fine," she said, her voice starting to waver. She knew he had a point.

"If you're boring or old," he retorted. "Take him to American Eagle, so he'll at least look cool and not stick out like a sore thumb like he already does."

"Okay. You win, but I'm not made of money." She searched through her dresser drawer and pulled out a wad of bills. She counted them and then said, "I've only got sixty dollars. That won't pay for a hair cut and outfit." She frowned.

"Don't look at me. I don't have any money," Jonah said, holding up his hands.

"I have some Confederate bills in my pocket but I don't right know that'll help you," Sam added and smiled once Ellie and Jonah looked at him to see if he were serious. "I can't have you paying for my clothing. You'uns keep discussing me like I'm one of Virginia's dress up dolls she used to play with."

"Sorry," Ellie said and added, "Quit worrying about me paying for the clothes. I don't mind. There's that whole Confederate money thing that won't do you any good."

"I still don't like it," he said.

She ignored his last remark and said to Jonah, "There's money in Mom's closet."

"How would you know?" Jonah asked skeptically.

"'Cause she told me about it. She said that it was important to have a stash of money for a rainy day. Dad doesn't know she hid money," Ellie said.

"Mom hid money?" he said in disbelief.

"Not in some Lifetime movie way. She just kept some cash handy in case she ever needed it."

"Well. Go get it," Jonah said, urging her.

"How about I tell you where it is and you go get it?" Ellie said, a look of concern crossed her face.

"Why? Is it up high? If so, tall man over here should get it then." Jonah pointed to Sam.

"I'm more than happy to oblige," Sam said, standing up. "Where is it?"

"I just can't deal with going in there right now. Okay?" she said, and her eyes welled up with tears.

Sam touched her on her shoulder and gave her a reassuring look. "I'll go get it," he said quietly, sharing an understanding look with her. "Tell me where it is." He pulled a handkerchief out of his pocket handing it to her. "Here."

She took the handkerchief and gave him a slight smile. "It's on the top shelf in a pink floral box," she sniffed. "Jonah, show him where Mom's room is."

***

Sam came back carrying the pink floral box, carefully and precariously, like he was handing the crown to the queen. He walked slowly and had a determined look on his face. He gently laid the box down on the bed and gave her a look. Ellie moved to the box and took off the lid. The box was full of greeting cards, photos, and pictures that were drawn by Ellie or Jonah. Ellie flipped through the box, taking out a card she had made for her mom. On yellow construction paper, Ellie had written "*To Mom. You Are the Best.*" Inside was a picture Ellie had drawn, a stick figure image of her mother in a white flowing robe complete with angel wings.

"Why did she save this?" Ellie asked, holding the card in her hand and looking to Sam or Jonah to tell her.

"Sentiment. Ellie, Mom was like any other. Think about it. When was the last time you made her something or told her she was the best?" Jonah said, unaware of his sting. He rummaged through the box and pulled out an old photo of him and Ellie in the bath tub—Jonah with a mask and snorkel, and Ellie with a pair of goggles. "What's up with the scuba gear?" Jonah asked, showing Ellie the picture.

She laughed inauthentically. She was more focused on the card, on the stack of cards and things she had made for her mom, and mostly on Jonah's words to her: "*When was the last time you made her something or told her she was the best?*" She couldn't recall. All she had was this as evidence. She pulled out another card, this one was pink construction paper with a big red heart drawn on front with the words, "*I Love You.*"

"She saved every card I made for her. Every last one," Ellie said, struggling to hold back the tears. The last thing she was going to do was break down into a blubbering mess. She had to hold it together.

"She loved you," Sam said.

"I should have made more of these for her," Ellie said, the sound of hurt and regret came to the surface.

"She knew you loved her. That is obvious to me," Sam said, trying to provide comfort.

Ellie wiped a few tears from her eyes. "I don't know. I wasn't very kind to her before she passed away."

"That don't matter. Love ain't about being kind all the time. Sometimes there's hurt and disappointment. If you don't love, you don't care and you don't fight back," he said.

"If that's the case then Mom definitely knew you loved her, Ellie," Jonah chimed in and then said to Sam, "She was always fighting with her."

Sam nodded his head, giving an understanding look.

"Who are you?" Ellie said in between tears.

"What do you mean?" Sam asked.

"You're Mr. Philosophy." A quick laugh came from the depths of her stomach, and a genuine smile flickered across her forlorn face.

"I've just seen things I'm hoping you never have to," he said pensively.

"Oh," she responded, not sure what to say.

"Look. There's no time to be all Doom and Gloom around here. You need to go into town to see what you can find out about this Ernest dude. Plus, he needs to shower," Jonah interrupted.

"He's right," Ellie said to Sam. "We don't have much time. My dad will be home in four days. Get in that shower." She pointed to the room. "I left towels out for you."

He did as he was told and entered the bathroom, leaving the door open. "How does this work?" he asked her, looking at the shower head and knobs.

Ellie walked in and turned the knobs on, water flowed out of the shower head. "This is hot." She pointed to the left knob. "This is cold. Turn them this way to get more or less." She indicated by moving the knobs around in different directions. "I'll give you some privacy. When you're finished, turn the knobs this way." She exited the bathroom, closing the door behind her. She sat on her bed and placed all of the contents, with the exception of the five one hundred dollar bills, back into the box.

CHAPTER 17

Ellie sat down in one of the chairs in the living room, waiting for Sam to finish taking his shower and get dressed. Jonah laid on the couch; Bosco rested on the floor beneath him. The TV was turned on, but the volume was low, and Jonah wasn't really watching the screen. Ellie let out a deep sigh.

"What are you going to do if you find out it's this Ernest guy?"

"I have no idea. It wouldn't make sense," Ellie said.

"Like it makes sense that Sam's from The Civil War era," Jonah said.

"True." She couldn't argue that.

He sat up and leaned against the couch arm, his legs still draped on the couch cushion.

"It shouldn't have been 10:00 a.m. when we got back," she said. "I checked the time on my watch when we left Sam's place and it was a little after seven. That hike doesn't take that long. Something is sketchy with the time. I know that for sure."

"Duh," Jonah scoffed. "There's obviously something up with the time. They're from the frickin' Civil War and your time has been all screwy since you met them."

"You know, you've always been a smart ass, but you've turned into a bitter, angry person since Mom," she started, saying things she had wanted to say for a long time.

"You're a hypocrite, Ellie," he spat out.

"How's that?" she leaned forward in a challenging stance.

"Who runs all the time? Who acts like nothing bothers her? Those were the first real tears I saw from you in a long time. If I had known it'd take a stupid box, I would have scavenged her closet when we got here," he snapped. "Quit criticizing me until you look at your own self in the mirror. You've got as many issues as I do," he said, refusing to make eye contact with her. He turned the volume up on the television and tapped the couch for Bosco to leap up and join him.

Ellie was stunned, speechless by her brother's brazen insults, by his accusations. She was dealing, wasn't she? That's what she told herself to believe. But beneath the surface of that facade she knew he had a point. She couldn't point the finger at him until she evaluated her own baggage. And some of it was lodged deep into her subconscious, waiting to unleash like a terrible storm.

Sam cleared his throat letting them know he was in the room. How long had he been in there, neither Ellie nor Jonah knew, but by the look on his face, she knew he had heard every single word.

"I'm dressed," he said, the jeans and shirt tight, accentuating every muscle.

Ellie jolted up. "Shrimp, if Dad calls, tell him I'm sleeping or in the shower or running. Make something up. Don't let him know I'm gone, k?"

"Got it," he chided. "I'm not twelve, Ellie."

"I know," she breathed. "He can't find out. He'd freak."

"Fine. Whatever. Bosco and I will be hanging out here having fun without the likes of you," he grumbled.

She ignored his insult and patted Bosco on the head and gave him a hug. "Sorry you're stuck with Shrimp. I wish I could take you with us boy, but I can't," she said to him while glaring at Jonah.

"Bosco and I will be just fine," Jonah said.

"It was a pleasure meeting you," Sam said to Jonah.

"Likewise. Sorry you're stuck with my sister," he said and then softened his tone, "Be careful, both of you." He looked specifically at his sister.

***

Sam trudged slowly with much hesitation toward the CRV. He gave it a strange look. He ran his fingers across the doors, stopping at the tires, and continued moving around the car, looking at it in wonder.

"And you just sit in it, and it'll take us somewhere, like a horse?" he said to Ellie, who nodded encouragingly.

"It's totally safe, Sam. Just get in. Trust me." She beamed.

She opened the door for him, and he sat down, gripping onto the armrest like he was on a roller coaster, climbing up hill about to roll down hundreds of feet. Beads of sweat formed on his forehead, and he wiped them off with the back of his hand. Ellie turned up the air conditioning and pushed the vents in his direction.

"You need to put your seat belt on." She motioned to hers.

He pulled on the seat belt unsure of what to do. She unstrapped hers and bent over, her hair touching his face. She could feel his breath on her ear—warm with a hint of chocolate and granola. He and Jonah had obviously been raiding the pantry while she showered. She latched the belt and moved back in driving position.

"I know sitting in here is freaking you out, but it's safe. Trust me," she said, trying to sound reassuring.

"I'm fine," Sam lied; he held on tight to the arm rest and scanned the interior of the car like it was an alien spaceship.

She plugged her IPOD into the radio and scrolled through her playlists. Once she found what she was searching for, she clicked on it and turned the volume up just a tad—enough that they could both hear the music but talk if they needed to.

The song started, and Sam instantly recognized the piano keys. He stared down at the radio and adjusted the knob, turning the volume up and down. "You can hear music in here, too?" he asked, and Ellie nodded. He hummed along and smiled. "I've heard this before on that device of yours. This is your favorite song."

"Yep, when we were in the woods," Ellie answered, impressed that he remembered. Most guys didn't pay that close attention. "It's Journey." She turned the volume up, and Sam began to sing along, his voice in harmony to the lead singer's. He caught on to the lyrics, singing them accurately and beautifully. They rolled off of the tip of his tongue with ease. The song continued to play and Sam's soft, alluring voice could be heard throughout the CRV.

Ellie let it all soak in—feeling a sense of overall peace at the sounds of his harmonious voice. Her favorite song and Sam's voice together—*what could be better*, she thought?

The song ended and Sam stopped singing.

Ellie said, "You sing so pretty." Her cheeks turned red, and she internally berated herself for such a stupid compliment. "I like your voice," she added.

"Thank you," he said with an air of humbleness.

"That song reminds me of my mom," she said. "I listen to it everyday."

"If I would have had something like this to make me think of my loved ones, I'd listen to it every day too."

They continued their drive on winding mountainous roads finding their way to the town of Mayfield. For a weekday, the town was thriving with business. A line of cars filled Main Street as Ellie pulled the CRV into the town's only gas station, the only one within miles. Tourists walked on the sidewalks, carrying shopping bags in one hand and ice cream cones in the other. Crowds filled outdoor tables, eating lunch and socializing, enjoying the impeccable weather.

Ellie rolled the windows down and turned the car off. "I have to get gas, and I'm thirsty."

"All right," Sam said, looking at everything around them.

"Stay in the car, k?" she said and flipped the gas tank lid open. She jumped out and pumped the gas, filling the tank. "I'm going inside," she said as if she were talking to a child. She almost added, "Don't move," but figured that would be too bossy. "Do you want anything?"

"No, thank you," Sam said.

Ellie walked inside the gas station and searched the refrigerator for a caffeinated beverage. She pulled out a bottle of iced coffee—packed with more than enough sugar—and grabbed a Cheerwine off the same shelf as a treat for Sam. On her way to check out, she also picked up a variety of candy for Sam to experience and made her way to the cash register. Once she paid, she left the store and returned to the car.

Expecting to see Sam, she was surprised her car was empty—all of the windows were down and no one was inside. She searched the gas station, seeing if she could find him, but came up short. He was nowhere in sight. She wondered if he had gone inside to use the restroom but knew she would have seen him if he had. She opened the driver's door, placed the drinks in their cup holders and threw the bags of candy down.

She scanned the parking lot one more time and turned around, facing the opposite direction, seeing if he had crossed the street.

Maybe he got hot and wanted some fresh air, she thought. She was trying not to panic.

A small, one story structure next to the Visitor's Information Center caught her eye. "Appalachian & Civil War History Museum. Free Admission," the sign read. Ellie knew if anything was going to cause Sam to venture out, it'd be a museum focused on that subject matter. Ellie hurried into her car and drove across the street, parking in front of the building.

She pushed the heavy door open and was immediately overcome by an odor of moth balls. The smell was a familiar one to her. Her grandfather had a penchant for placing mothballs in each closet of his house or anywhere else that he deemed necessary. Ellie's childhood memories of visiting her grandfather were filled with warmth and love, along with the terrible smell of those stinky moth repellants. She once asked her father what his obsession was with them. There wasn't a rampant moth problem in Florida. Her dad just shrugged his shoulders and said, "In Cuba it was hard to buy new clothes. He had to keep what he had in good condition. When he came to the US, he had the same mindset," he said and paused for a moment and then chuckled lightly. "He swore by those things. He said they killed silverfish, mice, and snakes. My mother was terrified of mice. I think that was the main reason he spread them all over the house, to ward off the critters."

The musty scent overpowered the antiquated building. A hand-written sign taped to a glass jar laid on an oak table near the entrance. "Donations accepted." Ellie felt compelled to place a dollar bill in the nearly empty jar.

A carpeted make-shift wall blocked Ellie's view of the rest of the museum. Tacked to it were posters of events and other goings on around the town. She didn't spend much time reading them and wandered her way around the wall and into the actual museum.

Sam was easy to spot. She could hear his deep slow drawl a mile a way. He was talking animately to the museum docent, an older man with a white mustache and white satiny hair. Ellie made her way over to them barging in on their discussion.

"Hi," she said, tapping Sam on his shoulder.

"Hello." He smiled and said, "This is Mr. Clyde."

"Hi." Ellie waved. "We need to get going, don't ya think?" she said to Sam.

"Mr. Clyde was telling me about his great-granddaddy who fought in the war," Sam began.

"Yes. This young man sure does know a lot about the war. Bet we could make a docent out of ya." He grinned broadly and nudged Sam on the arm.

"I don't right know about that. You're doing a fine job, sir. If I didn't know any better I'd think you had been in the war yourself," Sam said.

He chuckled and then coughed, hacking up phlegm. He cleared his throat. "I sure do look it, don't I?"

"No sir. That's not what I mean," Sam said with concern.

"I'm just kidding you boy." He laughed again. "I don't want to take up all your time. Y'all go on and look around. I'll be right here to answer any questions you have." He sat down in a folding chair and opened his large print book. Ellie could see the text from where she stood. He pulled a magnifying glass out of his pocket and placed it in front of the book, hovering close and leaning into it.

"I was worried," Ellie whispered. "When I came out, you weren't there."

"I apologize. I got out of that buggy to stretch my legs, and when I turned around I saw the sign, I had to see what was in here."

She decided not to correct him about calling it a car. That'd wait for another time. The last thing she wanted to do was seem too pushy. "Did you look around?"

He shook his head. "I've been talking to Mr. Clyde, but I'd like to if that is all right with you?"

"Sure," Ellie said, realizing the importance of what this place might mean to him. If she were trapped in a time warp and found a twenty-first century museum, she'd be into it, too.

To the right of them was a replication of Appalachian living. They walked through the entrance, and Sam touched the log siding as they entered the inside of a one room cabin. A faux kerosene lamp shined inside, allowing them to see the few pieces of furniture in the home.

Ellie caught her breath. Everything inside looked similar to Sam's, from the quilts to the table and chairs. "It's like your home," she said, and sat down on the lumpy straw filled bed. For a museum in the middle of the mountains with only the money from locals to support it, the curator had made sure it felt authentic. "Even the bed..."

"This is right correct," Sam said, sitting down on one of the chairs. He folded his hands and placed them on the table. He looked around and stared at everything.

"Did everyone live like this?"

"Yes," Sam answered, his voice distant and somewhere else.

Ellie gave him time to let it all sink in and watched as the faux dim lighting flickered in his gray eyes. He was lost in thought. "You miss home?" Ellie asked, knowing the answer to her question. She sat down across from him.

He nodded. "I didn't want to leave but had to. I was going to go alone, but after our town was ransacked by the Yankees and other vagrants, I found I wasn't alone. They stole our cows, hogs, and most of our food. Granny would have shot them all if she could. Taking her away from home was a terrible feat," he said. "She was the only one who wanted to stay. Everyone else couldn't see any reason to. The town had died, and our hearts along with it."

"That's awful," Ellie said. "I'm so sorry."

"It was the war. Horrendous things like this were common," he said, sadness filled his eyes. "No one knew who to trust. Some of our neighbors were on the side of the Yankees. Some weren't. One neighbor led a Confederate unit to a Yankee ambush. She said she hated the war 'cause it killed her son."

"But that was her own people?"

Sam let out a long, drawn breath. "We were fighting our brothers. Yankee or not, we all were from the same country. There were many like her—those that hated the war and would do anything to stop it even if it meant betraying their own."

"What happened to her?" Ellie asked.

"She was killed."

"Oh," Ellie breathed, feeling the weight of Sam's sorrow.

"Most of us in Sawyer were like her. We wouldn't betray our own brethren; but we opposed the war and all it stood for," he confessed. "We were a simple farming community and didn't have no qualms with the Union. The bigwigs and plantations owners were the ones who wanted to fight. Not us."

"I never knew. I guess I just assumed the entire south wanted to fight."

"Who wants to go to war— a simple man, perhaps. But an

intelligent man will always find a way to make peace," he said. "The men I killed will haunt me until the day I die."

Ellie reached across the table and placed her hand on top of his. She gently squeezed it and gave him a sympathetic look.

He blinked and his lips curled up, emitting a faint smile. "You're right nice to sit and listen to me."

"I want to know you," she said.

He stood up, his hand still clasped around hers and said, "Why don't we get out of here and see the rest?"

"Sounds good," she said, getting up and following him into the rest of the museum.

They stopped at each exhibit. Sam would confirm what they read or saw, giving her more details. His eyes lit up and a genuine smile crossed his face. It was the first time she had seen him so excited.

"Look, Sam," Ellie said in a hushed tone. "That picture looks like the one Virginia showed me." She pointed to an old photograph of two Confederate soldiers.

"It right does." He moved close to the photo to study it, analyzing it. He turned to face her. "I don't know them," he said. "They resemble me and Ernest though." He let out a soft, billowy laugh. "We all dressed the same. Most of us ain't had uniforms, and we all took things from home."

"For trinkets to remind you of home?"

"No. The army didn't give us nothing. We had to fend for ourselves. We brought what we could from home, what we thought we'd need—a spoon, a knife, anything," he said.

"Geez. Talk about getting the shaft," Ellie grumbled. "Fight for us and provide your own stuff too."

"Most of us that fought were poor. Ain't never had anything but our farms," he said.

He moved away from the picture and went on to the next exhibit. He stopped abruptly and jerked his head quickly, reading the inscription word-for-word.

"What is it?" Ellie asked, sensing Sam's tense body language.

"This looks like Jeremiah's knife," he said, bending over to closely examine it.

It was enclosed in a glass case. Sam pressed his face against it. He squinted his eyes and breathed against the glass: a cloud of fog covered it. He took his palm and rubbed the moisture off and moved close to it again. "This is his," he said with certainty.

Ellie moved toward him and bent over to inspect the knife. "How can you tell?" she asked, her breath moist against the glass. She could smell Sam's breath. If she turned to face him, their lips would be centimeters apart. She tried not to think about that.

Focus, Ellie, she told herself. *And get a life, for crying out loud.*

"I know 'cause I carved it for him," Sam said. "See that there." He pointed. A hawk's wings wrapped around the wooden handle that held the blade. A dogwood tree's leaves, the trunk's bark prominent, filled the rest. "He loved Dogwood trees. Said they were proof of God's existence—that nothing that beautiful could be designed by anyone other than God." Sam stood up and ran his fingers through his shaggy hair. He pulled at his scruffy beard and asked, "How did his knife get here?"

Ellie moved closer to the description next to it. "It says it was found.., " she said and continued reading. A look of horror struck her face, and Sam instantly noticed.

"What is the matter?" he asked.

"It says," she said quietly, almost breathing the words, "that it was found on a corpse in Pisgah Forest in the 1970s in pristine condition." She turned to face him, seeing that his reaction mirrored hers.

He jolted to the caption, reading what Ellie had just told him. "The corpse's clothes were found in excellent condition as well. They found this in the 1970s?" Sam said with a contorted face, confusion filled him. "If it was Jeremiah..." He continued to read the passage.

"Maybe it wasn't him," Ellie offered, knowing in her heart of hearts that wasn't the case. It was him. She knew it; Sam knew it.

He slightly shook his head. "Not likely. He held onto that knife for dear life. Our granddaddy gave us Bowie knives when we were younguns. They were real close." He leaned back against the wall and let out a deep breath. "This will devastate Uncle Caleb."

"I don't know what to say," Ellie said, a lump forming in her throat. She didn't know Jeremiah, but she knew about grief. She could feel Sam's agony. Guilt and blame were some of the worst feelings to have.

He peered down at her and placed his hand on her shoulder. "Ain't nothing you can say."

"We can't jump to conclusions. Maybe this person stole his knife?" Ellie was grasping at straws. The facts were in front of them; neither one of them wanted to admit it. Saying someone was dead made it final.

"He's most likely passed, Ellie," Sam said quietly. He ran his fingers through his hair, running his hands down to his neck and squeezing. His face was stressed. Ellie knew she couldn't say anything that could change what was right in front of them.

A museum patron stood close behind them, looking at the knife.

"We'll talk more about this in the car," Ellie said, peering over her shoulder and gesturing to Sam with a quick nod of her head in that person's direction.

They moved their way toward the exit, ignoring the rest of the exhibits. Sam was full of sadness and regret, and Ellie was distracted thinking of nothing but the time issues. She knew that if Jeremiah's knife was found in immaculate condition in the 1970s, that was more proof that time was on its own schedule where Sam and his family lived. Time ran by its own rules in his realm.

Ellie and Sam made their way toward the exit door. She quickly glanced at the last exhibit: a canteen from the Civil War belonging to an unknown soldier. It was made out of wood and had a cork top, a long cloth strap was attached to it. Sam had seen plenty of canteens in his lifetime so one more wasn't going to call his attention. Ellie didn't notice at first, and almost missed it. In big, black bold lettering a sign below the canteen read : "Donated by Ernest G. Price."

"Sam," she nudged him. "Look." She pointed.

He did a double take as he moved close to the name on the sign, making sure it was what he saw. "Donated by Ernest G. Price," he said out loud in a disbelieving tone.

"Think it's him?"

"I do not know," he answered. "That canteen can belong to anyone. Everyone I knew had one like that one."

"A canteen from your time period and donated by someone with the same name as your best friend? I highly doubt that's just a coincidence."

He nodded his head in agreement. "Who do you think can tell us if the Ernest you saw in the photo still lives here?"

"Maybe someone in the church we were planning to visit?" she said. "Old Clyde over there may know. He looks like he's been here since Christ."

"We can ask him, I 'spose," Sam said with uncertainty, ignoring her quip.

"Are you okay?" she asked and then shook her head, rolling her eyes. "Such a stupid question. Of course you're not. I don't know what to say. I'm not good at this."

For a brief moment his eyes flickered with a hint of happiness, and he offered her a crooked smile. "You are just what I need," he said in earnestness.

She smiled at him. "Thanks. Let's go see if Santa knows where Ernest might be." She pulled on his arm, heading over to Clyde who was talking with another patron. Ellie patiently waited for their conversation to finish.

"Do you know Ernest G. Price?" she asked. There was no sense in using social etiquette. Time didn't call for it. She wasn't going to beat around the bush.

Clyde looked up as if he were thinking. He scratched at his head. "That name rings a bell." He pondered for a moment, and then a look of recognition showed in his eyes.

"I'm related to him and wanted to meet him," she lied.

"He lived here back when my hair was black." He chuckled, and Ellie swore that he could play Santa Claus with his white hair and rosy cheeks. "That was a long time ago."

"Did you know him?" Ellie asked.

"Pretty good. We worked on the church restoration together. He was a loner type. A real docile man," he said. "He'd spend time with two men that no one in the town cared for particularly. Ernest was always pleasant, always willing to lend a hand. Those two riffraff he was friends with wouldn't lift a finger if their lives depended on it." He glowered. "They caused quite a raucous the short time they was here. Ain't none of us forgotten them. Thought it was odd a quiet, timid man like Ernest associated with them but..." he tilted his head to the side and his shoulders raised up then lowered, "sometimes people ain't too smart about their friends."

"Who were these men?" Sam spoke up.

"Rufus and Horace Boyd," he said with a look of disgust. "Made their neighbors lives a living hell. 'Course no one could ever prove it was them that did it, but we all knew it was them."

"What'd they do?" Ellie asked.

"Well..." He scratched at his chin. "For one, they killed Pastor Harmon's dogs."

Ellie and Sam's eyes widened, and their mouths were agape.

"Harmon had four blood hounds. When he wasn't at the church, he was hunting with them dogs. Loved them more than his own kids," he said. "Rufus and Horace used to complain about his dogs, gave Harmon a hard time about them. Said they barked too much. When they started showing up dead, Harmon suspected they had something to do with it." He frowned. "That ain't all they'd done. They stole Sue Stanton's chickens and messed up Hank Anderson's fence. Poor ole Hank's cattle were let out. Took a lot of us to reel them back in. A few were lost for good."

"That's awful," Ellie said.

Clyde nodded, his lips pursed. "Like I said. No one in the town liked them much. Were real glad when they left. They inherited some money from some rich relative. Lord knows who'd write them in their will," he said with a scrunched face. "We heard they bought a paper mill in Georgia. Thought it was right strange they bought the mill. Ain't much to the town they bought it in."

"Ernest went with them?" Sam asked.

"Yep. Lord knows why." He shook his head and then let out a sigh. "People do foolish things all the time. Ernest was a nice man but dumb when it came to them. He followed them around and did as they told. Like they had something over him. Whatever it was, it made him go with him."

"Do you know where in Georgia he moved?" Ellie asked.

"Rutherford," he said. "It's one of those mill towns near a river."

"You've been very helpful. Thank you," Ellie said.

"Thank you," Sam said with a serious expression.

CHAPTER 18

They sat in the car. Neither of them said a word. The realization set in for both of them.

Ellie started the engine, blowing the air conditioning on full blast and turning the volume to the radio off. She wanted to talk to Sam. She needed to. If they were in town in the 1970s and Sam said they left eight months ago, time moved slower than a snail's pace where he and his family were concerned.

That's why Dad said I was gone overnight when I was bit by a snake, she thought. *But for some reason time seems to be catching up.*

She wanted to offer comfort to him, to tell him she knew how he was feeling. She wanted to reach over to hug him and tell him everything was going to be all right because that's what she would want if she were him.

The way he looked at her, grief-stricken, the same expression that was glued to her face for months, she couldn't let it go. Despite the fear of being rejected or seeming too intrusive, Ellie leaned over and wrapped her arms around him, pulling him toward her, and hugging him tightly. Sam wrapped his arms around her, drawing even closer.

The coarse hairs from his beard rubbed against her face, tickling it. He breathed into her hair, wisps of it slightly blew. She wanted to cry but didn't know why. The emotion of it all was taking its toll. Allowing grief to be transparent and sharing it with someone was cathartic. She needed to be held like this as much as he did.

They stayed like that for a long time. Tourists and locals passed them by, seeing two people holding each other, sharing an intimate moment in the most public forum. As the world around them continued to pass them by, Ellie and Sam's stopped as they allowed what was inside of them to come out of its shell.

When it was time to let go, they both released their arms from each other and shared an understanding look, one that evoked appreciation and an inexplicable link that wasn't there before.

His hand touched the top of hers. "Thank you," he said.

She half-shrugged, unsure of what to say. You're welcome seemed so trite. "We're friends," she decided to say.

"I am thankful for that." He offered her a warm smile. "Why didn't he come back? Rufus and Horace—I understand, but Ernest? What made him go off with them? He knew Virginia was waiting for him." He grew silent, his face pensive. "And who'd they inherit money from?"

Ellie shook her head. "I have no idea. They wouldn't have known anyone," she said.

A look of frustration and anger overcame him, and he formed his hand into a fist and snarled his lips upward. "Ernest's got some explaining to do when I see him."

"First things first, we need to figure out where this town is and how far we are from it," she said. She opened up the atlas her father kept in the car and turned the page to Georgia, searching for Rutherford. "Where the heck is it?" She blew air from her lips and mumbled in frustration. She continued to study the map and finally found it. "There!" she squealed.

Sam leaned over. "It's in the mountains."

"Yeah," Ellie agreed. "I'd say it's a few hours from here, maybe more depending on how crappy the roads are. It looks like we have to take some 2-laners for a while. That can slow things down."

"I reckon we should get moving," he said.

"Not yet." She shook her head and gave a mischievous smile.

He formed a puzzled look.

"We're giving you a make-over. You can't keep traipsing around in those high waters," she said, pointing to his short jeans.

***

Ellie drove on the interstate heading to the nearest city, which was Asheville. It was a little out of her way, but there weren't any other cities within close proximity to Mayfield. Sam looked at everything as if seeing it for the first time. Each business, every single car that passed by, it was new for him, like he was a traveler to a foreign country. He couldn't stop gawking, his eyes and mouth wide open.

She exited the interstate and pulled into the packed mall parking lot. Summer time usually meant throngs of teenagers trolling the malls to pick up the opposite sex or to find something to do to occupy their time and take them out of the summer break doldrums.

She turned the car off and motioned for Sam to get out. They walked through the full parking lot, heading toward the mall entrance. Groups of people passed them, and Sam couldn't help but stare.

"Quit staring if you can help it," Ellie said through gritted teeth. "It makes you seem like a creeper."

Sam's gaze fell onto his shoes—tennis shoes that seemed one size too small—and he followed Ellie as they entered the mall. He was taken by it all—the noises, scents, crowds of people. The mall smelled of pretzels and chocolate chip cookies, brewing coffee and Chinese food.

"And people can just come here and buy clothes and leave with them? They don't have to have them made for them?" he asked, and Ellie nodded.

He couldn't help but look at each and every person, noticing body piercings, tattoos and unique hairstyles. "What's that mark on his arm?" He pointed and Ellie shushed him.

"It's a tattoo," she whispered. "Lots of people have them."

"And that silver thing in her lips?" He pointed again, and Ellie grabbed his finger bringing it down to his side.

"It's a body piercing."

"They're common too?" he asked.

"Not as much, but yeah, people get them. I wanted to get my belly button pierced but my dad wouldn't let me," she said.

The sound of a merry go round, whirling around in a circle, played the same annoying music over and over again. People chattered: their voices carried to his overworked ears. Ellie peered at him and saw that it may be information overload.

He went for her hand and held onto it, and Ellie didn't let it go. She liked holding his hand. It felt right, just as natural as breathing.

She peered at him. His face was contorted with anxiousness. "Is this all right?" he asked, his voice low, and he glanced down at their adjoining hands. She nodded, and he wobbled a bit and steadied himself.

"You okay?"

"Things are moving fast again," he said, and she clasped her fingers into his as they continued to stroll through the mall.

They walked into American Eagle and were immediately greeted by an overzealous sales person. Ellie gave her a quick "don't offer to help us" look and pulled Sam with her to the guys section. She picked up a t-shirt and held it up to him, seeing what the color would look like. "Blue is nice on you," she said, noticing that the lighter the color of blue the more his gray eyes popped.

"This works," she said and then meandered over to the shorts, pulling pairs of gray and khaki shorts off of the rack. "Both look good with this t-shirt." She laid the t-shirt down on the table and held both pairs of shorts up to it. "Which one do you prefer?" she asked, noticing that Sam was easily distracted, staring at everything and everyone.

She poked him on the arm. "Sam?"

He turned his glance in her direction. "Sorry," he said. "Whatever you prefer."

"Try them both on," she said and then walked back to the t-shirt table. "Try on this color too." It was a slate colored t-shirt.

"All of these clothes are available for people to purchase today?" he asked.

"Yep. That's how people shop."

She pulled him with her, still holding onto his hand. To any outsider looking at the two, they looked like a normal, playful couple out for a day of shopping. They made their way to the fitting room.

"Four," Ellie answered for him seeing that Sam was still in a daze.

The sales person handed him a number and unlocked the dressing room door to his right. "Go on in bro" he said to Sam.

Sam looked at Ellie who motioned for him to go on in the room. "I'll be right here," she said.

"My girlfriend is the same way," the salesperson said to Ellie. "She won't let me try on anything without her approval."

Ellie smiled, happy that someone thought she was his girlfriend.

She couldn't deny it: she wanted him to be her boyfriend despite the fact that they were from two different times and had a plethora of obstacles facing them.

Sam walked out wearing the light blue t-shirt with the gray shorts. He fidgeted and waited for her reaction.

Damn. Hot diggidy damn, she thought.

He tugged on his shorts and shirt and waited for her approval. "It looks good," she said, and she noticed a girl passing by gave him a double take. Ellie shot her a dirty look and then focused her gaze back on Sam.

He closed the door and tried on the other ensemble, looking just as good as he did the first time. Ellie knew Sam was in good shape, but his muscles were especially flattering in the vintage fit v neck t-shirts.

He left the dressing room carrying the stack of clothes, and Ellie picked up two pairs of socks and stopped at the boxers section on their way to check-out. "You need these," she whispered, feeling the color rise to her cheeks. "They're underwear."

"Oh," he said, his face showing hints of red. "Thank you."

"I'll let you pick these out by yourself," she said and moved away to another table while he sifted through the boxers section.

She saw him pick up the most basic three pack and he placed them under his arm, as if he were trying to shield them from her. They went to the check-out and purchased the items. Ellie checked the time on her phone, seeing that time was closing in on them.

"We still need to get you a hair cut, and you need a new pair of shoes."

"You do not have to do this," he said, showing a look of guilt.

"Please," she said brushing him off, and they left American Eagle in search of a nearby beauty salon.

When Ellie sat in that chair watching Sam's long brown locks getting chopped off, she pulled on her heavy, thick hair and begged the stylist to cut hers off too. The hesitant stylist trimmed it at first, reluctant to cut more of Ellie's beautiful "TV commercial" inspired hair. Ellie gave her a stern look and the stylist cut off the rest—leaving Ellie's hair hitting at the nape of her neck. She felt refreshed and new—like a monkey had just gotten off of her back.

She checked her reflection and then looked at Sam and said, "You look nice." She wanted to add, "*hot, really good, so good I can't believe I'm going to be in a hotel room with you tonight,*" but she didn't. His hair was cut shorter, and his face had a clean close shave, showing a much more youthful Sam, appearing more like his age than the man who lived in the woods.

"You look very pretty," he said. "I've never seen short hair like that on a woman. It looks real good on you."

"Thanks," Ellie said, trying to quell a smile. She was that girl now—hopeful for compliments and happy when they came from him.

Get a life, Ellie.

After buying Sam a new pair of tennis shoes, they grabbed a quick bite to eat in Chic Fil A. Ellie soon realized that Sam had a penchant for sweet tea and milk shakes.

"You've got a sweet tooth." She laughed, watching him slurp the rest of his milkshake's contents.

"This is incredible," he said, licking his lips and smiling. "I can't believe they can cook the food so fast."

They left Chic Fil A and got back onto the interstate. Several hours had passed, and Ellie knew it'd be dark before long. They'd have to check into a hotel first and visit Ernest Gosset Price in Rutherford the next day.

***

She exited the interstate, pulling into the Homewood Suites parking lot. She parked the car under the entrance and moved her way inside of the hotel with Sam behind her. The hotel was brand new, with shiny tiled floors and stain-free Berber carpet.

"This looks nice," she said to Sam. "I'd rather stay here than there." She gestured to shady, dingy motel across the street.

Sam didn't respond and followed her to the desk. The hotel clerk greeted them with a smile. "Welcome to the Homewood Suites," she said, her accent faint and barely noticeable.

"We'd like to check in for the night," Ellie said, feeling like an adult for the first time in her life. She never had checked into a hotel on her own, nor traveled by herself without her dad knowing where she was.

"Certainly," she said and clicked away on her computer keyboard.

It didn't take long to check into the hotel. Ellie was thankful she had reached the age of eighteen, otherwise they would have ended up sleeping in the car. She had wondered what the thrill in turning eighteen was all about besides being able to vote, buy a lottery ticket and get into a night club. Now she knew the other perk—she could check-in to any hotel, motel, or other accommodation across the country without question.

Once all of the paper work was completed, Ellie parked the CRV. Sam insisted on carrying all of their luggage: his American Eagle shopping bag, a brown paper bag full of junk food, and her back pack. Ellie told him that it wasn't necessary, that her hands were just as capable of carrying her own luggage, but Sam refused to budge. He told her it was bad enough she was paying for everything. They left the parking lot and trekked inside, heading into the elevator. Once the doors slammed shut, Sam leaned against the wall, holding on tightly to the bar.

"It's okay," she said to him.

He took quick, shallow breaths. The elevator began to move, and Sam's body language changed. He no longer gripped onto the bar, holding on for dear life, but let go, his face lighting up in response to the rapid movement.

"If you like the feel of this, you'd love a roller coaster," she said. "I'll take you to Six Flags sometime," she offered, hoping it wasn't going to be a broken promise.

The elevator dinged and they walked down the hall, heading for their room. She slid the plastic key into the slot and the green light flickered, making a slight noise as she opened the heavy, fire proof door.

The room was cold, and the air conditioner hummed quietly. It smelled new too. Ellie couldn't place the scent but it seemed like a mix of roses and lilac—floral and fresh. There was a couch, a table and four chairs, a kitchenette, and then an adjoining room and bathroom. The bed was king sized and covered in a white, fluffy duvet cover. The granite counter tops shined in the light's reflection, and the beige tiled floor glistened. The sage carpet looked good enough to walk on with bare feet. Ellie wanted to run her toes through the carpet's fibers.

"This is nice," Ellie said, referring to the room's basic but pleasant décor.

She plopped down on the couch and leaned her head back,

her body tired and achy. She hadn't run that morning, which was unusual for her, and her muscles and joints were stiff from the sudden change in her routine.

"I'm going to get out of these clothes," Sam said. "These are snug." He grimaced, and kicked off his shoes, placing them against the wall. He moved into the bedroom and closed the door behind him.

Ellie grabbed the brown paper bag and took out the bags of candy she had purchased at the gas station. She dropped a few Skittles in her mouth and chewed.

Sam came out of the bedroom, wearing a light blue t-shirt and khaki shorts. He sat down next to her and she handed him the bag of Skittles. He happily took more than a few and popped them all in his mouth.

She laughed.

"What?" he asked.

"You. You're totally addicted to sweets, and it's all my fault." She opened the other bags and took a few, gesturing for him to help himself. "Go ahead."

He happily complied, taking handfuls of candy. He smacked his lips and swallowed. She opened a bottle of soda and handed it to him. "You'll be asleep in no time. The sugar rush you've got now will turn into one, ugly crash."

He closed the bags and pushed them toward her. "I need to stop."

"Don't do it on my account. It's actually very entertaining," she said, snickering.

He stretched his legs out on the coffee table and leaned back. It was the first time Ellie had seen him so relaxed.

"This feels so good," he said.

"The sugar rush?"

"This." He pointed to the couch. He looked down at the candy bags and handled the Swedish Fish bag, taking a few more pieces out before closing it up again.

"Oh, the couch. Yeah. It's comfy," Ellie agreed.

"What is that?" he asked, pointing to the television. "I saw one of these at your house before we left."

"It's called a television. You can watch shows and movies on it." She picked up the remote control and clicked the television on.

He stared at it in amazement. He got up and moved closer to it, touching the screen.

"You'll go blind if you watch TV like that," Ellie teased. "That's what my mom always said to me."

"Is that true?" He slowly backed away from it, watching it.

"I don't know." She shrugged. "Here." She handed him the remote. "You push this to change the station, and this to turn it up louder."

Sam took the remote from her hands, his eyes squinting as he studied it.

"I've got to call Jonah." She pulled her phone out of her pocket and clicked on her contacts.

He answered the phone half asleep. His voice groggy, he croaked, "Hey."

"Hey yourself. We're staying overnight at the Homewood Suites. We found out Ernest lives in a town called Rutherford. It's in North Georgia," she said.

"So you're headed there tomorrow?"

"Yeah. Sam's a total sugar addict," she said.

Sam changed the station, an episode of *Friends* was on. He watched it for a few minutes and then channel surfed, showing no sign of focus. He turned the volume up and then down. Ellie walked into the other room so she could hear Jonah.

"What'd you expect? He's never had half the crap you fed him tonight. It's like sex. Once you have it, you don't want to stop," Jonah said.

"How would you know, Shrimp? Last time I checked, you're flying Virgin airways with me, and you've been single since forever."

"Just sayin'. Speaking of, Dad wouldn't be too happy about you sharing a room with a guy."

Through closed lips she whispered, "First of all, that's none of your business. Secondly, when did you become my second father? And thirdly, he's sleeping on the couch!" her voice raised. "Why am I defending myself to you?"

"Don't be so uptight. I'm just saying don't do anything dumb, Ellie. I saw how you act around him, all googly, batting your eyelashes and sticking that flat chest of yours out. You don't know him well enough yet," Jonah said and yawned.

Ellie recoiled, hearing the concern in her younger brother's bossy tone and said, "I get it, Shrimp, but I think I can handle making decisions on my own. I am older and wiser than you," she reminded him, a hint of smugness in her tone.

"Older maybe. Not wiser," he said. "I just don't want you getting hurt. He's nice and all, but don't go hooking up with him 'cause the opportunity is there." He yawned again. "I'm tired. Bosco and I have a bed calling our names."

"I'll call you tomorrow," she said.

She hung up and walked back in the room. Sam sat on the

couch sipping on his soda, watching an alien movie on the SyFy channel.

"How do you choose what to view?" he asked and changed the channel again. He grabbed the bag of Skittles and popped several more into his mouth.

"You just do." She plopped down next to him and leaned over to grab the bag of candy. Sam's eyes were glued to the TV. "What'd you do for entertainment back in your time?"

He turned the volume down on the remote and shifted so he could face her. "You mean when I wasn't tending to the farm?"

"Yeah."

"We didn't have the luxury of taking time off to enjoy things like nowadays. When I did, I'd read, or sing with my family. On warm summer's days, I'd go swimming. Sometimes I'd go fishing or practice with my bow and arrow."

"Did you have fun doing those things?"

"I didn't know any different. Weren't any other choices, not like what you have. I love to swim, especially in the summer months. There is nothing better than working outside in the heat and finishing off the day in a cold creek."

"I've never been fishing," Ellie said. "And you saw my archery skills."

"I will have to show you then," he offered. "And you just need practice with the bow and arrow." He touched her gently on the knee and then swiftly removed his hand.

"Were all men like you? You know, able to do all the stuff you can like shoot and fish." Most guys she knew that were his age couldn't do half the things he could. To her, Sam was a survivalist on so many levels. If Ellie was stuck on a deserted island with him, she'd be okay. She thought of him being so adept at most things: she couldn't wrap her fingers around it, but he intrigued her.

His eyes could barely stay open, and the further he leaned back against the couch, the more sedate he became.

"Sleepy?" she asked.

"Is this the crash you were speaking of?" He yawned, stretching his long arms above his head.

"Yep. You're crashing," she said. "It's too bad too. I'm wide awake."

"I'm sorry." He stifled a yawn.

"It's okay. Go on and sleep. I'll get you a pillow and a blanket," she said, going back into the room and taking a blanket from the closet and a pillow off of the bed.

She handed him the blanket and pillow. His hand brushed against hers and their eyes locked.

"Goodnight." He spread the blanket out over him and propped the pillow behind his head.

"Night, Sam." She turned the light off and went into the bedroom.

CHAPTER 19

She didn't realize she was screaming until Sam rushed into her room, shaking her awake, saying her name repeatedly. "Are you going to be all right?" he asked.

She couldn't see him. The heavy curtains shielded all the twinkling lights from outside, making the room darker than night. She lay in bed whimpering, feeling frightened, and trying to catch her breath. The nightmare had been the same as the last: someone was choking her, their hands wound tight around her neck, constricting her from precious air.

Her breaths were short and fast. Her heart beat a mile a minute, and she was perspiring all over. Everything about the dream felt real. All too real.

Sam sat next to her, leaning over her, his hand on hers. "Are you all right?"

"It was a nightmare," she said.

"You woke me," he said.

"I'm sorry."

"Don't be. You had me worried." His thumb rubbed the top of her hand, going back and forth, calming Ellie's nerves.

"It's the same nightmare I've had before," she told him. "I'm dying in it, and when I wake up, it's like I actually did die."

"Can I get you anything?" he asked.

"Could you..." she started, but was too afraid to ask.

"What?"

She could hear the eagerness in his voice. He wanted to help. "Could you stay in here with me for a while? Just till I get to sleep?" She felt ridiculous for asking, like she was a little kid asking her parents to leave the night light on. The thought of lying there alone frightened her.

"That wouldn't be right," he said, and she could hear him fighting with himself in the way that he answered her.

"Just until I get to sleep." She didn't want to beg, to seem desperate, but that's the way the conversation was headed.

He seemed to be having some internal war with himself. Debating what to do—what was right, what was wrong. But he no longer knew what the norm was and finally relented, got up off of the bed and walked to the other side. He lay down on his back, staring up at the ceiling.

Ellie turned toward him, seeing him laying there, and wondered what he had on his mind. She saw his chest rise and then deflate.

"Thank you," she whispered. "I never tell anyone I'm scared, but Sam, I am. Sometimes, I'm just so scared."

She reached for his hand and his fingers intertwined with hers. "I am, too," he admitted.

"How do you stop having regret?" she asked.

"I don't know. You go on. You keep living, I 'spose," he said and turned to face her.

Their hands were still clasped. Ellie let go and placed her palm up to his cheek, gently touching his smooth skin. The beard long gone, his cheeks felt soft to her touch.

"You are a good person," Sam said. He ran his fingers through Ellie's hair, making her stomach do somersaults. Her heart beat wildly.

"Not all the time, Sam."

"None of us is perfect," he said, and he moved his hand back to his side, leaving Ellie feeling disappointed.

"Are you ever going to tell me what happened to you, Sam?"

"I'm not ready to tell you. I want to, but not yet. Can you accept that?"

She could hear the vulnerability in his question. "For now. But know that nothing you say can make me hate you. No one is flawless." She held his hand again. This time he didn't let go.

"You feel this way because of your momma," he said, bringing up a topic Ellie didn't know if she was ready to discuss.

Ellie took a deep breath and exhaled.

"I could have been a better daughter," she admitted. "If I had gone shopping with her that day, she might not have died." The stages of grief had clawed their way to the surface. Ellie was still somewhere between the stages of bargaining and guilt. Like most people who are dealing with loss, there is always that sense of "if I had done something different" then they wouldn't have died— as if to say they held a special power to keep that person from meeting their fate. Ellie had yet to realize that she didn't pull the strings—that her mother's fate had already been sealed and she had no control over it. "She died that day in a car accident. The truck driver swore he never saw her coming. If I had been in the car with her, maybe it would have been different," her voice trailed off.

"We all make wagers with ourselves– what we could have done, should have done. I do that. I think about what I could've done differently that wouldn't have placed my family in danger. But deep down, I still would've made the same decision even though it wasn't the best for anyone but me," he said, a tone of hurt in his voice.

"It's not the same, Sam. I chose not to go shopping with her or do anything with her for that matter 'cause I'm selfish. I loved her and treated her like crap," Ellie said bitterly, rolling over on her side, her back facing him.

"I'm selfish too. I choose what I think is right despite the consequences. We are the same in that sense."

Ellie tossed back over on her side. "I guess that makes us awful people." She let out a long winded sigh. "More me than you."

"It makes us human. Tell me one person who is perfect."

She thought of the people she knew, what mistakes they had made. Even her mother wasn't impervious to character flaws. No matter what angelic image she had of her in her mind, she knew that there was no such thing as a perfect human being. It was part of being human—to have imperfections.

It was like he read her mind. "Your momma, was she without flaws?"

"No. She had a terrible temper." Ellie laughed, thinking about all of the times her mother shouted the F bomb when household items and other gadgets didn't work. "She'd curse like a sailor and say the most awful things. Then she'd say sorry, and all was supposed to be forgiven. Bosco hated it when she'd get mad—he always thought it was directed at him."

"Now I know where you get your mouth from," Sam joked, lifting the solemn mood.

"Jonah's worse than I am. Since she died..." it was the first time Ellie used the word "died" when referring to her mother. "Since she died, he has the foulest mouth."

"He is coping in his way," Sam said.

"But he's so angry," she argued.

"And you, you're guilty, like me, I 'spose?"

"Were you like the smartest person in your class? 'Cause you're going all Dr. Phil on me."

"I don't right know who Dr. Phil is, but I ain't that smart, Ellie.

I just say things out loud that you already think." He took a hold of her hand again. "You're just as smart, if not more."

Even though it was too dark in the room to see anything, she could feel him staring at her. She wondered if he was thinking the same thing as her. She had a choice: lay there and continue to ask herself that question or be bold and go for it. What did she have to lose? Her self-respect? He could reject her, but she didn't care. Ellie had never been one to just go out and kiss a guy, but with Sam laying there next to her, she knew if she didn't she'd regret it. She didn't think about all of the "what ifs." Instead she went with her heart and raised her hand to the nape of his neck, touching the short strands of his hair and moved in, pressing her lips against his. Their lips parted and their tongues moved together in unison. It was as if they were born to kiss each other.

He suddenly broke from their embrace. His lips were no longer on hers. "We shouldn't."

"It's okay. I want to," she said, leaning in to kiss him again.

He quickly pulled away from her and got out of bed. "I don't think you'd feel this way if you knew the kind of man I was. If you knew what I had done." Standing at the edge of bed, he said to her, "I cannot allow myself to take advantage of you."

He started to walk out of the room and stopped at the threshold, turning to face her. He opened his mouth, about to say something, and then sealed it shut, exited the room and left her alone again.

Ellie lay there feeling confused and conflicted. A part of her yearned for things to continue, but the other half was terrified by his admission. *What did you do, Sam, and will I forgive you once I find out?*

***

Ellie woke up and shuffled to the bathroom. She brushed her teeth and took a shower, then dressed in a pair of white shorts and a pink t-shirt. She put on a pair of tennis shoes and wandered into the adjacent room.

Sam sat at the table. He wouldn't look her in the eye. Not right away anyway. It was easier in the dark to do the things that their heart desired, to strip away any formalities, and lay inhibitions aside. Darkness gives the illusion that nothing is forbidden. That all will be forgiven. But morning comes, and everything changes.

"Hi," she said, as if it were a question. She had no idea how to act. Kissing him only to be rejected filled her with embarrassment and insecurity.

"Hello," he answered.

There was an awkwardness between them. They both wanted to discuss what was right there in front of them, yet neither would take the first step. She sat across from him, studying him. He didn't look like a man from the 1800s. If she hadn't known, she'd swear the man sitting across from her was a fellow college student. His short hair needed to be matted down with water: strands stuck up haphazardly.

Her mother used to lick her own palm and pat Jonah's hair down, fixing it with the wet surface of her hand. She wanted to do the same to Sam. She wanted to gobble him up and keep him close to her heart even though he told her he had done something unforgivable. Common sense told her to be wary, but she hadn't listened to that part of her brain since her time with Sam began.

"Have you eaten?" she asked, attempting to create conversation, ridding the room of the stagnate state. Food was a safe subject in any situation. She imagined heads of state often chose this topic instead of discussing nuclear warheads and threats of war. Everyone could agree on food—it was a necessity for life.

"No. I waited for you."

"Thanks," she said. "We can grab a bite to eat downstairs and then get going." She grabbed her backpack and purse, and motioned for him to follow her out the door.

After eating a continental breakfast in silence, they got into the CRV and headed toward Rutherford, Georgia, in search of Ernest Gosset Price.

"How are we going to find his home?" Sam asked, referring to Ernest.

"The world wide web," Ellie said, flashing a grin. It was the first smile she had offered him that morning. *Maybe things would go back to normal*, she thought, but she knew they wouldn't. How could they? She'd made it obvious that she was attracted to him, and he didn't reciprocate. The thought of him being so disdainful that he wouldn't allow himself to get close to her concerned her, but she kept telling herself to put that thought in the back of her mind. They had to find this man that could explain things that no one else could.

"Nothing is hidden is it?"

"Nope. It's all out in the open, Sam, for millions of people to see. It's become a powerful tool for bullying by every mean girl across the nation. Do something stupid, someone takes a picture and posts it for the whole world to see and ridicule you for."

"That's a shame. I've made enough mistakes in my life, I would not want everyone to know about them."

"Well. It is what it is. There's good and bad with everything," she said. She wasn't going to pry, but if he didn't tell her soon what he had done, she'd force it out of him.

***

As they entered the town of Rutherford, Georgia, Ellie slowed to the town mandate of twenty miles per hour, not twenty-five like most town speed zones were, but a slow, turtle's pace of twenty miles per hour. Ellie drove down the two-lane road which led to the center of town. Rutherford didn't appear to have much to offer. Centered in a remote area nestled in the Blue Ridge mountains of Georgia, it faced the Chapatuga River—a polluted body of water inundated with chemicals from irresponsible corporations. No one dared to swim or fish for fear of toxic poisoning. In Rutherford, the Boyd Paper Mill owned a large pocket of the Chapatuga. Waste and other byproducts from the paper mill had tainted the once fresh, pristine body of water, turning it into a murky playground.

Rutherford didn't have the flare or pizzazz that other mountain towns had. There wasn't a draw, nothing that would peak someone's interest to stop by and visit for a while. It wasn't an overly-friendly town, either. Ellie was used to driving through small towns where old people sat on rocking chairs on their front porches waving at anyone who passed by. All she and Sam were greeted with were looks of distrust and scowls on faces both young and old.

"This place gives me the creeps," she said, checking her speedometer, making sure she followed the speed limit. The last thing she needed was a speeding ticket.

"It's quite desolate, ain't it?" Sam said, noticing the bare streets and lack of cars.

"Yeah. Where the heck is everyone?" She turned her head in both directions seeing nothing but emptiness. A few kids rode their bikes outside, but everyone else seemed to have disappeared.

She pulled the car into an open parking space—one of many—and dropped several quarters in the meter. "This should last us a few hours," she said. She scrunched her face and grimaced. "Holy mother of god it smells out here." She plugged her nose.

Sam cupped his hand over his face.

"Must be the paper mill. It reeks," she said.

"It has a distinct odor about it."

"Yeah. Like poop," she said, and he laughed.

"You have an eloquent way of saying things."

"I can say the same for you," she teased, happy that the awkwardness they felt earlier that morning had disappeared.

They walked toward the library. A group of children passed them, peddling on their cruiser bikes, giving them strange looks and whispering to each other.

"What was that all about?" Ellie said, turning around and seeing the kids had stopped to watch them.

"I don't right know. Think this town has many visitors?"

"I think we may be their star attraction."

"About last night..." he began.

"That can never be good," she said.

"Why?"

"Because it sounds like the beginning of one of those speeches where you tell me it was all a mistake and let's forget it ever happened." She kept walking, purposely avoiding all eye contact with him. If she didn't look at him, she could handle the rejection.

He placed his hand on her shoulder which caused her gaze to meet his. "I don't regret what happened, and I won't forget it ever did."

She gulped.

"I want to remember. I would be a fool if I didn't."

"But?" Ellie asked.

"I promise to tell you about me once we finish here," he said.

She couldn't argue with that. He was putting himself out there for her with no guarantee. She nodded, and they continued their trek toward the town library.

Ellie pushed the creaky wooden door open. The floors were battered oak wood, in need of restoration, and there was a musty smell about the place. The building was cramped. A two-room structure in dire need of a paint job, it lacked an adequate selection of books and technology. There wasn't a sign of life inside, either. Ellie noticed that besides a couple of librarians, there wasn't anyone else in the library.

"The whole town stinks," she said to Sam.

They stopped at the front desk and were met by an older woman with white curly, over teased, and definitely, over sprayed, hair. If polyester had died and gone to heaven, then this woman would have angel wings. Her blue polyester suit was reminiscent of a Don Knots ensemble from *Three's Company*.

"Can I help you?" She had a chubby, grandmotherly face, but her voice was shrill.

"We need to use the internet," Ellie said.

"Who are you?" the woman asked in a flippant sort of way. "Ain't never seen y'all here before."

"We'd like to use a computer, please," Ellie said, feeling slightly annoyed. She wasn't going to explain who they were. It was a public facility. Anyone off the street was welcome to use it. That was what libraries were for—the public.

"Hold on." She held her index finger up at Ellie. "Go in that room." She pointed and went back to flipping through her tabloid.

"She was sweet," Ellie said facetiously as they moved their way to the other room. Shelves were sparse, and the few books that were on them were dated. A decayed paper smell was prevalent in the room. Three lone computers from the late 1990s were all the room had to offer.

"This search could take forever. Something tells me they're on dial up, too," she remarked to Sam.

"Dial up?" Sam asked.

"Long story," Ellie said.

They sat down in front of one of the computers, and Ellie quickly typed Ernest's full name on the keyboard. The globe icon spun for what seemed like an eternity. "Told ya," Ellie said in frustration. She sat back, tapping her fingers against the table.

The search results finally popped up, and Ellie was able to retrieve his address. "I wish I had a GPS," she said, more to herself than to Sam. "Thanks for being so cheap, Dad," she grumbled. She typed in the address on the computer in Google Maps and waited impatiently for the results to show. "I could have never used the internet back in the day."

"I know what you mean," Sam teased, and Ellie shook her head while laughing.

The results finally surfaced. Ellie clicked the print button, and they made their way to the printer. "Ink jet?" she said in disbelief. "It's like we're stuck in the 1990s." The sound of the print arm moving back and forth filled the confining room.

She pulled the paper out of the printer, and said, "Come on. Let's go."

CHAPTER 20

Ellie handed the directions to Sam. "I need you to be my navigator, k?" she said.

"All right," he agreed. "I'll do my best." He scrunched his face and stared down at the paper.

"Just tell me when to turn and which way," she said. "Follow these directions. I'm thinking we'll be there in, like, fifteen minutes."

"This internet is incredible," he said with a look of awe.

"Yeah. I guess it is," Ellie said, never having thought much of it. Since she was born, she always had access to the world wide web. She couldn't imagine a life without the luxury of being able to look up anything and everything at the drop of a hat.

"Turn here," he said.

Ellie made a right turn and drove on, waiting for Sam's next instruction. "What's next?"

"It says to turn left on Boyd Boulevard," he said. "Think that has to do with Horace and Rufus?"

"I don't know, Sam. If Horace owns the paper mill, and by the look of things that seems to be the only source of income for this cruddy town, I'd bet it does," she said, changing the air conditioning to inside. "It stinks!"

"I thought that was you," he joked.

She lightly punched him on the arm and laughed. "Nah. It's your upper lip."

***

Ellie pulled into a gravel driveway and parked behind a white Datsun pick up truck. The house was bare of any paint, each piece of lumber exposed, weathered and without a stain or paint to protect it. Hedges needed to be trimmed, and weeds had taken over flower beds long ago. Rusted patio furniture sat in tall blades of grass. An old car without tires sat on top of concrete blocks.

"Think anyone lives here?" Ellie said to Sam, referring to the lack of care and attention the home received. "Everything about this town gives me the creeps."

They were greeted by a few cats on their way to the front door. Ellie knocked more than once and waited for someone to answer. "I don't think anyone is home," she said to Sam. He gestured his head toward the window, and Ellie saw an older man peering at them behind beige curtains. "Looks like I was wrong," she said.

Ellie knocked again. "Is he hiding from us?" she asked Sam. "Hello! We'd like to speak with Ernest Price." She pounded against the door.

The door slowly opened, and an older man in his late fifties greeted them. He was thin and definitely a smoker. The smell of stale cigarette smoke filled the air. Lines surrounded his thin upper lip and his brown eyes. His skin had a yellowish tint to it—the kind that only a life-long smoker could inherit.

"Can I help you?" he asked, his face expressionless.

Ellie wasn't going to play along. No way. Not at this point in the juncture.

"Hi. I'm Ellie and this is Sam. Do you recognize him?" She pointed to Sam and watched him as she asked the question, waiting to see his response.

He answered, "No," but his facial expression was too exaggerated.A small bead of sweat formed on his forehead, trickling down toward his muddy brown eyes.

"I don't follow you," he said and cleared his throat. She watched as one of his hands twitched. He placed his other hand on top of it, but it continued to shake. He was a basket full of nerves.

She looked at Sam and mouthed "say something" to him.

Sam's head was tilted to the side, and he studied the older man. "You look just like your daddy did before he passed," he said.

"I think you'uns better get going," he said. He was trying to intimidate them, but Ellie wasn't afraid in the slightest.

"How do you know its him, Sam?" she asked, ignoring Ernest's threatening stance.

"That scar above his lip. He got that when we were younguns," Sam said, still staring at him.

"I think it is best you two leave now before you end up in jail," Ernest said.

"Is that some kind of threat?" Ellie said. "'Cause we're not doing anything wrong."

"Virginia is heartbroken, Ernest," Sam said, trying to get through to him.

Ernest looked down, and Ellie thought she sensed regret, and then he lifted his head, glaring at them both. "I don't know who you think I am, but I'm not that person. I suggest you both leave my property now," he raised his voice.

"She can't sleep. She can't eat. She can't do nothing 'cause all she thinks about is you," Sam said as Ellie pulled on him, motioning for him to leave. He jerked himself free from Ellie's grip. "Tell us what happened. How you're as old as you are and I'm still young."

Ernest took his cell phone out of his pocket and began to punch in a phone number. "You have ten minutes until the Sheriff gets here."

Ellie stared him down. "You're hiding something. Why?"

"What about Jeremiah?" Sam asked. "Is he dead?"

A look of pain shot through Ernest's eyes. He blinked a few times and then said, "I've asked you more than once. I suggest you get off my property and find your way out of town." He slammed the door shut, leaving them both angry and confused.

Still reeling, Sam said through gritted teeth, "That was him."

"I know," Ellie said. "It was written all over his face. He's hiding something and is scared shitless of you."

"I don't understand why," Sam said. "Although he should be now." He had a look of malice that made Ellie afraid.

"Sam." She touched his arm, and he flinched.

He breathed heavy and banged on the door. "Be a man and come out here!"

"Sam," Ellie pleaded. "We don't need to get arrested."

He pounded his fists against the door, screaming for Ernest to come out.

"Please, Sam," Ellie begged.

Sam lowered his fists. Still breathing heavy breaths, he took Ellie by the hand and stormed off toward the car.

Ellie sped off, leaving his property as fast as she was able. Once they reached the main road, she slowed down and parked the car off to the side of the road. She turned the car off and rolled the windows down. The paper mill's putrid scent of rotten eggs permeated the air as a warm breeze blew in.

She plugged her nose and rolled the windows back up, starting the car up again, and blowing the air conditioner on them.

"Sam," Ellie said quietly.

He turned to look at her. "I want to know what happened, to see if he can explain."

"I know, Sam, but you may not be able to. We can try going back to his house," she said, doubtful that they'd ever learn the truth. "Maybe he'll talk?"

"He has to. I'm not leaving until he does."

"Let's grab a bite to eat, and then we'll come back," she said, trying to say something, anything that could make that wrong situation right.

***

There was one restaurant in town, which didn't surprise Ellie. Judging from her stroll down Main Street and the sparse number of businesses she found there, she thought the town lacked any sort of substance of modernization.

The odor of onions blew up Sam and Ellie's noses the moment they opened the glass door. A bell rang, alerting all of the customers that they were there. Everyone looked in their direction— expressions of curiosity and skepticism showed on all of the strangers' wary faces. It was almost as if Ellie and Sam had a big red A on them. She felt like she was wearing the "Scarlet Letter for Newcomer to Town."

"I think they know we're not from around here," Ellie mocked with a fake southern accent.

"I agree," Sam said. "That smile of yours is giving you away," he kidded.

Ellie had grown to appreciate Sam's sense of humor. Despite what had just happened, he managed to lighten the mood.

"Yours too. Wipe that grin off your face. We need to fit in," she teased in a low voice.

A thin woman greeted them with a frown. Her dyed fire-engine-red hair was up in a hair net, and age spots covered her wrinkled skin. Grease stains were all over her faded pale blue uniform. Red lipstick stained her crooked teeth. "You can sit anywhere you want," she said.

They sat at the first empty table they could find. She handed them a one page menu and poured water into their empty glasses. Water splashed on the table, and she took her grimy apron and wiped the spill.

"Whatcha want?" she asked.

"A hamburger," Ellie answered. It seemed like the safe thing to order in a place like that. After touching the greasy menu, she wiped her hands on a napkin.

"And you?" she asked Sam.

"The same," he said with uncertainty.

"You sure?" she said to him. "'Cause you don't seem like it."

"No, I am," he answered.

"Whatcha want to drink?" she asked them both with impatience, as if they were wasting her time.

"Tea," Ellie said.

"Tea," Sam repeated.

"Harry, two hamburgers!" she shouted to the cook in the kitchen as she made her way to another table.

Ellie felt the rest of the crumbling restaurant's patrons' eyes on them. "They're still looking at us," Ellie whispered.

"What is a hamburger?" Sam asked, unconcerned with all the eyes burning holes into his back.

"Only the best food you'll ever have," Ellie said. "It's ground beef between two pieces of bread. I wish you could try it for the first time somewhere else." She frowned.

He took a sip of his tea and then gulped the rest down.

"Easy there," Ellie said, snickering.

He wiped his lips and smiled. "It's good."

"I know, but ole Midge over there isn't going to rush over to refill your glass."

"People don't seem very pleasant here, do they?" He moved his head, looking at everyone.

Ellie scanned the restaurant, noticing some people who continued staring at them. They averted their eyes when she looked in their direction. For the only restaurant in town, it felt eerily quiet, too. Too quiet. Given the number of people, it should've been a struggle to hear Sam, but it seemed as if Ellie and Sam were the only people talking. There was a jukebox in the corner, but no music played from it. It was as if everyone was on a schedule—eat lunch, then get back to whatever it was they were doing. The life of that town had been sucked out into another vortex.

The waitress took her time coming back to their table. She dropped their plates in front of them. "You need anything else?"

"More tea please," Ellie answered, motioning to the two empty glasses.

She grabbed their two glasses as if she were being inconvenienced and filled them up, bringing them back to the table.

Sam stared at the hamburger with a fork in hand, ready to cut into it.

"Hold up." Ellie held up her hands. "First off, you don't eat it with a fork. You hold it with your hands. And secondly, you need ketchup and mustard." She picked up the nearby bottles, took off the top bun, and poured them both on it. She placed the top of the bun back on the hamburger. "There. All better." She gave a smile of satisfaction.

He picked it up and bit into it. He chewed and then swallowed. "Good," he said.

"It'd be better if we weren't eating it here," Ellie said. She took a bite of hers and swallowed. "Yep. This is like a two star hamburger."

"Is that bad?"

"Totally. Two out of ten stars is pretty pathetic. No wonder everyone looks pissed off. They're eating crappy food," she said and bit into her hamburger again.

"I don't right know that he'll talk to us when we go back," Sam said, his forehead wrinkled with worry.

"I know Sam." She looked around and saw a few people were eavesdropping on their conversation. "Let's discuss this in the car. There are some big ears around here."

***

They walked down the isolated sidewalk heading toward the car. Ellie noticed Ernest coming from the police station. He appeared agitated, raking his fingers through his thinning hair, and his lips were semi-pursed.

"Sam." Ellie nudged him and pointed at Ernest.

Sam charged toward Ernest. His stride was long and fast—he was on a mission. Ellie worried that he was libel to do anything— especially something drastic that could make them wind up in jail or worse.

"Sam!" she yelled, but her warning was like a poof of air that quickly disappeared.

She ran toward him and grabbed a hold of his arm. She couldn't make him stop. He kept moving. "Just step away, Ellie," he warned.

"Don't do anything stupid," she begged.

Ernest heard them and rushed the other way, quickly hurrying toward his car. Sam bolted after him and gripped his arm. Ernest tried jerking the hand off of him, but Sam was too strong.

"What do you think you're doing?" Ernest said, trying to get Sam's hand off of him.

Sam took a photo out of his pocket, showing it to Ernest. Ellie didn't know he had brought it. Ernest's eyes cast down. He wouldn't look at the photo.

"This is you and Virginia before we left for the war. Remember she begged that photographer to take this picture 'cause you'uns were engaged?"

Ernest turned his head. It was like the photo was an electric fence shocking him every time he glanced at it.

Sam shoved it in his face. "Look at this!" If he could have held onto Ernest's head and forced him to look, he would have. The look of intent and boiling anger in his eyes sent a shiver down Ellie's spine.

Sam tightened his grip around Ernest's thin arm. His loose skin jiggled, and he winced in pain.

"Sam, you're hurting him," Ellie said, a look of frenzied worry on her face.

"The way he has hurt Virginia. Leave us be, Ellie," he said through gritted teeth. He shoved Ernest, who moaned in agony as his back slammed against a building's brick wall.

She placed her hand on Sam's hand that was clung against Ernest's chest, stepping in front of him. "Stop it, Sam. Think about what you're doing!" She looked into his eyes, hoping he'd see reason.

Sam took a moment to consider what she said. Ellie watched as his gray eyes dashed back and forth in deep thought. His breath was heated like fire, heavy and fast. He flared his nostrils and his eyes narrowed to Ernest's frightened brown eyes. "You will talk to us," he commanded, his voice even-keeled, this concerned Ellie even more.

Maybe Sam was right? Maybe he was a bad man with a past she didn't need to know about? Had she ever been that angry? No, she hadn't and witnessing Sam's wrath right there and then told her what people were capable of. What Sam could be capable of.

"Sam," she pleaded one more time.

He lowered his palm from Ernest's constricted chest and gave a look to Ellie. "I apologize."

"I know, Sam. I know," she answered. "We're causing a scene," she said and nodded her head toward the few onlookers that had stopped to see the commotion.

"Will you talk to us?" Sam said to Ernest, his tone softer but his eyes still shooting darts at him.

"Yes," he answered. "But not here." He looked around, biting onto his lip to the point that it bled; sweat poured into his eyes. "Follow me back to my house," he whispered.

CHAPTER 21

Ellie stepped over a stack of newspapers and made her way from the foyer into Ernest's living room. She was immediately overwhelmed by the mildewy, fetid scent. She heaved, tasting bile in the back of her throat. A cat rubbed up against her leg purring and then jumped up onto an old, tattered velour green couch. Ellie swatted at a few flies that swarmed around her.

"We can sit in here," Ernest said, indicating the wicker chairs in his dining room.

It was the only uncluttered room in the entire house. Two cats jumped up onto the glass table and sat down near Ernest. He mindlessly petted them; the low, rumbling purrs resonated throughout the small room. A brass chandelier gently swayed above their heads. Cobwebs were etched onto it and to the four corners of the ceiling. Ellie was glad she had worn tennis shoes and not flip flops for fear of what lived in the hideous shaggy carpet beneath her squeamish feet. She grew immune to the smell, finding she no longer had the urge to throw up.

"I didn't ask if you wanted something to drink?" Ernest said.

"Nothing for me, thanks," Ellie said.

"No," Sam said in a quick, clipped tone.

"It's been so long since I've had company," Ernest said apologetically, well aware of his shabby surroundings. He fidgeted, and his fingers tapped onto his other hand. "No one comes around here. Guess it's a little isolated." He laughed nervously. "And messy."

"Thank you for talking with us," Ellie said, trying to ease the tension that filled the room. "I know we must have taken you by surprise."

"That's putting it mildly." He let out a laugh. "Never thought I'd see you again," he said to Sam.

"Why did you act like a stranger to me when we first visited you?" Sam asked with an distrustful expression.

Ernest cleared his throat and scratched his peeling, chapped lips. Life had gotten the worst of him, aging him. "I'm not sure," he said, his brows furrowed. He took out a cigarette from his pack of Marlboros and placed it in his mouth. He lit it with a sterling silver lighter and inhaled. A puff of smoke filled the room.

"That ain't the truth, and you know it," Sam huffed. He folded his arms against his chest and raised an eyebrow. "You're hiding something."

Ernest squirmed in his seat, shifting nervously from side to side. He took another drag of his cigarette and lowered his head, quietly uttering, "I wanna tell you the truth; I'm not so sure you're ready to hear it."

Sam breathed heavily and pointed his finger aggressively in Ernest's direction. "You don't get to dictate when I'm ready to hear something."

Ernest slowly got up and ambled to the kitchen. "This is strange for me," he said as water flowed from his faucet into a large plastic cup—the souvenir kind that should be thrown away. "Talking to you right here and now." He walked back into the room and took a long, hard swig of water. "Seeing you frozen in time and me," he shrugged, "well, looking like my Daddy. I'm an old man now, Sam."

"I can see that," Sam snapped. "I don't right care how you're feeling, Ernest."

Ellie placed her hand on his arm. "You have to let him talk." She urged with her eyes.

Sam sighed and gestured for Ernest to continue.

"I can't explain any of it. How you're young; how I'm old. How time passed us all by for so many years."

"I'm not asking you to. We might never get the answers to those questions," Sam said. "What I want to know is what happened to Jeremiah and why you didn't come back. These are questions *you* can answer."

"This has weighed heavy on my heart for years," he said remorsefully. "Do you know what it does to a man to have something eat him up from the inside out?"

"Do you know how it feels for a young woman to wait day after day for her fiancé to come back to her? Each day she is hopeful to see him. She goes to bed crying that he didn't come home," Sam retorted.

Ernest winced, shuddering slightly. "I think of her every day." He didn't make eye contact, focusing instead on fidgeting hands that rested on top of his jittery legs. He took out another cigarette and lit it. He sucked on it like it was air.

"Thinking about someone ain't the same as being with them," Sam said, leaning forward in an intimidating stance.

He scratched at his scalp and moved his head slightly. He let out a deep breath and said, "I knew you weren't gonna make this easy on me."

"Why should I? You owe us an explanation," Sam said.

"If I tell you what I'm gonna tell you, you're likely to kill me. I don't have nothing to live for anyhow, so do what you're gonna do but know this," he said, looking directly into Sam's eyes for a brief moment, "I have always loved your sister and am sorry for what I did to her."

"If you loved her as much as you claim, why didn't you come back?"

"Sometimes you do what you gotta do. You know that," he said, his eyes searching Sam's for commonality.

"Don't compare what you done to what I done. They ain't the same."

"I'm not," Ernest clarified. "I was just trying to point out..." He let out a frustrated sigh. "Oh, who am I kidding? You're never gonna forgive me. What's the point in explaining myself?"

"Because I deserve an explanation. We are, were, best friends," Sam said. "That should count for something. I don't recognize the man you've become now. I'm hopeful that the old you is in there somewhere."

"People change, Sam. The war changed you. Made you stop seeing things idealistically," he said.

Sam didn't say anything.

"Changed all of us. You for the better. Rufus, Horace, and me for the worse," Ernest said with a mournful expression.

"Quit stalling and tell us what happened," Sam said impatiently.

Ernest lay his cigarette in an ashtray and stood up, walking back into his kitchen. He poured bourbon into his bulky cup. "Thirsty?" he asked them. Ellie shook her head no, and Sam rolled his eyes in frustration. "Gonna need this with what I'm fixin' to tell." He pointed to the glass.

"So you're a drunkard?"

"It eases the pain, Sam," Ernest said unapologetically and gulped the rest down. He grimaced and let out a breath. "Whoo wee, gets me every time."

"Virginia is too good for you," Sam said.

"True," Ernest agreed as he poured the rest of the bottle's contents into his cup. "Always was. Even when I was a decent man. Never knew how I got someone as pure as her to love me. I ain't pure, Sam. Even then." He drank the rest of his bourbon and set the glass down on kitchen counter and headed back into the dining room. His fidgeting stopped, and he had an overall relaxed look about him. "Better." He smiled at them. Neither of them reciprocated. He grabbed the cigarette and took another drag.

Ellie felt sorry for him. He was a lost man and nothing was going to bring him back. And although she didn't really know Virginia, the thought of her loving a man like him broke Ellie's heart. He was broken.

He sat back and gave a sedated smile. "Remember when we used to go huntin'? You were the best aim. Never missed a shot. I miss those times. I've tried going by myself, but my hands ain't steady anymore so I can't use a bow and arrow so good." The alcohol had taken its toll. Words were slipping from his tongue, all formalities were gone, and Ernest was becoming an open book. His muddy brown eyes were less lucid.

"I ain't going to sit here and rekindle our times together," Sam said. "For me that was eight months ago. For you that was years ago."

"Inexplicable ain't it?" Ernest said.

"What?"

"Why time froze for us all those years. If we hadn't left Sawyer we could've lived out our lives normally," he said with a regretful expression. "I daydream a lot, about Virginia and me. I imagine us living together as husband and wife, raising younguns of our own, having grand babies, and dying in each other's arms. It's all I can do."

"I don't sympathize with you if that's what you're searching for,"

Sam said.

"Ain't seeking your sympathy. Just telling you how I feel. I've had this bottled up forever. I need to get it out," Ernest said, putting the cigarette butt out in the filled ashtray. "You'uns in love?" he asked Ellie. Ellie didn't know how to answer and looked at Sam with embarrassment. "I'm not trying to make you blush. If he loves you, hang onto him. He's a good man. A better man that I ever was."

"How we feel about each other doesn't concern you. Leave her out of this," Sam raised his voice.

Ellie noticed he didn't deny or confirm what Ernest asked. *Was she in love with him? She wasn't sure. Did she feel strongly for him and would she be devastated if she couldn't be with him?* Yes.

"I apologize. I forgot it ain't my business. I still think of you as my best friend," Ernest said. "After all this time."

"We ain't here to reminisce," Sam said.

"I know. Let me have this moment because what I'm fixin' to tell will change things," Ernest said. "We fought together in the war. Did he tell you that?"

Ellie said quietly, "Yes."

"We did everything together. There wasn't a place he was that I wasn't. Everyone teased us for it. Guess that's why I started getting sweet on Virginia, 'cause of Sam. I was around him so much, and she was always there. Never understood why it took me as long as it did to fall in love with her," he said and looked out distantly. He brought his gaze back to Ellie's, "She was an angel. So honest and kindhearted. I miss her." He frowned and said, "That picture you showed me. I regretted not taking one of her with me when I left. I'll never forget what she looks like, but if I could see it every day, that'd be something to get out of bed for."

"Are you telling me this so I'll feel sorry for you once you've confessed? I won't, Ernest. You left my little sister. She spends her days pining for you, waiting for you to return. It's all she lives for," he said, hurt brimming in his gray eyes. "Don't tell me how difficult it's been on you."

"The day we left. I had this feeling I'd never go back," he started. "It is a shame I was right."

"What happened to Jeremiah?" Sam asked in annoyance.

"None of us knew what to expect when we left that day. We kept wondering if the Yankees were gonna get us but after walking for over a day and no sign of them, we began to think maybe the war was over." He stood up and went back into the kitchen.

Sam gave a look of disgust to Ellie as Ernest sloppily poured rum and Coke into his glass.

Ellie leaned into Sam and whispered, "He may get too drunk to tell us what happened to Jeremiah."

"I'll force it out of him so help me," Sam gritted through his teeth.

"You need to chill the hell out," Ellie commanded in a low voice. "You're starting to scare me."

Sam turned to look at her, surprised by her statement. "I don't want to," he said with sincerity.

She placed her hand on his arm. "Promise me you'll calm down."

"I will," he said.

Ernest slogged his way back into the room. He swayed a little, and almost spilled the contents of his glass onto the nasty carpet. "Whoa," he said. He plopped down on the chair and stared at Ellie and Sam. "Where was I?"

"You were in the woods," Sam quickly answered, his hands balled into two fists. His leg began to tap back and forth impatiently.

He took a sip from his glass. "We kept walking and made camp when it grew dark. We thought it was odd we didn't hear or see nothing in the woods. Scared Jeremiah. He kept saying the Yankees were gonna kill us in the middle of the night. That they were just waiting for us to get to sleep. But the rest of us thought the war might be over. At least we hoped it was."

He continued with a frown, "None of us knew where we were headed. The woods were thick with brush and trees. We couldn't see the sun to find out if we were going north or south. Me and Jeremiah thought we should go back the other way, but Horace didn't agree. He was in command and made sure we knew he and Rufus had the rifles."

Sam leaned forward. "They threatened you?"

"Not at first. Horace is real good at getting you to do what he wants. That's why he runs this town. He makes you believe he's on your side, that he cares about you. Then he stabs you in the back, and by the time you figure it out, you're in his debt too deep to dig your way out." He took another cigarette and lit it, taking a long drag off of it. "Everyone is scared of him," he said, smoke blowing out of his thin lips. "It's how he likes it—ruling by fear. Rufus ain't any better. He does what Horace wants, and since he's the sheriff, there ain't much law here except theirs." He finished off his drink. His face was flushed, and his words were slurred together. "I ain't any better I 'spose since I'm their lackey." His lips twisted into disgust.

"Maybe you should drink coffee instead," Ellie said, noticing he didn't seem very steady. She could smell the alcohol on his breath, and his pupils were dilated.

He smiled at her. "It ain't going to sober me up if that's what you're aiming at. I ain't been sober since the day I left Virginia," he said.

"That's something to be proud of," Sam spat out.

"Wasn't bragging," Ernest said. "Just confessing my sins. Feels so good to tell you'uns." He picked up his empty glass, frowned, and placed it back down on the table. "Jeremiah decided if we didn't get nowhere by sunset, we'd part ways with Rufus and Horace. I wanted to get back to Virginia, and Jeremiah wanted to be with you'uns. I don't know how long we walked. Several hours?" He shrugged his shoulders. "It felt like a long time. Nothing was out there. And when I say nothing, it was virgin forest. Ain't even a trail out there. I'm sure it's changed since that time."

"When was this?" Ellie interrupted.

"1973," he answered. "I remember the sun was starting to set so me and Jeremiah decided we were gonna go our separate ways the next morning, but fate had other plans for us. I didn't notice him, but Jeremiah did. He's the one who called out for us to come see."

"Come see what?" Sam asked.

CHAPTER 22

"All of us had seen plenty of dead bodies since we fought in the war, but the sight of this shocked us. The man was hanging by his parachute in a tree. 'Course we didn't know what the parachute was, thought it was a queer contraption. We figured he was a criminal that had been hanged by some vigilantes or the law. Horace and Rufus wanted to cut him down from the tree. Never understood why. It weren't out of respect for the man. I think they wanted to see if he had anything on him that they could claim as their own. Gave me the chills." He shook slightly. "Stealing from a dead man has to be a sin. They told Jeremiah to give 'em his knife. He didn't want to. Rightfully so too. A man's weapon is all he has to protect him." He raised his eyebrows and let out a sigh. "Horace forced it off of him in so many ways. When a man is holding a rifle, you don't argue," he said and paused for a moment. "Rufus climbed up, 'cause Horace told him to, and cut the parachute strings. The man fell to the ground, and Horace and Rufus hovered over him like vultures."

"How long had the body been there?" Ellie asked.

"Can't right say." He scratched at his head. "Not too long. A week I 'spose. His flesh was rotting away, and he stank real bad," he grimaced and continued, "Rufus and Horace went at him like a wolf on its prey. Dug at him, took off his watch, and talked about taking his clothes, too. That was one of the other things we noticed that wasn't right. He was dressed right strange, and his watch wasn't like anything we'd ever seen."

Ellie and Sam didn't respond and waited for Ernest to continue.

"Thought that was going to be that but it weren't." His lips cast down, and his forehead wrinkled. "Rufus came running over to

Horace, carrying a large black bag. He was so giddy, shouting 'Look what I found!' while he held up a wad of American dollars. 'Course Horace told him to quit acting like a girl on her wedding day 'cause the money didn't look right. It didn't resemble the money from our time anyhow." He cleared his throat, the sound of phlegm coming to the surface. "Lord, I'm thirsty." He got up and poured more rum in his glass than Coke and sat back down. "Sure you don't want nothing to drink?"

"Yes," Sam said in a curt tone.

He guzzled the drink down. "Rufus found a newspaper article inside the man's jacket. It was dated in 1973 talking about a man who robbed one million dollars from a bank and was on the run. We figured the money that was on the man had to be the same money stolen from the bank 'cause the the description in the newspaper matched him. You can imagine Horace and Rufus' delight in finding that much money." He shook his head in a one swift movement, and steadied himself from falling over on his side. "None of us did or said anything for a while. It was a lot to take in. Jeremiah was the first to speak up. He wanted to go back to you'uns," he said, looking at Sam. "He said he wanted to tell you what we discovered about the time. He was fearful adamant that the money be turned in to the law, that it wasn't theirs to keep."

"It wasn't their money," Sam cut in.

"True, but Rufus and Horace didn't see it that way. They got very angry with Jeremiah. Said the money was theirs and they weren't returning it," he said. "Scariest sight to see when the light in a man's eyes flickers out. Jeremiah saw it; I saw it. He knew there was no getting through to them. He tried to leave, but they wouldn't let him."

Ellie lost her breath, and Sam leaned forward, his fists pounded against the table in a loud thud. The rattling didn't startle Ernest, he was too far gone to care.

"What did they do?" Sam shouted.

"You see... Rufus still had Jeremiah's knife. He held it up at him, like he was gonna use it on him." He wiped the sweat off of his forehead with the back of his hand. "I'll never forget what Horace said. 'Give me the knife,' he told Rufus, and he handed it over to him without question. He has always obeyed his brother on command. I ain't no better though," he said regretfully. "I thought that maybe Horace was going to give it back to Jeremiah and let him leave peacefully. That he hadn't lost his soul. He strolled over to him, smiling even, like all was good. He even said, 'We'll return the money.' It didn't hit me at first. The way he was holding the knife, the empty look in his eyes. I thought it was a peace offering. That he had come to his senses." He continued to look down, avoiding their eyes. "But then I heard a sound that haunts me to this day. And I knew. Horace had done it."

"He killed him?" Sam said in disbelief. He sat back against the chair, his mouth wide open. Ellie mirrored Sam, surprised by Ernest's admission.

"Yes," he said quietly. "Jeremiah wasn't dead though. He was bleeding something fierce from his stomach. And Horace just stood over him, watching him moan in pain. He was possessed at that point. There weren't no turning back for him."

Ellie and Sam sat stunned, trying to digest Ernest's confession.

"Horace and Rufus were keeping the money and told me I could have a portion too. But I didn't want it. It was blood money, and I didn't want any part of it. Horace gave the knife to Rufus and told him to stab Jeremiah, to finish him off for good. I ain't never seen someone so eager to kill in my life," Ernest said, crying.

"They killed him, and you stood there and watched? Why didn't you grab one of their rifles?" Sam asked indignantly.

"Once I realized what Horace had done, it was too late. Rufus had the knife, and I didn't have any weapons to fight them back with. Horace and Rufus knew they held the power, and they told me to join them or die," he said. "Said they'd kill me and all of you'uns if I didn't prove I was with 'em."

"How did you prove it?" Sam asked, knowing something more nefarious was at the surface of this horrible tale.

"You don't wanna know. Done horrible things for them since that time. I was stuck," he said.

"How so?" Sam said. "You could have left them and come back to us."

Ernest shook his head. "Life played one of its cruel tricks on me. I tried going back more than once and couldn't find you'uns. My sense of direction ain't never been good. You know that. Jeremiah's the one who could've taken me back."

Sam leapt across the table, his hands balled into two fists. His jaw clenched tight. He was within inches of Ernest's face. "You are a weak man!" he shouted.

"I know," Ernest agreed. "Just kill me. Put me out of my misery," Ernest begged, moving his face closer to Sam, hoping he'd do just that.

"Sam!" Ellie warned. "Don't!"

Sam looked into Ernest's cloudy eyes. It took all of the strength that he could muster to move his fists away from his withered face. "Killing you does nothing but save you. Your punishment is living with what you've done," he spat and moved away from Ernest and next to Ellie.

"I'm sorry," Ernest said, tears streaming down his face.

"I don't accept your apology. I'm glad Virginia ain't with a man like you," he said with bitterness. "It's time we left, Ellie." He took a hold of Ellie's hand and stormed out the door.

"Sam, tell Virginia I'm sorry!" Ernest cried as they left. "Tell her I didn't mean to hurt her!"

Ellie and Sam sat inside the car wondering if the world around them had crumbled and if there was any way to pick up the pieces. Her hands shook. She struggled to get the key into the ignition. Her skin was damp, and she was perspiring all over. The thought of driving didn't seem probable. She didn't even know if she'd be able to make it out of the driveway, let alone drive several hours home.

The keys slipped from her shaking hands to the car floor. Tears in her eyes, she picked them up and laid them on her lap. Sam's heavy breaths were all that she could hear. The inside of the car grew warm, sweat trickled down their foreheads, but neither of them bothered to wipe it off.

"Ellie," Sam whispered. His face was distraught and his tone unrecognizable.

She sniffed, the tears continuing to fall. "It's so awful," she said, horrified by the truth. That there were people like Rufus and Horace who existed in the world. People who did terrible things and got away with it. People who traveled through life without a conscience to guide them.

"I know," he agreed, his voice low and full of an emptiness she had never heard before. "I never should have gotten you involved."

She turned to face him, struck by his statement. "You didn't get me involved," she said while sobbing. "I wanted to help you. And I'd do it all over again too." She swiped the tears off of her face with the back of her hand.

He reached for her hand and brought it to his lips, kissing the tips of her fingers, then brought it down to his hand, intertwining his fingers in hers. "In this dark world, you are my light, Elisabeth," he said.

She tried to catch her breath. It was the most beautiful string of words any guy had ever said to her.

"Thank you," she said, wishing she were more astute. What she really wanted tell him was that he made her heart leap out of her chest. That it no longer belonged to her; it was his.

Her hands had stopped shaking, and she placed the keys in the ignition, starting the car. As she backed out of the narrow driveway and looked in the rear view mirror, she swore she saw someone hiding behind a tree. She looked again, and the figure was gone.

CHAPTER 23

"I can't drive anymore," she said. "We're gonna have to stay somewhere overnight."

"Whatever you need to do," Sam said, feeling just as much on edge as she was.

Traveling on a two-lane country road at nighttime and in the middle of the mountains of Georgia made their prospects of finding accommodations even more of a challenge.

Ellie squinted her eyes and leaned forward. "It's so dark out here."

She drove slowly, afraid she'd run over a wild animal running across or veer off the unmarked road from lack of good vision. A light shined in the distance giving her hope that some sort of civilization was ahead.

"Finally," she said, turning into a parking lot. "This isn't the Homewood Suites, but it'll do for tonight. Plus, the rooms are super cheap," she said, pointing to the sign.

The Mountain Inn was the only accommodation within miles. Built in the 1960s, it was probably once a nice place for families to stay whiled they vacationed in the mountains. With the onset of newer, more plush hotels nestled in the Blue Ridge Mountains, The Mountain Inn became less of a first choice, and more of one out of desperation or sheer frugality. Her dad would love the affordable price: $29.99 a night, plus HBO. Ellie figured it was better to stay in a motel far enough away from Rutherford. She wanted to forget everything about that dreadful town. Plus, she was just plain tired. The prospect of driving further while they searched for a better place to stay was out of the question.

They checked in, discovering they had their choice of rooms.

Most were unoccupied, and the owner tried to persuade them to take the "The Honeymoon Suite," which was available for an extra ten dollars a night. Ellie kindly objected. Hearing the words "Honeymoon Suite" made her think of vibrating heart-shaped beds with pink velvet bedspreads and carpeted ceilings.

"If you're hungry, we got a restaurant here on the premises," the owner said. "Good food, too." He smiled too eagerly.

"Thanks," Ellie said.

Fireflies lit their path as they made their way down the sidewalk facing the long strip of rooms in the one-story structure. Coyotes howled in the distance, and a full moon glowed in the dark night sky. Cicadas chirped incessantly, and the fragrant scent of jasmine filled the warm summer night air. It was a pleasant night given what they had been through. The kind of night to sit outside on the front porch and sip iced tea, hold hands and stare up at the stars. The type of night good for stolen kisses and whispers of sweet nothings.

She put the key in the lock and turned, pushing the door open. The room wasn't as bad as she had expected. A fresh, clean piney scent permeated the room. The carpet, although old, was clean and didn't show signs of wear or tear. There was one double bed with a floral bedspread, two yellow swivel chairs, a round formica table, and a boxed television set that was at least twenty years old. The bathroom was just as dated as the room but recently cleaned. The room had a vintage feel about it, like something Ellie had seen when she watched reruns of television shows from the 1970s.

"At least the room is clean," she said, her fingers running against the table without a spec of dust clinging to them. Her stomach grumbled loudly, and she laughed in embarrassment.

"I'm famished too," Sam said.

"Let's get something to eat then," she said. "I'm calling Jonah first." She walked outside and clicked his name on her phone.

"Hey, Shrimp," she said, walking down the sidewalk.

"Dad is coming home in two days. He's getting a little suspicious that he hasn't talked to you both times he's called."

"Yeah, I figured," Ellie said with worry. "I'll call him when I get home tomorrow. What'd you tell him this time?"

A painted white bench sat against the wall. Tired of pacing, she sat on it and watched as a few cars high beamed headlights passed by on the road in front of the inn.

"That you were in town at the library using the internet, something about your schedule for school," he said, chewing food.

"At least that sounds believable," she said.

He swallowed. "More believable than the fact that you're traveling the country with a guy from the Civil War. Yeah, I'd think so," he said.

"How's Bosco?"

"Hungry and sleepy. A total sloth."

"Like you," she said.

"So, another night in a hotel with Johnny Rebel?"

"What's that got to do with anything?" Ellie said, her cheeks ruddy and warm.

"Just be smart, Ellie. I'd hate for you to become a part of the statistic and end up on that stupid MTV show. Just sayin'." Before Ellie had time to reply, he added, "Listen, *CSI* is on, so I'll talk to you later." He hung up the phone.

***

The restaurant was thriving with hordes of senior citizens. "It's the blue hair convention," Ellie whispered to Sam as they entered. They sat down and ordered drinks, watching as couples danced on the raised wooden dance floor below a gaudy disco light shimmering a spectrum of colors. The DJ played tunes from the sixties and seventies, songs that caused the rowdy crowd to cheer vigorously and clap their hands attempting to relive a part of their long gone youth.

"They're a lively group," Ellie said.

Sam bopped his head back and forth and tapped his foot to the beat of the music. "I like this," he said loudly, talking over the music.

"It's the Supremes," she said. "Motown is the best. I'll have to introduce you to more music."

"I would like that." He offered her a crooked grin and studied the menu."What is a grilled cheese?"

"An awesome sandwich. It's melted cheese between two slices of bread. You have to get it," she pushed. "Trust me." She raised her eyebrows and grinned. "When I need comfort food, I love a grilled cheese with tomato soup."

"It says it comes with that," Sam said, pointing to the menu.

"Then get it," she said.

Ellie scanned the restaurant, noticing the 70s décor was a constant theme throughout the Inn. The walls were painted an avocado green and had kitchen inspired root vegetables as the border wallpaper. The booths were a dark emerald green and in need of replacement. Duct tape covered the tears, and every table had a red checkered table cloth. The ugliness factor didn't deter the older customers from patronizing the lackluster restaurant.

They finished their dinner and sat quietly, watching everyone else moving to the beat of the music. Ellie felt like she was back at her senior prom sitting like a bump on a log.

Going with Zane Elders had been a mistake—a mistake Ellie wished she could have wiped from her memory. Zane was decent looking, popular, and seemed like the safest choice for a prom date. They shared a few classes together, and he always had the class laughing with his antics. He was the quintessential class clown. He couldn't talk about anything without making a joke out of it. That was part of the appeal to Ellie.

Prom was just a few months after her mom had died, and the last thing she wanted was to be with someone that made her think, that noticed she was numb. Zane was the perfect choice: vacuous and incapable of having one deep thought. On the dance floor, he lacked confidence. Clumsy and stiff, he proved to Ellie that there was such a thing as someone having two left feet. His ego had been wounded. In the classroom, he was the court jester. On the dance floor, unmemorable. He refused to dance with her—even during the slow songs. Dancing would have taken some of the pain away. It would have made her forget. Instead of spending time together, Zane left Ellie watching all of her friends dancing with their dates, having the time of their lives while she sat back and let life pass her by. She stole a few dances with friends but not enough to keep her occupied through the night.

Hours later, and after too much drinking, Zane resurfaced. He was beyond drunk; inappropriate words slipped from his tongue. His hands wandered too much. Ellie refused to get in the car with him and called her dad to come pick her up. Zane eventually found a ride home with one of his friends. He never called Ellie to see if she made it home okay. He never apologized for being a jerk. When they saw each other in class, he'd look the other way, and Ellie would glare at him, hating herself for ruining her prom by going with someone like him. She was better than that. In life's big moments, she hoped that prom was a small spec soon to be forgotten.

The DJ switched up the tempo and put on a slower song. His deep voice resonated through the microphone. "This one is for all you lovebirds out there," he said, playing The Bee Gees' *How Deep is Your Love.*

Sam stood up, offering Ellie his hand. "Would you like to dance?" he asked.

Surprised but pleased, she answered "Yes," and walked with him to the dance floor. She gazed up at him as they stood a few inches apart from one another. "You sure you know how to dance?" It was a reasonable question. Did they dance back in his time? Then Ellie remembered all of the period piece movies where peopled danced the Virginia Reel and other types of dances.

He smirked. "I know how to dance." He wrapped his arms around her waist.

She leaned into his chest, hearing the pounding of his heart, and feeling his warm breath on her hair. Wisps of it blew in front of her eyes, sending a long line of goosebumps up and down her body. They swayed back and forth to the music, feeling the weight of the words to the song's lyrics about love. Sam brought Ellie closer to him, his hands on the small of her back. She moved hers up and around the back of his neck, looking into his eyes, wondering if he was going to kiss her. It was killing her. This was the perfect moment.

Sam could dance. His feet moved smoothly, and he took the lead, confident in his movement, in what he was doing.

This is how prom should have been, Ellie thought.

The song ended, and they made their way outside of the restaurant, wandering to a small courtyard area filled with wooden benches; a working fountain was centered in the middle of paver stones. They sat and heard the sound of water flowing endlessly and the thumping of the music coming from the speakers in the restaurant. The full moon cast a gleam of light on them, giving them a peek at each other's faces.

"I need to tell you about me before this goes any further," Sam said seriously.

"Okay," Ellie said, reaching for his hand. She had waited all this time, and now whatever he said wouldn't matter, she thought. But then she second guessed herself wondering if he had done something terrible, could she forgive and forget? Everyone had flaws, didn't they? But what if he had done something so heinous there was no forgiving him?

"I'm very fond of you," he said, and Ellie let out a laugh. He looked wounded. "What do you find so humorous?"

Ellie felt a pang to her heart. She didn't want to hurt him, but sometimes she forgot she was dealing with someone from another time, and saying things like "I'm very fond of you" seemed almost comical when they shouldn't have. It was better than, "I like you. Do you like me? Check yes or no; now let's go out."

"I'm sorry, Sam." And she was. She wanted him to be fond of her, more than fond, and in extreme like with her leaning close to love. "It's just nowadays guys usually say 'I like you' when they like a girl," she tried to explain delicately.

"Oh," he said; hurt lingered in his eyes.

"Really, Sam, I'm sorry." She tugged on his hand, trying to get him to see the sincerity in her eyes. "I like you, Sam. More than like actually," she admitted and looked down. "I'm way more than fond of you."

He smiled at the sound of her words. "We would be courting if this were my time."

"Well...since it's my time, we should date," she said. "You know, call each other boyfriend and girlfriend. But only if you want." She shrugged, trying to feign indifference but she was waiting, hoping he'd agree.

"I would very much like that, but I need to tell you this about me first, and if you don't share those same feelings after, I understand." His smiled faded to a more serious expression. "I," he started and sighed through his nose.

He sat for a moment, contemplating what he was going to say. He'd start but no words would come out. He sighed through his nose again, and opened his mouth, wanting the words to come out.

"It's okay," Ellie said, weaving her fingers into his.

"I didn't fight in the war that long. Six months and thirteen days," he said with a frown.

"I guess I figured you were in longer," she said, trying to follow him.

"I was supposed to be. My time was meant to be a year."

"What happened?" Ellie asked, shifting so that she was sitting cross legged and facing Sam.

"I left, Ellie," he confessed. "I just left."

"You deserted?" Ellie asked, allowing what he told her to sink in.

"I hated everything the war stood for. Watching young men die and for what? To keep slaves? To keep the union out of southern politics? I didn't have no qualms with the union, and I certainly didn't think it was right to own slaves."

"What happened?"

"I told Ernest I was leaving. He said he wouldn't fight if I wasn't there. I told him to make his own decision."

"Did he?"

"Yes and no. A part of me thinks he left because of me; the other part thinks he left because he wanted to be near Virginia again. Ernest ain't a fighter."

"Are you?"

"A fighter?" he asked, and she nodded. "Yes. I will fight for what I believe in. I'll fight for my loved ones. But fighting for something I think is wrong— I can't do."

Ellie realized the similarity she shared with Sam. She'd fight for her family no matter what the price may be. But having the guts to walk away from a war? She didn't know if she'd ever be that self-assured.

"I planned to leave later that night. It was easier to escape unnoticed in the dark. Ernest decided to come with me, and I thought it would be just the two of us. But Horace and Rufus said they were going, too. And Jeremiah.."

"Did they object to the war?" Ellie asked.

"No, I don't believe so. I think Horace is an opportunist, and he knew the south was losing. We all knew it. Horace wanted to be on the winning side. And Rufus? Well, he did whatever his brother did."

"What about Jeremiah?" she asked, noticing Sam hadn't mentioned why he chose to go with him.

"He wanted to stay but decided to leave because of me. I regret that. I made him lose a part of himself."

"You didn't make him leave, Sam. He made his own choice,"

Ellie said.

"Oh, I don't know, Ellie. Jeremiah was young. He didn't have a mind of his own yet."

"He chose to join, didn't he?" Ellie cut in.

"If I had stayed, he would have stayed. It was as simple as that. I am the reason he left. That's why Uncle Caleb blames me because he knows Jeremiah would follow me to the sun and I should have set a better example."

"You showed him that you stood up for what you believed in. How is that bad?"

"I'm not right sure about that. My decision cost my family everything. It's one of the reasons we left, because we were known criminals. Leaving the army was against the law, and all of us had broken that law. On top of that, I was hiding Moses, who was a runaway slave, which was a serious crime. There wasn't a day that went by where I wasn't peering over my shoulder." He looked down, slowly shaking his head. "I just hope Caleb will come to forgive me in time."

"He can't keep blaming you," she said. "Is that how Moses came to live with your family?"

"Yes," Sam answered. "He escaped from a plantation in the town next to Sawyer. I couldn't turn him in. None of us could. So we thought if we let him hide out with us for a while, we'd help him find his way up north. I was planning to go with him to Chicago."

Ellie was surprised by what Sam told her. "You were going to leave?"

"I always wanted to travel, and me and Moses decided Chicago would be a good place to start."

"You're good friends," Ellie stated.

"He's become a member of the family."

"How come he doesn't talk?"

Sam took a deep breath. "He had a real mean plantation owner. Meaner than a snake and the devil himself. Let's just leave it at that," he said with a grimace. He grew quiet for a moment and turned his gaze to meet hers. "Do you still think I'm a good man even though I left the war?"

"Sam, you are a good person. What you did took courage— leaving the war, helping Moses, all of it."

"Most would beg to differ. I didn't honor my commitment."

"It's not about honoring a commitment," she said, leaning into him. "You did what you thought was right. That makes you a man with a conscience in my book. If I had been in your shoes, I would hope I'd do the same thing."

"You do?" he asked hopeful.

"I'd like to think I would, but I've never been in a situation where I've had to make that kind of choice. I'm not sure I'm as brave as you."

"You are the most courageous woman I've ever met," he said seriously. "I hope this hasn't changed your opinion of me." He waited for her answer.

"I don't judge you for what you did, Sam. It makes me like you even more. In fact, you just earned a few extra brownie points." She smiled assuredly.

"Brownie points?"

"It's a figure of speech. It means it makes me like you more." She grinned too broad.

"I hope that I tip the scale in brownie points then." He leaned closer to her and whispered in her ear, "Now if you don't object, I'd like to kiss you."

She answered him with her eyes, and he pulled her closer to him. His fingers grazed the back of her neck, touching the soft baby hairs that curled up on the ends. His thumb gently caressed her cheek, and his lips barely touched the surface of hers. He kissed her slowly and carefully, as if he was afraid to be careless.

After several minutes of kissing, they stopped and shared an understanding look. Their feelings were raw and fresh and out in the open. Ellie wanted to tell Sam how much she enjoyed the kiss, how it was toe curling—the kind of kiss she daydreamed about. She wanted to wake up in his arms and hear his slow deep drawl whispering "good morning" in her ear.

***

Ellie stopped in the restaurant's restroom on their way out. She stared at herself in the mirror. Her hair was unkempt; her face was blotchy and covered with pink spots. She tucked her hair behind her ears and was mortified at the sight. They were red as a strawberry.

"Crap!" she said, checking herself. She splashed some water on her face, hoping the difference in temperature would shock her face back to normal. She waited a few minutes. No way was she going to go back out there looking like that.

She checked her reflection one more time, and noticed the white box hanging up on the wall behind her. She spun around, and took a few steps heading over to it. Like any other dispenser found in a woman's restroom, inside of it were tampons, pads, and condoms sold at low prices for emergency instances. Ellie opened her purse, and slid four quarters into the slot. She hesitated for a moment, thinking of the repercussions of what she was doing. This was it, she thought. If she bought this, it meant things could go as far as she wanted them to.

She thought long and hard, studying that dispenser like it was the ACT, and then she clicked on the button. One packaged condom came out. She carefully placed it in her purse, and left the bathroom, meeting Sam outside.

***

Ellie dressed in her Pj's. She emptied all of the bags of candy on the bed and motioned for Sam to sit down next to her. "Your choice," she said.

He grabbed a few Twizzlers and shared a smile—the goofy, love struck kind.

"Here," Ellie said. "Use one as a straw. It's so good that way." She took two Twizzlers and plopped them down in the two Coke cans. They drank and ate candy until their bellies were full to the point of feeling sick. It was well after midnight, but time didn't matter. They were too busy getting to know each other.

"I got this scar from falling off a fence. Jonah and I used to climb it to use the community pool. Dad was too cheap to pay dues, so we'd hop the fence to sneak in." She pointed to her knee.

"I got this scar from chicken wire catching onto my britches." He ran his finger across a long, pale pink mark on his calf.

They continued to share more stories, hoping to soak up as much information about each other as possible. "When was your first kiss?" Ellie asked.

"You don't ask a man that type of question," Sam answered.

"Why not?"

He shrugged. "You just don't."

She rolled her eyes at him and said, "I was thirteen and it was with Bobby Jenner. It was terrible. He had a cow tongue and tasted like cheese." She made a squeamish face.

"Cheese ain't bad," Sam said.

"It makes your breath stink."

"I was a lot older than you when I first kissed a girl—sixteen. Her name was Pamela, and no, Ellie, my first kiss wasn't as bad as yours."

Ellie wondered if he was teasing her. "Well, lucky you." She stuck her tongue out a him.

He laughed and then grew more serious. "It wasn't my favorite kiss," he said. "That would be tonight with you." He ran his fingers through her hair. They found their way down to her cheeks. Slowly, his fingers trailed to her parted lips, outlining the shape of them.

"Your lips are the shape of a heart," he said, and he leaned in to kiss her.

This time it was neither slow nor careful, but much more hectic, reckless even. They couldn't get enough of each other and forgot to come back up for air. He kissed her with hunger, devouring her completely, nibbling her ear lobes and applying the lightest of kisses from her throat to her shoulder blades. She rolled over onto him, straddling him, and his hands tightened their grip around her petite waist.

He tugged on her shirt, slightly lifting it, as his fingers brushed the surface of her flat stomach to the lower part of her back. Goosebumps formed in an instant. "Is this all right?" he whispered.

"Yes," she breathed. Her full weight on him, she moved in motion with him, their hands and mouths exploring each other, finding places that were once off limits, now open and yearning for each other's touch.

"Ellie?" he questioned, his voice husky and deep.

"Uh hmm," she murmured between kisses.

He looked into her eyes. His breath rapid, and his voice evoking desire. "Are you certain this is all right?"

"Yes," she said with one hundred percent certainty.

***

Waking up in each other's arms felt natural. Ellie realized it was the first time she had slept through the entire night since before her mom died. She watched as Sam slept, his face composed of a sweetness and gentleness that she had grown attached to. There was no going back. She was falling fast and hard.

He opened his eyes, and offered her a crooked smile. "Good morning," he said, his fingers finding their way to her face. "This is the most beautiful sight I've ever woke up to."

"Sam," she started, wondering what would be the perfect words to convey how she felt, to express what he meant to her.

"Elisabeth," he said her name slowly, pronouncing each syllable as if he were trying to bottle it up like a treasure.

She searched his gray eyes trying to read what was behind them. God, she was frustrated. She was the sickening epitome of *that* girl— just like all others she couldn't tolerate back in school— insecure and overly sensitive. She could kick herself for laying there wondering what he was thinking, desperate to know if he was into her as much as she was into him.

"What are you thinking?" he asked, his fingers still running through her hair, soothing her.

"Last night meant a lot to me," she started. She might as well open up. If he ripped her heart into shreds, she wanted it done sooner than later.

"And to me as well," he said.

"What I mean is... I haven't done that before," she admitted, feeling the warmth rise to her cheeks and ears. Sure, she made out plenty with Russell Thompson, her boyfriend of three months. But not the way she and Sam had.

"The same is true for me," he said.

"It is?" Her eyes widened.

"Of course, Ellie. I told you, I didn't court but one girl, and we weren't ever *that* intimate."

"Did you want to be?" Ellie pried.

"I'm a man, Ellie." His answer gave her in a yes in so many ways.

"Oh," she said, her lips curved downward in an instant. She rolled on her other side, facing the window, feeling an overwhelming sadness. She had been kicked in the gut.

He touched her shoulder. "Ellie. What is the matter?"

"I get it. Things happened between us because you're a guy," she said, trying to fight the tears. She felt so stupid, so vulnerable.

His grip tightened, but was gentle, and he turned her over, facing him. "No, you don't understand. I was never like that with her, like I was with you, because I have feelings for you."

"You do?" Ellie asked. She couldn't help but smile.

"Yes. Do you?" he asked. He was just as vulnerable, which made Ellie love him even more.

"Sam, I want to hold your hand and go to the movies together, and share spaghetti like they did *Lady and The Tramp*." He gave her a strange look. "It's a movie" she explained and continued, "I want to run in the rain with you, and kiss you at my front door, and then wait for your call the minute I get inside."

She knew the odds were against them. That they had more

upfront conflict to deal with than most couples, but if they could get past that, they were going to be okay. That's all she wanted, for it all to be all right.

He laughed. "We will do that all and more," he said. "I would do anything to be with you. You are my passion."

"Promise?" she asked, taking an uneven breath. She was trying hard to stay composed by what Sam had just said to her.

"I swear on it," he said and brought her closer to him.

She looked up at him, and he kissed her on her forehead. To Ellie it felt as intimate as the other kisses they had shared. The way he looked at her mirrored her own feelings for him. To be so into someone that you can't take a breath without thinking of them. She now knew what it felt like to be crazy, senselessly in love.

They lay there holding hands, listening to the sounds of traffic on the road, and hearing the owner talking to someone outside.

Ellie looked over at Sam and saw his smile had faded into a frown.

"What is it?" She moved closer to him.

"We need to go back and see Ernest," he said.

"Why, Sam? It's over, isn't it?" She knew it wasn't. *Why'd I even say that*, she thought.

"No." He shook his head sadly. "He needs to be the one to talk to Granny and them. They won't believe me about the time. They were skeptical when we left, and they need to hear it from him. They need to see him in person to believe."

"And he and Virginia need closure," Ellie added softly. "She won't ever get over him otherwise."

"I want her to move on," Sam said. "All of them need to. I'm beginning to..."

"I don't want to go back."

"I know, but he owes this to us."

"Back to Rutherford we go, then." She grimaced. "We should buy nose plugs before we go."

He laughed. "It does have a stench about it."

"It's like sewage." She made a grossed-out face. "I don't want to stay too long. That place gives me the creeps, and knowing what we do about Rufus and Horace, the less time we're there the better."

CHAPTER 24

They pulled up into Ernest's driveway. His truck door was wide open. The engine chugged as it idled in park. *In Dreams* by Roy Orbison played on the truck's antiquated radio, and several of Ernest's cats sat perched on the hood and inside on his worn bucket seats. The cats shrilling meows mimicked the sound of sirens. Their tails swayed back and forth against droplets of blood that were splattered all over the white hood. The keys danced and jingled, hanging from the ignition—the sound of an irritating buzz added to the array of noises.

Ellie turned her car off, and looked to Sam for guidance. "Do you think it's safe for us to get out?" she asked.

He turned around, and climbed over to the back seat, and pulled the Bowie knife which was hidden on the floor. "I'm going inside. You stay here."

"Sam, don't," Ellie warned. "I don't think it's safe."

Sam jumped out, gently closing the door behind him. He held the knife upward and out, treading carefully and quietly, moving like an animal in search of its prey. Ellie knew there was no way she could wait in the car and allow Sam to take all the risk. She took her keys out of the ignition and placed them in her pocket. She got out of the car and ran swiftly to catch up to him. The song echoed in the background—the reverb amplified. She felt the hairs on the back of her neck stand up.

"Ellie," he whispered with unease. "I told you to stay there."

"Sorry, but we're in this together."

He gave her a look, pursing his lips. He sighed heavily. "You are obstinate."

"If that's the worst thing you can say about me, then I'm not so bad, am I?" she whispered back to him.

"Get behind me," he said, moving her behind him, shielding her from whatever lie ahead of them. His height and size blocked her from seeing anything.

She stared down at her feet; a trail of blood led them to the inside of Ernest's house. His door was wide open, and the inside had been ransacked. Furniture was broken. The once neat stacks of newspapers were now spread sporadically on the floor. Things had been knocked over, like a tornado came and unleashed its powerful force.

They heard a loud thud, and Sam instantly moved Ellie further behind him. He held the knife out. An orange cat trailed past them, meowing, and then ran outside.

"Stupid cat," Ellie grumbled, her heart beating wildly.

They walked further, and Sam suddenly stopped. "Ellie," he said frantically, and bent down to Ernest, who laid on the floor half unconscious.

Ellie gasped.

Sam leaned his head against his heart. "It's still beating," he said to Ellie.

"There's blood all over him," she said, noticing his shirt and pants. Blood oozed out of his nose and mouth. His left eye, puffy and swollen, was turning violet. An open bottle of rum laid on the floor next to him.

Ernest moaned. He squinted his right eye, trying to regain focus.

"What happened?" Sam hovered over him.

"Got beat up," Ernest croaked.

"By who?" Sam asked.

"Rufus and his boy." He tried lifting his head but shrieked in pain from the sudden movement. "They jumped me outside and beat on me all the way in here." He groaned again.

"Don't try to move," Ellie said. She got up and walked to the kitchen, soaking several paper towels in water. She wrung them out and placed them on his face, wiping the blood away as it trickled down his body.

"I think they broke a rib." He squinted, inhaling a harsh sounding breath, his chest rattling. "Help me up," he said to Sam, who put his arm behind his shoulders and slowly sat him up. Ernest wailed in agony, showing his discomfort. "Yes. I'd say they did."

He took a wet paper towel, held it against his bloodied lips, and grimaced from its bitter, metallic taste. He spat, blood splattered on his shaggy carpet. His palms against the floor, he heaved, pushing himself up. Sam and Ellie helped lift him and sat him down in a chair.

He breathed out, exhausted by the movement.

"Do you have asprin?" she asked.

"In my cabinet over the sink," he answered.

She went back into the kitchen, opening the cabinet door. An array of bottles filled it, both prescription and nonprescription pills. Whatever the ailment, he had a pill for. She moved the bottles around, searching for asprin, and found it in the back of the shelf. She took two pills from the bottle and filled up a nearby glass with water, and carried them to Ernest.

"Here." She handed him the pills, and he popped them in his mouth and swallowed without drinking water.

"Thank you," he said, coughing with his arm tight against his chest. He doubled over, and groaned. "I thought the rum would help, but I passed out before I could drink any."

If Ellie didn't know about him or his history, she'd think he was a harmless old man living like a recluse trying to hide from life before it found him.

Sam sat on the chair across from him. Ellie stood behind him, too anxious to sit. All she could think about was the fact that one of the men Ernest spoke of was a murderer and had just beaten him. There was no explanation for inflicting that amount of harm on another human being.

"Why did he do this to you?" Sam asked.

"Said it was a warning. That if I told you'uns anything, the next time I'd be dead and you'uns with me."

Ellie found herself sitting down next to Sam. Jaws dropped, and mouths wide open, they both let what Ernest said sink in. This wasn't a game. This was real, and their lives were in danger.

"How did he know we talked?" Sam asked as Ellie realized the figure she saw in the rear view mirror could have been one of them. The thought gave her the chills, and she instantly shuddered. Sam noticed and asked with concern, "Ellie?"

"I'm okay," she breathed. Fear filled her to the core. Never in her life would she think she'd be a part of something as dangerous as what she was involved in now. "I saw something... someone when we left, but I didn't know for sure." She bit on her lip.

"It was them," Ernest said. "Waiting till you left. They knew you were here. When you'uns met me in town, I had just been to the police station. I told Rufus you'uns weren't meaning no harm. He must have followed you'uns out here and saw us talking."

"What did you tell them?" Sam asked.

"Didn't get much time to speak. They laid into me real good, right in my good eye too," Ernest said, pointing at his swollen eye.

"Told them you were trying to see if we knew about the time issue. Didn't mention I told you'uns about Jeremiah and what they had done but Rufus forced it out of me."

"Do they remember where we live? Did you give them Ellie's name?" He shook Ernest, and he moaned in pain.

"No. I don't even know her name," he cried. "They don't know where you live. They tried going back and got lost each time. Just the fact that you'uns knew the truth about them, they would've killed you'uns long ago if they knew their way back."

Sam sat down, taking his hands off of Ernest.

"Do you have an ice pack?" Ellie asked. She had to do something. Sitting there and hearing it all was too much.

"Don't know," Ernest answered and coughed again. He spat blood onto a wet paper towel. "That can't be good." He frowned.

Ellie got up, making her way back into the kitchen. She opened the freezer door. The interior was covered in grime and appeared as if it hadn't been clean in a very long time. She grabbed a paper towel and used it to rummage through the freezer, searching for an ice pack. There wasn't one. She grabbed a frozen bag of peas instead and closed the door, handing it to Ernest.

He brought the bag of peas up to his eye. "Better," he said, attempting to smile.

Ellie tried not to pity Ernest. He was like Bosco had been when he showed up on her front lawn: tattered and torn on the outside. She wondered if beneath the exterior was a good man. *He had to be*, she thought. He was once best friends with Sam, which meant he had to have been a decent person at one time. The remorse and guilt that consumed him was evidence he had a conscience.

"Why did you come back?" Ernest asked. "Ain't safe for you'uns to be here now. They could be out there hiding and watching."

"I need you to come back with me—to set things right. They need to hear everything from you," Sam said. "But I don't right know that it is a good idea." He looked over at Ellie. "This has gotten dangerous."

"You said he's the only one that would make them believe," Ellie said to Sam.

Ernest turned his aching head. "Virginia don't need to see me like this no how."

"This ain't about you. It's about making things right," Sam said.

"Sam's right, Ernest. She needs closure, and the rest of them won't believe our crazy story even if it is the truth," Ellie added.

Ernest thought for a moment. "I got nothing to live for. They're coming back, and when they do, they'll finish me off," he said, sending a shiver down Ellie's spine.

"They'll hurt you again?" Sam asked with concern.

"Hurt me? They already done that. They're aiming to kill me. I'm nothing to them, and they know they'd get away with it." He coughed again and moaned in pain. "Gonna need to tape up these ribs before we go."

Ellie asked Ernest, "Do you think they would follow us?"

"Hard to tell. If they knew you was here, yes."

Ellie looked at Sam with fear. He tried to reassure her, but she could see he was just as worried as she was.

"It will be all right," he said. He turned his attention to Ernest and said, "We should leave."

Ernest steadied himself as Sam helped him up from the chair. "My cats," he said. A few had circled around him.

"You won't be gone that long," Ellie said.

"A day there ain't the same as it is here," he said to her.

"No." She shook her head. "Time's speeding up somehow. Or going back to normal?" She scrunched her face in contemplation. "Either way, it's moving faster."

One of the cat's jumped up on the table and Ernest petted him dotingly. "Still gonna leave food and water out for 'em. I got me a pet door so they can come and go as they please. But some of 'em are older and ain't so inclined to leave the house."

"We need to tape up those ribs too. Do you have a first aid kit?" Ellie asked.

"In my bathroom. I'll get it," he said.

"No. Let me," Ellie offered. "Sam can help you with the cats."

Ellie walked into the other room; it was just as much as a disaster as the rest of the house. The bed was covered in piles of clothes. The floor was just as cluttered with unopened cardboard boxes scattered throughout. The room had a distinct odor about it too: cat urine and cigarette smoke. Ellie noticed cat droppings and bowls of food on the floor. She dry-heaved and ran into the bathroom, thinking she'd throw up any moment. A few cockroaches crawled on the sink, and Ellie jumped back. Whatever nausea she had before had dissipated. All she could think about was finding the first aid kit and getting out of that room. She opened the medicine cabinet and pulled out a rusted box with the words "First Aid" printed on the front. She ran out of the room, scratching at her head, arms, and legs, hoping that none of the insects or other things latched onto her.

"I don't want Ellie to get hurt," Sam said to Ernest.

Ellie hid behind the wall, listening to their conversation, knowing it was wrong to spy but she wanted to see where the conversation was headed.

"I know," Ernest said.

"It's my fault she is involved. She is the best thing that has ever happened to me," Sam said, more to himself than to Ernest.

Ellie entered the room, holding the first aid kit. "Let's doctor you up and get going."

***

Ellie was wound up and feeling edgy. She wanted to take Ernest back to Sam's, let him tell his side of the story, and then drop him back home, never to think about him again. But she couldn't do that; Sam couldn't either. Leaving Ernest to be eaten alive by the vultures wasn't something they could do with a clear conscience. Ellie couldn't lead a man to his own death. She'd never live with herself if she did. And Sam? He felt enough guilt about Ellie being involved. If another person died on his watch, he'd surely blame himself, and their relationship would start off with martyrdom.

Ernest sat in the back of the CRV, drifting in and out of sleep as Ellie drove with Sam by her side. Ernest had taken more than enough pain pills and found it hard to keep his eyes open. Ellie's adrenaline was at its highest peak. She drove fast and struggled to keep her hands steady. She constantly checked in the rear view mirror to see if any suspicious cars trailed her.

"Try not to worry," Sam said, noticing Ellie was on edge.

"I just don't want them to hurt you."

"You heard Ernest say they couldn't remember how to find their way back to where I live. Don't fret," he said.

She breathed and tried to relax. They rode in silence for a while, listening to the hum of the tires on the pavement and the radio playing an old tune.

"I know you're mad at him, but he may be able to give you some advice."

"What advice could *he* give me?" Sam asked petulantly.

"He went through the same thing you're going through now. You know, adjusting to a new time. You should ask him how he managed."

"He didn't look like he was managing to me," Sam retorted. "You saw the state his home was in."

"He's a mess. I know," she said. "But he is the only other person you know who has been in the same shoes that you are wearing right now."

"Your phrases confound me sometimes." Sam smiled crookedly.

"Don't knock my way of talking, Mr. Poor Grammar. Last time I checked, 'ain't' wasn't a word."

He leaned back in the seat and folded his arms against his chest, smirking. "Been using it my whole life. It's a word."

"Just because *you* use it, doesn't mean it's a word."

"Always have to win." He shook his head slightly and laughed.

"And that's why you love me," she teased, and her face turned scarlet wondering if she used the word "love" way too soon.

"It *ain't*," he emphasized, "the only reason, Ellie."

She couldn't help but smile.

"Ellie," Sam started, his tone had taken a different turn, much more serious.

She looked at him in a questioning way.

"Once we get back to your house, I'm going with Ernest by myself."

"No way, Sam."

"I'm concerned about your safety," he said. "There ain't no

reason for you to get more involved."

"Look, I get it, but I'm going. Okay?" she said.

***

Ernest grimaced in pain as he got out of the car. Jonah ran out to meet Ellie as soon as he heard the car pull up into the driveway.

"Don't freak," Ellie said to him as he looked at her more as the stern father than an impressionable younger brother.

"You brought the guy here?" He sighed, looking Ernest over and threw his hands up in the air. "Ellie, what are you thinking?" He paced back and forth in frustration.

"We're taking him back to Sam's place so he can explain," she said as Sam stood beside her. "Now do you believe that Sam is from another time?"

Jonah rolled his eyes. "I didn't doubt it before."

"Yes, you did."

"Fine," he huffed. "I did a little. Anyone would. This whole world has gone bat shit crazy!" He threw his hands up in the air again in frustration and uttered a string of curse words.

Ellie grabbed him by the arm. "It's insane, I know, but I gotta take him to Sam's." She motioned with her head.

"What happened to him?" Jonah asked, noticing Ernest's fresh bruises that covered him in various places on his beat up body.

Ellie hesitated.

"What kind of crazy shit have you gotten involved in?" he asked.

"He got beat up," she answered with a lump in her throat. "By these two men that used to live with Sam."

"What?" Anger flashed through his eyes. "Why would they beat him up?"

She let out a long drawn breath. "Because they don't want

anyone to find out what they've done."

"What'd they do, Ellie?" Even his tone sounded parental. The roles had somehow changed between Ellie and Jonah in the past few days.

"Something bad, okay." She didn't want to tell him. "I'd rather not get you involved."

"That's it!" he shouted and spun around, storming into the house. "I'm calling Dad, and we're getting the hell outta here and going back to Florida."

She ran after him, nearly tackling him. She wrapped her arms around him snugly. "Don't, Jonah!"

"Or what?" He jerked loose in one easy swooping motion. "I've been riding this crazy train with you, but I'm getting off, and so should you before you get hurt."

"Jonah," she pleaded.

"I get it. You like Sam, and he's a nice guy, but Ellie, this has gotten dangerous." He grabbed the phone from the receiver. "You have to see that."

"Go ahead and call Dad," she said. "I'm going with Sam, and you can't stop me."

Sam entered the house solemnly. "He's right, Ellie. You don't need to involve yourself any further." He placed his hand on her shoulder.

She shrugged him off. "Not you, too." She shook her head in disbelief.

"Ellie," he started in an apologetic tone. "It's best..."

"It's not best," she protested. "I'm going with you whether you like it or not. We're in this together."

"Please," he begged. "Listen to me and stay here with your

brother. Go back to Florida and forget you ever got involved with me."

She felt punched in the stomach and stepped back a few steps. A look of hurt showed in her eyes. "I can't believe you just said that."

"I'm trying to protect you. You need to stay here," he pleaded. "Please."

She ignored him, turning to face Jonah. "Go ahead and call Dad, Shrimp. I'm going with Sam without anyone's approval."

"I won't allow you," Sam said, and Ellie didn't like his tone of voice.

"You don't get to tell me what I do," she snapped.

"Listen to me, please, Ellie."

"I'll follow you, and I won't give up. I'm in this, Sam, and once I'm in, I'm in for good," she said, walking out the door.

CHAPTER 25

Other than hearing Ernest moaning in pain as they slumped their way up hill, no other words were uttered. Sam and Ellie were too angry with each other to speak.

Ellie didn't care if her dad found out what she was doing. Jonah could tell him the whole story for all she cared. She knew once he got off the phone with him, her dad would be on the first plane out of Florida and on his way back to North Carolina. He'd be ticked—mad at her for lying, for traipsing around the country with Sam, for being so irresponsible, for putting her life in jeopardy. She could deal with his anger. She'd have to. With love, she knew she had to take the good with the bad.

"None of this looks familiar to me," Ernest said when they stopped to rest.

"It's been a long time," Ellie said and wondered if it'd be the same for her. If she was forced to leave, could she find her way back to Sam again. The aspect of leaving didn't seem plausible.

The closer they came to reaching their point of destination, the more Ernest lagged behind. Ellie turned to look at him—weary and worn out. It was taking every ounce of strength he had left in him to continue.

"Do you need to rest?" she slowed down to ask.

"No." He smiled at her appreciatively and frowned. "Just dreading what I've gotta do. It's the only way to set things right though," he said thoughtfully.

"It'll be hard for you to see Virginia again," Ellie said more as a statement than a question.

"Yes," he answered quietly. "When I left, I was a different man."

Not broken, Ellie thought.

"And now... well, she ain't going to like what she sees and hears. That's the toughest part about this."

She could only imagine what he was feeling. If she left Sam and came back old and broken like him— seeking his forgiveness for her past sins—she'd struggle just as he was.

"It's getting dark out," Sam interrupted, pointing to the sky. "We need to keep moving."

***

It was night time, and the wind was blowing ferociously. Ellie could sense a storm was coming. The smell of rain was in the air. A dim light flickered inside Granny's cabin. The sound of a fiddle could be heard.

Ernest stopped to listen to the music. His eyes closed, and his lips curled upward into a smile.

"We need to get inside," Sam said, and Ernest opened his eyes. His jaw was tense and he hesitated to move.

A loud beep interrupted them. Ellie pulled her phone out of her pocket with a look of confusion. "It doesn't sound like my phone." She clicked the phone on and squinted her eyes. "It's not mine. I can't get service up here." She held her phone up in the air and brought it back down to her. "Nope. No service."

Ernest placed his hand in his pants pocket and pulled out his phone. "It's mine," he said and clicked the phone on to unlock. "It's a text from Horace," he said and gulped.

"You have an IPhone?" Ellie said in disbelief. "My dad refuses to buy me one."

"Horace bought it for me. So I could take their phone calls when they need me to run errands," he explained.

"What does the text say?" Ellie asked, peering over his shoulder.

Sam followed her, doing the same.

Horace: *Rufus told me what he done. It wasn't my doing and he's being dealt with. Where are you?*

"Should I reply?" he asked them.

"No," Sam answered quickly. "You said Rufus doesn't do anything without talking to Horace first. He knew Rufus hurt you. I'd wager it was his idea."

Ernest stared at the phone contemplating. "I gotta text him back. He'll know something is wrong if I don't." He thought for a second. "I'll just text him that I'm at the hospital." His fingers had already begun typing before Sam or Ellie could object.

Horace: *I'll take care of your bill. I'm on my way to the hospital.*

Ernest read the text out loud to them. "He ain't gonna like it when he shows up and I'm not there," he said with an expression of concern and then shrugged. "Oh well. Don't care no more."

Something about Horace texting Ernest unsettled Ellie, but she kept those feelings to herself. She'd bring it up to Sam once Ernest told his side of the story to the others and they were alone.

***

They followed Sam inside of Granny's cabin, and the room immediately fell silent. One look at Ernest, and Virginia collapsed, hitting the floor in a loud thud. They all hurried over to her and shook her, trying to wake her.

"Get outta of my way," Granny ordered, placing smelling salts under Virginia's nose.

Virginia awoke, choking for air, and her eyes widened as she stared at the man looking down at her with regret. "Ernest?" she said with uncertainty, rubbing her eyes.

"Virginia." He blinked back tears.

They helped her up off of the ground, and she stood in front of Ernest staring at him as if it were the first time she'd ever seen him. Her head titled to the side, and her mouth was partially open. She gazed at him as if he were a stranger. Tears fell from her eyes.

"Where have you been?" She cried. "Where have you been all this time?"

"I couldn't find my way back," he said, tears filled his eyes. "I tried to so many times, but I couldn't find you."

"Why are you so old?" she asked, her finger trailed against the lines on his face. She moved her hand up to his hair, rubbing it between two of her fingers. "It's gray. And your face," her face scrunched from confusion and revulsion, "it's like Granny's."

"I'm an old man, Ginny," he said. "I'm come back to explain," as he started, tears fell from his eyes.

"I waited for you, Ernest," she said. "You didn't come back to me." She sobbed, and

Sam moved protectively between her and Ernest and then guided her by the arm to one of the chairs circled around the table.

She looked up at Ernest. "What happened to you?" She glanced up and down at him. "You ain't the man I knew."

"I wish I was," he said solemnly. "I come here to make things right."

"You never came back," she repeated. "I waited for you, and you never came back."

"I'm sorry," he said. "I'm so sorry."

"It's best if we all sit for what he's fixin' to tell," Sam interrupted.

***

Granny and Caleb's stunned expressions hadn't changed since Ernest entered the room.Caleb hobbled to the table and formed a suspicious frown. Granny joined him, her lips puckered and her eyebrows furrowed. Virginia's face was pale as snow, and her eyes wouldn't leave Ernest's. Tears streamed down her face.

"I know this don't seem right, but this is Ernest," Sam said, and Granny shook her head skeptically while Caleb glowered. Moses formed a confused expression. "The Ernest we knew eight months ago, only now he's older."

Granny reached across the table, squinting her blue eyes at him. She smacked her lips. "That's the same scar Ernest got when he was a youngun."

"It's him, Granny," Sam said.

Ellie noticed that through this all, Ernest's eyes remained locked on Virginia's.

"How?" Granny asked Sam.

Sam let out a long winded sigh. "I wish I knew. Ellie was telling us the truth. The war is over, and we've been here for over one hundred and fifty years."

Caleb got up, jostling the table. "I ain't gonna sit here and listen to these lies."

"They ain't lies, Uncle Caleb. Look at him." Sam motioned. "It's him."

Caleb bent down studying Ernest's face and shook his head slightly. He scratched his head in confusion. "I don't understand how this is possible."

"It's me," Ernest said. "Your name is Caleb Gantry, and you fought in the war in 1861 until you were shot at and lost your leg. You had a wife named Clara, and my daddy and you used to go squirrel huntin' together," he stated the facts like a recording.

Caleb got into his face, his hands on Ernest's blood stained collar. "Where is my boy? If that's you?" He studied him like a slide under a microscope. "Tell me where my boy is!"

Ernest flinched and took a deep breath; his chest rattled.

"What happened to my boy?" He asked again.

Ernest closed his eyes and cried, "He passed, Caleb. He passed."

Caleb grabbed Ernest by his shirt collar. "Tell me what happened to him!" he screamed desperately.

"Caleb, stop it!" Granny shouted.

Caleb let go of Ernest's collar and collapsed into the chair. He had a blank stare, and his hands were slightly trembling. "He's gone," he cried. "My boy is gone."

Granny turned to face Ernest. "Tell us what you came to tell us. I reckon this ain't a pretty story."

And so Ernest began to tell them the same tale he'd told Sam and Ellie.

***

The rain had begun to pour and the crack of lightening repeatedly whipped in the dark sky. Granny, Caleb, and Virginia were too stunned to say anything about the news Ernest had just given them. It was a lot to digest—the amount of time that had passed since they had been there and that Jeremiah was killed by people they considered to be their friends.

Ellie worried that Virginia was in shock. She had a vacant expression, and her skin didn't have any color. She stared through Ernest—not at him—and had no reaction to what he told her. Ellie nudged Sam, motioning for him to look at Virginia.

He formed a look of concern and mouthed, "Is she all right?" to Ellie.

Ellie shrugged and peered back over at her.

"Granny," Sam said. It was the first thing he had said since Ernest began to tell his story. "Virginia." He pointed.

Granny scooted her chair closer to Virginia. She waved her hand in front of Virginia's face, narrowing her eyes as she studied her. "She ain't here." She snapped her fingers, and Virginia continued in her frozen state. Granny picked up her limp hand. "It's damp and her finger nails are blue." She brought her ear to Virginia's chest. "She's breathin' all wrong."

"What can we do?" Sam asked.

"Get me my kit," she said.

Sam hurried over to the table where Granny's box full of homemade remedies laid. He frantically picked it up and brought it over to her. She sifted through the box and pulled out two bottles of herbs. "Lavender and Passion Flower should help her." She crushed the herbs onto the table. "Sam, pour some water into that thar cup and put it on the fire for a spell. We need it warm."

Sam did as he was instructed and waited patiently by the fire place as the water in the cup began to bubble. He grabbed his handkerchief and wrapped it around the hot cup, and carried it to Granny.

Granny scooped the herbs into the cup and swirled them around with her spoon. She held the cup up to Virginia's lips. "Drink this," she said, opening Virginia's lips slightly and pouring the liquid down her throat. Most of it spilled onto her dress.

"Will it help?" Ellie asked.

"Give it time," Granny answered, pouring the rest down Virginia's mouth. "Let's lay her down."

Sam gingerly carried her over to her bed, gently placing her down. Ellie brushed Virginia's wet hair back away from her clammy skin. "Can I do something?" she asked Granny.

Granny shook her head. "Ain't nothin' to do right now."

Ernest rushed to her side, kneeling beside the bed, and clamped his hands together like he was praying. "I'm so sorry, Virginia," he said. "So sorry."

***

Discovering Jeremiah had died, that Horace and Rufus were filled with cruelty, and that there had been a stagnation in time, sent them into silence. Learning that the days were lost and they would never come back caused them to question their purpose. It was the first reaction Sam had when he learned the truth, but somehow he managed to pull himself out of depression. Ellie gave him hope.

None of them slept. Ernest refused to move from Virginia's side, hoping she'd wake up with a forgiving heart. Caleb isolated himself into his grief for the loss of his only child, and Granny realized that the extension she had received on her long life was coming to an end. Moses was filled with joy, knowing that he was finally a free man. He didn't need to hide from the law anymore. Sam knew that nothing was holding him back now. His life was his to live as he wanted.

Ellie sat with Sam outside, facing the fire. An owl hooted up in a tree—the branches moving to the shifting of the wind. "What will everyone do now?" Ellie asked.

"I'm not right sure," he said pensively and then quietly added, "I'd like to see the country." He waited for her reaction.

"Me too," she said, and she wondered if they'd see it together.

"I don't right know what I'm going to do. Acclimate, I guess," he said. "We'll all have to learn to adjust, which ain't going to be easy."

"You're already doing that."

"For some of them it'll be a challenge. Virginia's heart is broken, and Granny is too stubborn to change her ways. Some people can't deal with change no matter how strong they seem," he said.

"About earlier..." she started.

"I ain't mad at you, Ellie. I just wish you'd listen to me. I don't want you harmed."

"I know, Sam. But you have to allow me to make my own decisions even if you don't agree with them. I'd do the same for you."

"I can't argue that."

The fire illuminated the night sky. The stars twinkled above them, and a crescent moon glowed above the darkness. The wind continued to howl, threatening a storm, but it never came. Ellie and Sam continued to sit around the fire as dawn approached them.

The sun was rising, and rabbits hopped across the grass, nibbling on berries and other sources of food. A doe stole food from Sam's garden and ran when it heard a noise. The scent of morning dew filled the air.

Ellie rubbed her eyes, yawning from exhaustion. "I'm going to have go home." She let out a sigh.

"I know." He blinked.

"I don't want to."

"I don't want you to, but you have to. Your father..."

Ellie sighed again. "He won't be happy with me," she fretted.

The feeling of exhilaration she had the morning before was coming to an end. Love was like being on a ride at an amusement park—going up and down, waiting for the next drop or quick unexpected turn to throw her off guard.

She slowly rose from the tree stump, squeezing the back of her sore neck. Her knees buckled, and she stretched, feeling pain in her lower back. "What are you going to do about Ernest?"

"I don't know," he said.

"We can't take him back to his house. You heard him. He said they'd kill him."

"He can't stay here. Virginia and him can't patch things up," he said. "I don't know where he's going to go. I don't know what will happen to any of us. So much has changed in the last couple of weeks. I'm trying to get through today, then I'll worry about tomorrow."

"I know, Sam, but you all will have to figure this all out sooner rather than later," she said.

She thought it was just another doe stealing food from the garden, but as she turned to see where the noise was coming from, the sight of two men came into her view. She quickly lost her breath.

"Hello, Sam," one of the men said.

CHAPTER 26

They both held guns and pointed them in Sam and Ellie's direction. Horace was bigger, meaner looking and more intimidating than Ellie had imagined. He was a stout, well built man for his age, with graying dirty blonde hair and beady blue eyes. Wearing jeans, a cowboy hat, and a beige button down top, he was dressed like a man from a bad western, complete with a bolo as his tie. His face hinted at older age but didn't show clear evidence like Ernest's did. A few creases accentuated his forehead, lips and eyes, but they were faint lines, and anyone looking at him would call him a handsome older man with lips that faced down into a consistent frown. Rufus, thinner and not as good looking as Horace, bore a striking resemblance to his older brother. He was less stout, much more muscular and dressed similarly with the exception of a knife hoisted at his firm waist.

Horace tipped his Stetson at Ellie, and she shot him a dirty look. "Ain't you cute?" His voice was higher pitched and sinister sounding, almost as if he had sucked on helium earlier and its remnants were still lingering in his voice box.

They moved closer to Sam and Ellie, with their fingers on the triggers of their guns. "She is." Rufus licked his lips and eyed Ellie, making her feel sick to her stomach. She shut her eyes and flinched as he tugged on her hair, his long fingernails trailing against her cheek. "Real cute," he said, and Ellie grimaced.

"Get your hands off of her!" Sam shouted.

"Calm down." Horace taunted Sam, pointing the gun at him. "He ain't gonna touch her." He laughed devilishly and added in a menacing voice, "not yet, anyway." Horace glanced sideways at his younger brother and put the gun up to Rufus' cheek.

"Quit gawking at her and get your head out of your pants!" he commanded.

Rufus peered down and looked back up at them with malice.

"You'll have to forgive my younger brother. He has a weakness when it comes to young girls," Horace said.

Ellie tried to stand, but her knees felt like they were going to buckle, and she couldn't stop her hands from shaking. She could feel her heart beating violently against her chest.

Rufus let out a laugh—the kind that was monotone and sucked air as each sound was let out. "I like 'em young and feisty like her. Bet she tastes good too."

Sam rushed toward Rufus, and Horace quickly grabbed Ellie's arms. He pulled them up and behind her back. She screamed, and he slammed his palm against her mouth.

"Better be quiet," Horace whispered to her and then said to Sam, "I'll break her arms. Coming at Rufus when he's holding a gun ain't too smart," he said. "What were you going to do, punch him?" He let out a quick laugh. "I'd shoot you if you did. I'm the only one who gets to hit Rufus."

"I oughta punch you for that," Rufus said to Sam.

Sam breathed heavy and said through gritted teeth, "Let her go."

Horace loosened his grip on Ellie, releasing her. She brought her arms against her chest and tried massaging them. The pain lingered.

"Are you all right?" Sam asked her.

She nodded.

"Young puppy love. Ain't that sweet?" Horace quipped. "Too bad it has to come to an end."

"Leave her out of this. She ain't a threat to you," Sam pleaded.

"Oh but you see, she is. You'uns know how we got our money,

and I'm not willing to risk losing it. I've built myself a little empire in Rutherford." He gave a proud smirk. "Run the whole damn town. I ain't a poor farmer's son there. I'm the boss." He pointed to himself. "I'm the one who calls all the shots. You think I'm gonna let the likes of you or her take that away from me?" he scoffed. He rammed the gun into Sam's chest. "Stupid, Ernest." He shook his head slightly. "He never knew we put an app on his phone that we could track him with. If I own someone, I need to know where they are and what they're doing at all times."

"She don't know anything," Sam lied.

"You're lying, Sam." He made a tisk, tisk sound. "We know Ernest told you'uns. He confessed to everything. Rufus can be purty persuasive when he wants. Can't you, brother?"

Rufus let out another menacing laugh. "It didn't take much till he squealed like a little girl. I'd like to hear her squeal," he said.

"You better not touch her!" Sam shouted.

"Or what? We've got the weapons," Rufus retorted.

"My very astute brother is right, Sam. You've got nothing. Quit putting up a fight," Horace said.

"She'll be missed," Sam argued. "I may not be, but she will. She's got a family expecting her home any minute now."

Horace blew off Sam's last remark. "We can make it look like a hunting accident. Got a few people that owe us some favors. It ain't that strange for someone to get shot by accident. It's happened before."

Ellie's heart sank to the soles of her feet. Her life was flashing before her eyes—right at the time when she had just begun to live again. She'd never see her brother or father again. How would they cope with her loss, too? Two deaths in her family in the same year would send them over the edge. That was what bothered her the most. Not that she wouldn't see another sunset, run just as the sun was rising, or feel the comfort of Sam's touch, but that her family would suffer the most. They would be alone and left to pick up the pieces. At that moment, their happiness was more valuable than her own precious life.

"Her father knows people too," Sam lied.

"You sound desperate," Horace said. "Women will do that to you. They'll mess you up. Look at you now, begging for her life when you should be begging for you own." He pursed his lips. "Move," he ordered with his gun pressed against Sam's back.

Sam looked at Ellie apologetically. He took a hold of her hand. "I'm so sorry," he whispered.

What could she say? That it was all right, because it wasn't. They were all going to die and there was nothing she could do to stop it from happening.

It felt like the longest walk in the world. Knowing that death was imminent, Ellie slowed to a snail's pace.

Virginia was sitting up in bed; Ernest sat in a chair beside her. Their hushed tones silenced the moment Ellie and Sam entered the room with guns pointed at their backs. Caleb reached for his knife, but Rufus' reflexes were too quick, and he snatched it from Caleb's hands. "You too." He eyed Moses, aiming his gun at him. "Carefully now. Don't do nothing stupid."

He dropped both knives in an empty sack and kicked it behind him. He kept the gun pointed at them, waiting for Horace's next instruction.

"Where you keeping that rifle of yours?" Horace said to Granny.

"We ain't got one no more," she lied.

"You're lying. I don't like it when I'm lied to," he said and stormed over to Virginia, yanking her out of bed. He dragged her against the floor and slammed her slim body up against the wall. She wailed from the sharp pain. "Give it to me or I'll do much worse than that to her."

Ernest charged toward Horace. "Don't you hurt her!" Horace swung his gun toward Ernest's head and knocked him to the floor. He placed his hands up to his head and moaned. Horace kicked him in the stomach with the tip of his pointed snake skin boot. "Stay out of this!" He spat down at him.

Granny shot him a disgusted look and got up to get the rifle. She shoved it against his chest. "Always knew you were no good," she said.

He sneered and handed the rifle to Rufus. "Don't really matter what you think," he told her.

Ellie knew that was their last form of defense. Everyone's weapons were gone, and there was no way they could defend themselves. They weren't going to win this fight.

Everything was intensified—her five senses were keenly aware of every sight, sound, touch, taste, and scent. She noticed that the cabin smelled of chicory and cloves. That Sam's hand was free of hair and soft to touch. That the red in the quilt popped more than the other colors, which showed signs of aging. That maple syrup lingered on the tip of her tongue from the waffle she had the day before. That Sam had a radio voice: even when he whispered, his accent was music to her ears. All of these thoughts raced through her mind as she took one step closer to her death.

"You'uns need to sit down," Horace commanded, forcing Ellie and Sam down against the wall. "The rest of you, over here." Rufus sat them all against the wall in single file order.

Granny folded her arms against her chest and sat on a chair, refusing to budge. "Ain't moving an inch." She smacked her lips hard and glared at them.

"I told you to sit over here." He pointed to the floor.

"I am too old to sit on that dern floor. You wanna kill me, do it now. I've lived my life." Some would call the old woman crazy or stupid for refusing a man with a loaded gun, but Ellie envied Granny for her courage. To stare death in the eye and have the strength to challenge the person who was going to end her life was a fearless act in her opinion.

Horace didn't know what to say. People rarely said no to him, and those that did usually suffered from his brother's hands. He turned to Rufus and gave him a signal. Rufus kicked the legs out from Granny's chair, forcing her to fall back against the floor.

She brushed off her shoulders and sat up straight. "Always said you'uns were nothing but trash but never thought you'd be this evil. Greed makes your worst traits even more visible. You're worse than the Devil himself," she pointed to Horace and then to Rufus, "and you're the dumbest boy I ever knew."

Rufus' waved his fist in Granny's face. "Gonna enjoy putting you out of your misery," he seethed.

She didn't even flinch and hacked up saliva, spitting it at him. "You're lost, boy. Whatcha goin' to do once you're done with us? Keep livin' your miserable life until it all catches up to you one day, cause it will."

"We've gotten by this long," he said with a smug face. "No one will miss any of you."

"You don't think Horace wouldn't turn on you if he had to

save himself? You're sadly mistaken, boy," Granny said. The angrier Rufus grew, the more calm Granny became.

"I think you need to shut your mouth or I'll shut it for you," Rufus yelled.

"I ain't afraid of you, boy. I've done lived my life." She leaned forward and squared her shoulders back.

"Enough of this squabbling. Always were an annoying nag. Nag, nag, nag," Horace whined in a mocking way. "I wanted to forget about all of you'uns. We found that money fair and square. It was our ticket out of this god forsaken place. Livin' day after day thinking the war was being fought while we waited for it to end." He chuckled, the sound of his laugh made Ellie shiver. "All that time wasted. Then we got lucky and now you'uns want to go and ruin it for us? We're not gonna have it."

"No way," Rufus added.

"Shut up, Rufus," Horace said. "We got a special thing goin' on in Rutherford. I make all the rules, and he makes everyone follow them. You think I'm gonna let that kind of power go just 'cause you'uns have a conscience? That was the problem with Jeremiah. He didn't know when to shut up for his own good."

"It's not your money, and our lives are not yours to bargain with," Sam said.

Horace turned to face him, his face contorted into disgust. "Always thought you were an uppity know it all. Just 'cause you're intelligent don't make you have common sense. If you had enough sense, you wouldn't have poked your nose in our business. You couldn't leave well enough alone. You and doin' the right thing all the time. Ha," he said with a sly smile. "Left the war 'cause you thought it was wrong." He scrunched his face and said "boo hoo" to

Sam, taunting him. "Couldn't stand the sight of you after a while. Always thinkin' about things."

"You are not the man I knew who saved my life," Sam said.

"Saved you," he scoffed. "You think I did that for you? I wanted to kill that Yankee. It was all for the kill, Sam."

"You're a lost soul. I pity you," Sam said.

"Pity me all you want. When you're dead, I'll still be the most powerful man in Rutherford, and there's nothing you can do to stop that. Nothing."

"Have you ever heard of Karma?" Ellie said. "Because Karma will make damn sure it catches up to you."

"You're a feisty one, aren't you? Was gonna save you for last for Rufus, but I can't stand that yap of yours." He stretched his arms out wide, "'But I was like a lamb that is brought to the slaughter; and I knew not that they had devised devices against me, saying, Let us destroy the tree with the fruit thereof, and let us cut him off from the land of the living, that his name may be no more remembered,'" he said. "Time to say bye bye."

"That ain't what the good Lord's verse means," Granny said.

"I get to say what it means." He jerked Ellie off of the floor and wrapped his arm around her neck narrowing her path for air. "Your fate is sealed." He held his gun up to her head. She tried to fight him off. "I wouldn't do that if I were you." He squeezed harder. She gasped, choking for air. Blood pounded in her ears.

"Don't hurt her!" Sam shouted, getting up off the floor only to be knocked down by Rufus.

Ellie's life flashed before her eyes: her first day of school when she cried for her mother and she ran back to hug her one last time before the bell rang; blowing out the candles on her cake and then sharing a special dance with her dad at her quinceañera; starting her period and staying home with her mom sharing hot fudge sundaes and watching *Pride and Prejudice* more than once; her father teaching her how to parallel park so she could get her driver's license; Jonah saving up all of money from mowing neighbors' yards and buying her favorite bottle of perfume.

Images continued to pass through her mind as if she were changing television stations with the click of her TV remote. A new scene popped up, and then faded to another, and then another— each memory once forgotten, now lucid, like they happened yesterday. The air in her lungs was withering away, and everything around her was turning darker and darker. Horace's grip wasn't getting any looser. The nightmare she had over and over again had become her reality.

Their voices sounded distant, like her body was sinking down below the surface of water. It was just like those hot summer days in Coral Gables when she and Jonah would jump the fence to swim in the community pool and she'd sink down to the bottom, sitting crossed legged, waiting for her brother's buoyant body to try and meet hers. He never could. Jonah was born to float in the water.

"Ernest!" Virginia shouted, her voice was like an echo in a cave.

Before Ellie had time to blink her drooping eyes, Ernest pulled a knife from his work boots and jabbed it across Horace's neck. Blood splattered all over the left side of her face, and Horace's arm went limp. He fell back against the wall. Ernest thrust it in further, deeper. Horace's blood gurgled, and his body shook violently. He brought his hands up to the open slit in his neck, touching the head of the knife, begging for air.

"Horace!" Rufus screamed. Ellie felt a whoosh of air sweep by her as Horace fell to the ground. She gasped for air, coughing over and over again while trying to remain upright. The taste of blood filled her mouth.

Less than a second later, the deafening sound of a gun shot rang throughout the cabin. Barely missing Ellie's head, the bullet from Rufus' gun pierced Ernest's boney shoulder. Ernest tumbled to the floor, wailing in pain.

The blast of the gun was louder than a firecracker. The percussion of sound waves caused Ellie to drop to the floor. She cupped her ears and screamed in horror. It felt like someone had shoved a sharp metal rod into her ears accompanied by the sound of an angry swarm of bees. The buzzing was loud and muffled all other sounds.

"Ellie?" she heard Sam say. "Ellie, are you all right?" She felt his hand on her, but his voice sounded as if she were submerged in water. She tilted her head up to look at him. His face was an abstract canvas. Dizzy and lightheaded, her vision was hazy.

She wiped Horace's blood away from her eye, cheek and mouth, and saw Virginia hovering over Ernest, sobbing hysterically. A shrill ringing sound pervaded her ears. She tried to utter something, but she couldn't hear herself speak.

Rufus pointed his gun at Ellie, pulling the trigger back. "I'll kill you all!" he cried hysterically.

Sam leapt in front of Ellie as another gun shot blasted.

A look of terror filled her eyes. "No!" she screamed, but it felt like an exercise in drama class where everyone had to speak and act in slow motion.

Sam collapsed in front of her. Moses and Caleb charged at Rufus, toppling him to the ground. They struggled, wrestling as they tried to get the deadly weapon out of Rufus' hands. Moses pinned Rufus to the ground, and Caleb freed the gun from Rufus' hand. Instantly, without a moment's hesitation, Caleb shot straight through Rufus' callous heart. Caleb dropped the gun to the floor and scooted away from Rufus, watching as his body convulsed.

Ellie looked down at Sam. He clutched onto his stomach, and his hands were doused in blood. "No," she cried. "Help!" she shouted.

Granny perched herself over Sam and pulled up his shirt. Ellie winced, seeing the bullet had lodged itself in his stomach. Blood streamed out. They both knew that if he continued to lose that much blood, he'd be dead.

Granny tore Sam's t-shirt, bundling it up, and pressed it hard against his stomach. He groaned. "Need to stop the bleedin'," she said. "I don't right know if I can save him." She frowned to Ellie.

Ellie crawled over to Ernest. "I need your phone," she said.

Virginia held him in her arms, her hand was pressed against his shoulder, blood covered her small, delicate hands. "Pocket," he murmured.

She stuck her hand in his left pocket and pulled out his phone. She tapped in her home number, her hands shaking uncontrollably. "Jonah!" she screamed.

"Ellie, lower your voice," he said. "Dad's home, and he's beyond pissed."

"He needs to get here quick." She sucked air. "Sam's been shot. You need to bring him here. There isn't much time!"

"Shot?" he said in disbelief. "Oh my God, Ellie. Are you okay?"

"Quickly, Jonah. Get him here as fast as you can!"

CHAPTER 27

Granny removed the bullet from Ernest's shoulder. Unlike Sam, he had luck on his side. The bullet had barely broke through his skin and was easy to remove, even with Granny's antiquated tools. She sewed up the wound with a needle and thread and applied a mixture of cinnamon and cloves onto it. She brought the same mix over to Sam, who had been moved to one of the beds.

Her lips turned down into a frown. "Don't right know if this'll do much."

"We have to try it," Ellie said as Granny compressed it against his skin. Her voice was still loud and she couldn't hear well.

He let out a groan. Beads of sweat trickled down his forehead. His gray eyes were half open.

"You have to stay awake!" Ellie shouted. She shook him. "Sam. Dammit! Stay awake!"

Blood continued to flow from his body. Her palms pressed flat against his stomach, she exerted all of her weight against his wound hoping that amount of pressure would stop the bleeding or at least slow it down. Her hands were red all over, and she continued to hear a persistent ringing in her ears. Everyone's voices sounded far off and distant, as if they were speaking through a bullet proof glass wall.

The hands of time were ticking in her head. Each minute felt like an excruciating hour. She wondered how long it would take Jonah and her dad to get there. She knew Jonah would remember the way; he had a photographic memory. He could get there blindfolded. It was just a question of when. Would they move in haste? Her dad was an avid runner like Ellie. Could he make it there in time? Was time on their side anymore? Did it still move to its own rhythm where Sam and his family were concerned?

Sam was writhing with pain. Ellie felt so useless. She looked to Granny for guidance, who shook her head sadly, feeling just as lost as Ellie. "The cloves and cinnamon are 'spose to slow the bleedin'."

"We should add more," Ellie insisted and watched Granny amble to the table to whip up another mix. The rest of them were hovered over Horace and Rufus' bodies trying to figure out what to do with them. Ellie could not care less. Let their bodies rot away, she thought. They didn't deserve any respect for what they had done. Sam's life was at stake, and nothing else mattered.

***

Her dad barged in, pushing the door wide open. Social niceties such as knocking on the door, shaking hands and introducing himself were trivial to him at that moment. He scanned the room and saw Ellie and rushed toward her. He nearly tripped over Rufus and Horace's lifeless bodies. He gazed down and instantly looked back up, his face filled with frenzied worry—his eyes fixated on Ellie.

Panic stricken, he ran to her and wrapped his arms around her, squeezing her tight. He finally let go of her. "Are you injured?" he asked. He held her arms and turned them over, searching for any cuts, scrapes or bruises. "Were you hurt?" he repeated, still checking her over. He cupped his hands against her cheeks and ran his hand across her forehead. "Can you hear me?" he raised his voice, his eyes focused on nothing but her.

She held up her hands to stop him. "Dad, I'm fine. I'm fine," she repeated. She showed him her hands and spoke slower, "This isn't my blood. It's his." She pointed to Sam. "He needs your help. He's been shot."

"But you're not hurt?" he said, checking her over once more.

"No," she breathed. "Please, Dad. He's lost a lot of blood."

"Jonah said someone was shot, and I feared the worst." He let out a sigh of relief. "Thank God you're all right," he said and then frowned. "We will discuss this later." He gave her a look that she had grown to know very well that summer. If she were her parent, she'd react the same way. Gun shot wounds and dead bodies were not what a parent wanted his child to get involved with. It wasn't what Ellie had bargained for either. She imagined the summer was going to be the way her life had been headed since her mom died—dull, without much change in her routine. Love sent her down a different path. She had always heard the stupid cliché "love made me do it." Now she knew exactly what those trite words meant.

"What's his name?" Her dad's tone of voice sounded distant and formal. He was in doctor's mode. He put on his surgical gloves and pulled up the cloth covering Sam's wound.

"Sam," Ellie answered, a lump formed in her throat. "Sam Gantry." She was on the verge of tears. "Can you save him, Dad?"

***

Her dad worked feverishly to save Sam. His skills as a surgeon were tested with the inadequate medical supplies he had in his doctor's bag and the setting in which he had to perform this miracle. He was a fine surgeon—a well-respected doctor for his steady hands and overall survival rate—but to save a man's life without the right tools or medicine was a feat he wasn't sure he could accomplish. Granny assisted him as well as she could, trying hard to keep her only grandson alive. Sam was her favorite. She'd never admit it, but if he was gone for good, her life would have less meaning.

Ellie paced the floor. She wobbled a bit from vertigo, wondering if her feet were unsteady from lack of hearing ability or due to post traumatic stress. She had almost been killed, watched the man she loved get shot, and saw two men murdered. She wondered how men in combat were able to overcome their stress. How did they go on with their daily lives after witnessing so much death? She knew once she got out of this, her life wouldn't ever be the same. How could she go back to living a normal, simple routine life? How would things go on as they were? How was she supposed to start college in the fall as if nothing ever happened?

As more time passed, Ellie grew tired from pacing and sat down on the floor near the fire place. She wrapped her arms around her knees and drew them close to her chest. Her head down, she wept silently onto her arms, praying that Sam's life would be spared. A man as good as him deserved to live. She'd never forgive herself if he died from saving her. She took a deep breath and tried to control her crying, but it was an epic fail. Jonah sat down next to her and wrapped his arms around her. She raised her head slightly and gave him a look of gratitude and then lowered her head, sobbing into her arms.

Her father's voice broke her sobbing. She wiped at her eyes and felt a fresh burning sensation from salty tears and looked up at him, hoping he was going to relay good news. She bit on her lip in anticipation and crossed her fingers like she used to do when she was a little girl. She knew something as silly as that wouldn't save Sam, but it gave her false hope, and if anything, she needed hope. It was all she had left in her.

He pulled off his bloodied gloves and dropped them into a sack Granny had brought over. He wiped the sweat from his brow with his forearm, and exhaled. "He lost a lot of blood," he said to them all;his face was a blank canvas, and his tone was monotone. "But he will pull through. I'm leaving this bottle of antibiotics to keep him from getting an infection. If that bullet had gone any further, he most certainly wouldn't have made it."

Ellie jumped up and ran over to her dad, hugging him. "Thank you!" she shouted, smiling, with tears streaming down from her brown eyes. "Thank you!"

He released her and said in the same serious tone, "Who are those two dead men, and why are you involved in this?"

***

Trying to explain to her father that time had slowed down for Sam and his family sounded preposterous out loud. Even she could hear the ridiculousness of it. Time didn't pick and choose favorites. It didn't decide to prolong lives for some and not others. How could she persuade her father to see that in this case, where Sam and his family had been, time worked by its own set of rules?

Her father's expression never altered. He was incredulous. Ellie hoped that he'd believe her. It'd take a leap of faith and having faith meant believing what you couldn't see.

"Time cannot slow down," he argued. He sat on a chair in front of the fireplace, his leg folded over the other, and his hand up to his chin. He looked like a psychologist analyzing Ellie.

"I'm not delusional. I was just as skeptical as you, Dad. But it's true. I can give you proof," she said. She knew that there had to be a record of him in a Confederate army log somewhere that she could show him, and Ernest could corroborate the story. But in her father's eyes, in anyone's eyes for that matter, Ernest was an old man with a hankering for alcohol.

"I'd like to see it," he said and lowered his voice, "Do you think that these people may be unsettled?" It was his politically correct term for crazy.

"At first I did. But not now," she said. "You have to believe me," she begged.

"Ellie, what I don't understand is how you got involved with these people, in all of this. You could have been killed!" his voice raised. He placed his palms against his cheeks. "I could have lost you." He sighed. "This is all my fault."

"Your fault? Dad, this has nothing to do with you."

"If I had sent you to a counselor when your mother died, you wouldn't have been drawn to all of this." He shook his head slightly. "Grief sends people over the edge all the time."

"First off, I'm not over the edge. I'm a little shaken by what happened today, but I'm sane. And secondly, I didn't go looking for this. I went for a run in the woods, like I do every day," she said. "And these people—they're good people. Sam has helped me get over Mom's death. He has been," she added carefully, "a better help than any counselor ever could."

He sighed. "They may be nice, but they can't be all that good if there are two dead men laying on the floor."

"They were bad men. Not Sam. Not his family. He saved me from being killed!"

He leaned forward. His hands balled into fists resting against his knees. "Listen to yourself. What type of man are you involved with that you are thankful he saved your life? You sound like those women who make excuses for their abusive husbands."

"I am not making excuses for him. There is nothing to excuse. Sam is a good man, and he saved my life tonight."

"Once I know for sure that he is stable," he gestured to Sam, "we are getting out of here, and we are not looking back. We're going back to Florida, and when we get home, you are not leaving my side. Do you hear me? You will go to school and come home, and that's it!"

"You may be able to control what I do, but you can't control my heart or how I feel," she said. "You can't stop me from loving him."

Ernest shuffled over to them. "Sorry to interrupt," he said. "We've been talking and I've decided to call the police. I wanted to let you'uns know."

"What? You can't. How will you explain who they are?" She motioned to Sam's family.

"It's my fault we're in this situation. I aim to make things right," he said.

"If you want to make it right, then leave them out of it," she said, pointing to Sam's family.

"Elisabeth Sophia, this is not the way I raised you. Wrong has been done here, and you can't cover it up with a band aid," her dad said, a look of disappointment crossed his face. "*No eres la hija que yo te crié a ser.*"

That was a double whammy. Ellie felt crushed. To hear her dad say that she was not the daughter he raised her to be was the equivalent of being disowned. For the first time in her life, her father was disappointed in her. Ellie was learning what it meant to grow up—to make decisions on her own that her dad may not agree with. She was doing what she thought was best even if it meant he'd be crushed and ashamed of her. Part of becoming an adult, becoming her own person, would mean disappointing loved ones because their ideals for her weren't necessarily her own. Part of forming her own identity meant making her own choices no matter what the cost.

"If I may," Ernest started, and they stopped talking to listen to him. "I've done decided I'm calling the police."

"But you'll be arrested?" Ellie said.

"I know, but that's all right." He gave her an assured smile. "I got to pay my dues. I placed you'uns in this situation and I'm aim to get you'uns out of it."

"But it'll bring attention to them." She gesticulated at Sam's family.

"I'm taking Horace and Rufus out to the woods, far enough away from here. I'm gonna tell the police we were going huntin' and had a bad fight." He raked his fingers through his thinning hair. "I figure that's the best way to handle this all."

"So you're going to move them to the woods?" Jonah interrupted.

"Yes," Ernest answered. "I'll make sure it's far enough away from here so you'uns don't have to be involved."

"Does anyone else see a problem with this?" Jonah asked.

"Son, I have issues with all of this," Ellie's dad said.

"I know you do, Dad, but for different reasons than I'm asking," he said. Look," he faced Ernest, "you need to plan ahead. They're going to wonder where the all of blood is. If there's no puddle that raises more questions."

"He's right," Caleb chimed in—the first words he had said in a long time. "Look at all that blood." He pointed to the blood soaked floor. "Gonna 'cause more questions if there ain't any of it."

"When Sam and me were in the war together, the worst place to fight was in shallow water 'cause all the blood would flow by you. Ain't nothin' more frightening than looking down and seein' you're knee deep in bloody water." Ernest grimaced. "The water flushes the blood away."

"Exactly." Jonah snapped his fingers. "Move them down to that creek along the trail. The water's high from all that rain, and it's far enough away so the cops won't snoop around up here."

"That's what I'll do then," Ernest said.

"Caleb? Moses? You'uns help Ernest move them out of here," Granny said.

They nodded their heads.

"Who fired the gun?" Jonah asked.

"I did," Caleb answered.

"You need to wipe your fingerprints off it," Jonah said. "It won't add up otherwise. Ernest you'll need to make sure your finger prints are all over it." Caleb picked the gun up and used his shirt to clean it off.

"What have you become?" Ellie's dad said to Jonah with a horrified face.

"Dad, sometimes what seems right isn't, and what appears to be wrong is closer to right," Jonah said.

"You are not the children I raised," he said.

"We are, Dad. We're the same people you taught to be good and treat others like we want to be treated," Ellie said.

"No." He shook his head in dismay. "If your mother were here..."

"If Mom were here, she'd tell you to quit blaming yourself. She'd tell you to wake up and become alive again," she said. "She'd tell you to quit laying on the couch night after night. This," she pointed, "may not look pretty, but it's woken me up. I'm alive again."

Ernest and Moses left carrying Horace and Rufus' bodies out of the gorge, through the cave and into the woods, far enough away from their cabins. Ellie watched as Ernest said goodbye to Virginia. Virginia's heart was broken after seeing the man that she loved for so long wither away to nothing, only to lose him for good. They had their closure, Ellie thought, but she knew Virginia would never be the same again. They would have to carry on with their lives. Virginia would have start hers all over in a new century, and Ernest would live out his days in prison, paying his penance for his past mistakes. He was going willingly, and Ellie thought that at last, Ernest was no longer a broken man but a healed man.

Things were never going to be the same with Ellie and her dad. He didn't trust her, and even though Granny had told him what she had done, in his eyes, she lied to him. "If it weren't for your daughter, we would have kept on livin' here unaware that the world had changed around us," Granny said. "Your daughter saved us."

Ellie didn't regret what she had done. She would do it over again in a heartbeat.

Ellie's dad took one last look at Sam, checking his vitals to ensure that he was in stable condition. "He's going to be okay. Make sure he takes those pills," he said to Granny. "Time to say your goodbyes." He gestured to Ellie and Jonah. "We're leaving."

Virginia reached over to hug Ellie and whispered in her ear, "Thank you for bringin' Ernest back. I don't have to wait for him no longer. I can try to go on now," she said and hugged her again. This time, Ellie was the last one to let go.

Granny gave her a quick hug. "You're a good girl. Good enough for my Sam," she said, and those words meant more to Ellie than

Granny would ever know.

"Thank you," Ellie said. She walked slowly over to Sam who lay awake in the bed. He tried to sit up, but the pain was unbearable. "Don't," she said. "It's too soon for that."

"I want to see you," he said.

She peered down close to his face and tried to smile. "This isn't goodbye, Sam," she said, fighting off tears. "You hear me. This isn't goodbye."

"Elisabeth," he said her name softly. "You gave me my life back." He offered her a warm smile, and she leaned down to gently kiss him on the lips.

"I'm not saying goodbye," she said through tears. "I will see you again, Sam."

"You can count on it," he said. "I promise."

***

She walked several feet behind her father and Jonah. She moved slow. Her body ached, and she still couldn't hear that well. The buzzing sound was prevalent. Tears streamed down from her brown eyes. It was hitting her all at once.

Her dad turned to look at her. His anger subsided, and he took her by the hand. "You need to go home and rest," his tone was soft.

She didn't respond but held onto his hand, following him toward her house and away from Sam, wondering if she'd ever see him again.

CHAPTER 28

Packing everything away made it final. Her dad insisted that they leave North Carolina as soon as possible. He was taking his children back home, where he believed they all belonged, and getting them away from it all. Ellie begged him to stay, just a little while longer, but he was just as stubborn as she was and believed a change in scenery was exactly what his children needed.

It had been two days since she had seen Sam and already she felt heartache. Knowing that she may never see him again was killing her. She tried not to sit around the house and mope, but the constant reminder of their hurried goodbye was on her mind.

"Things are going to change," her dad threatened. "Your curfew for one. I will know where you are at all times."

Ellie let him scream at her. At least it was a reaction, she thought. At least he was showing signs of life for the first time in a long time. If being angry at her made him come out of his paralyzed state, then she could deal with it.

***

The knock on the door surprised her. They weren't expecting company. No one came to visit—not that far out in the sticks.

"What are you doing here?" her dad said in a curt tone.

"I came to thank you and to see if we could set things right," he said.

Ellie jumped off of the bar stool and raced to the front door. "Sam!" she said through heavy breaths. It was him. He had come back just as he had promised.

"Hello, Ellie," he said to her and then said to her dad, "You saved my life Mr. Morales, and I wanted to thank you." Moses stood beside him. Bosco charged toward Sam, and he bent down to pat him on the head.

"You're welcome," her dad said being terse. "You shouldn't have walked here so soon."

"It wasn't too painful," Sam said, standing up right and facing him. Ellie noticed his hand was clutched to his side where the bullet had been lodged. No matter how strong Sam was, trekking several miles two days after a near fatal gun shot wound had to have been more than excruciating. Sam took a deep, quick breath. "I knew I had to make things right with you, and Granny said you'uns weren't going to stay here too long."

"She was right. We were getting ready to leave soon," he said, pointing to the suitcases near the door and the sheets that covered the furniture. Her dad had sworn the house off, telling Jonah and Ellie that they wouldn't be back for a very long time, if ever. "I may sell it," he threatened.

"If I could talk to you for a few minutes, I sure would appreciate it," Sam pressed.

Her dad let out a sigh and thought for a moment. "Five minutes," he said reluctantly. "Come in." He gestured to Sam and Moses. "We'll talk in my office."

Ellie watched as Sam followed her dad into his office. She heard the door close shut.

"Do you want something to drink?" she asked, and Moses nodded. She poured him a glass of water, and he drank it all in one big gulp. "How about another?" She giggled. He smiled at her, and she felt warm all over. Something about Moses made her feel happy—the way his broad grin took up half of his face and his dark eyes lit up.

"What are they discussing?" she asked him. She glanced toward the room and back at Moses.

He pointed to her.

"Me?"

He nodded.

"Why?"

Moses made the shape of a heart with both of his hands and pointed to her.

"Love?"

He nodded again.

Her cheeks turned pink and she beamed. "I'll be right back," she said and tiptoed toward her father's office door, pressing her ear against it.

Her hearing still wasn't one hundred percent. Her dad had told her that it would be hopefully be restored within forty-eight to seventy-two hours and advised her to stay away from loud noises. Their voices were low and muffled through the heavy wooden door. Her mother had not spared any expenses on home accents, and the doors weren't the cheap, luan board that most were made of. These were made of solid oak.

"What are you doing?" Jonah asked, coming from behind her.

She screeched. "Jonah, you scared me!" she whispered.

Her dad opened the door. "Ellie?" He cocked an eyebrow. "This is a conversation between Sam and me."

She back peddled, her head lowered, and she failed to meet his gaze. "Sorry," she said, feeling embarrassed.

***

Their conversation had well passed the five minute mark. They had been in that room for almost an hour. She knew because she hadn't stopped looking at the clock. She sat on the couch in the living room, her legs dancing in place, going up and down. She was jittery and nervous. Moses sat calmly in one of the chairs. Bosco rested at his feet.

Jonah plopped down next to Ellie and rolled his eyes. "You're making me sea sick with all that moving. Quit being so antsy."

"I can't help it. They've been in there forever."

"So." He shrugged his shoulders.

"So," she repeated. "What are they talking about?"

"You, dummy." He slapped her on the head and turned the volume up on the television. "This is called a television," Jonah said to Moses, speaking loudly.

"He's mute, not deaf. Who's the dummy now?" Ellie said with a smirk.

Moses laughed.

"Whatever." He changed the channel, trying to find a show to watch.

"How long are they going to be in there?" she whined.

"Till he decides if he gets a goat or just a donkey for you," Jonah said.

"For what?"

"For your dowery. I'd trade you to the Greek Army Battalion for a goat if I could."

Before Ellie had time to give a snide remark, the door opened, and she instantly stood up, meeting them halfway. She couldn't read either of their faces. She felt like one of those girls in the period piece films where the man asks the father for his daughter's hand in marriage.

"Thank you for hearing me, sir," Sam said, shaking her dad's hand. "It means a lot to me."

"You are very welcome, Sam" he said. "Be sure to change that bandage, and finish all of those antibiotics. You can get an infection otherwise."

"Yes sir. Granny gave me some of her home fixings to put on it too," Sam said. "She said I need it after I take all those pills you gave me."

"Your granny will have to share her secret remedies with me some time," he said and smiled. Ellie noticed her dad's grin and felt hopeful. Maybe they had called a truce and all would be forgiven and forgotten, she thought. He turned to face Ellie. "You can say your goodbyes now."

"Now?" Ellie said.

"Yes now," he said sternly, but with less anger. He was warming toward her, she could feel it. "He has somewhere to be, and we need to finish up around here."

If anything, she was not about to say goodbye to him in front of her dad and brother. She wanted privacy or the semblance of it. She took a hold of Sam's hand and said, "Let's go outside and talk."

She walked toward the back of the house and opened the french doors, stepping onto the back deck. With a back drop of the Blue Ridge Mountains, the view was spectacular.

"It's beautiful out here," Sam said, seeing the peaks standing tall above the horizon. The afternoon sun beamed down on them. Ellie noticed natural golden highlights in Sam's brown hair. A scent of juniper breezed by them, as squirrels wrestled in the trees, securing acorns for later.

"So, you and my dad?" Ellie started.

"He's a good man. He really loves you," Sam said.

"What'd you talk about?"

"You, me, everything. He said he knew what I was going through," Sam said.

"How's that?"

"When he came here from Cuba. He said he had to start all over like I'll have to." Sam stood against the rail of the deck and faced the mountains. Ellie moved beside him and clasped her hand into his.

"I never thought of it that way," she said quietly.

"He said I deserved a fair chance in my new life, and he gave me some money. I didn't want to take it, but he insisted. I told him I'd repay him as soon as I could," he said. "He's just as stubborn as you." He placed his thumb under her chin and rubbed it gently.

"If he gave you money then he must adore you," Ellie said. "He doesn't hand out money that often."

"I hope I have earned his respect," he said and was quiet for a moment. "Ellie, I'm going away for a while."

Ellie shifted so she was looking directly at him. "You are?" she said, hoping she didn't sound desperate or sad. She knew they had to go their separate ways—she had to go to school and he had to start his life. It just didn't hit her until that moment.

"Me and Moses are planning to travel the country." He beamed brightly. "We've got a list. Look." He took a folded piece of paper out of his pocket and showed it to Ellie. "Chicago; St. Louis; New York...all the big cities. I've always wanted to travel."

"You're going to places I've never been," she said, feeling the bittersweet taste of happiness and sorrow at the same time. She wanted the best for Sam but would selfishly miss him with all of her heart. She knew he needed to do this, and love meant letting him go.

"That's great, Sam. It really is." She gave him a warm smile and then it faded. "What about Granny, Virginia and Caleb? What will they do?"

"Granny says she's too old to adapt. She's staying put up in the holler. She's aiming to die there I 'spose. I don't think Caleb is planning to leave either. He don't mind the quiet, and he's got some healing to do over losing Jeremiah. And Virginia...she's gotta mend her broken heart. She'll come around eventually. It may take a while, but when she does she'll adjust fine. I can already sense a part of her wants to see what else is out there. She's asked me a lot of questions since I came back from my time with you."

"Will they be all right without you?"

"They never needed me, Ellie. I needed them, and now, I'm standing on my own. I have you to thank for that."

"Me?"

"You opened my eyes to a whole new world. I'd never be planning to travel the country if it weren't for you. Speaking of," he clutched onto the list and pointed to it,"I need to add another city to the list," he said.

"Which one?"

"Coral Gables," he answered and smiled. "There's a girl that lives there that has stolen my heart." He bent down to kiss her on the lips.

Ellie pulled away and said, "You should move it to the very top of your list." She brought him close to her and kissed him.

"I just might." He smiled. "I just might."

OTHER BOOKS BY THIS AUTHOR:

The Summer I Learned to Dive.

Since the time she was a little girl, eighteen-year-old Finley "Finn" Hemmings has always lived her life according to a plan, focused and driven with no time for the average young adult's carefree experiences. On the night of her high school graduation, things take a dramatic turn when she discovers that her mother has been keeping a secret from her—a secret that causes Finn to do something she had never done before—veer off her plan. In the middle of the night, Finn packs her bags and travels by bus to Graceville, SC seeking the truth. In Graceville, Finn has experiences that change her life forever; a summer of love, forgiveness and revelations. She learns to take chances, to take the plunge and to dive right in to what life has to offer.

The Year I Almost Drowned.

In this continuation of "The Summer I Learned to Dive," nineteen-year old Finley "Finn" Hemmings is living in Graceville, South Carolina with her grandparents. She's getting to know the family that she was separated from for the last sixteen years. Finn and Jesse's relationship seems to be going strong until they're forced to deal with obstacles that throw them off-track. As Finn prepares to leave for college, she has to say goodbye to the town, her friends and family, and the way of life that she has grown to love.

At college, Finn tries to acclimate to a new setting, but quickly falls into an old pattern. Just as things start to become normal and Finn begins to fit in, something unexpected happens that takes her back to Graceville where she is forced to deal with one challenge after another. Her world nearly collapses, and she finds herself struggling to keep from drowning. Through it all, Finn discovers the power of love and friendship. She learns what it means to follow her heart and to stay true to what she wants, even if what she wants isn't what she originally planned.

ABOUT THE AUTHOR

Shannon McCrimmon was born and raised in Central Florida. She earned a Master's Degree in Counseling from Rollins College. In 2008, she moved to the upstate of South Carolina. It was the move to the upstate that inspired her to write novels. Shannon lives in Greenville, South Carolina with her husband and toy poodle.

Did you enjoy *The Days Lost?* Please consider supporting the author by writing a review on Amazon.com or Goodreads.com.

Learn more about upcoming projects by becoming a fan on Facebook at www.facebook.com/shannonmccrimmonauthor, or follow me on twitter@smccrimmon1

ACKNOWLEDGEMENTS

Chris, I love you with all my heart and soul, thank you for everything. Laurin Baker, my editor, thank you for your heart-felt honesty, enthusiasm, constructive feedback, and for all the frowning faces. You make me a better writer. Sheila Lutringer, thank you for illustrating a beautiful book cover. You are so talented! To my betas: Peggy Ambler, Mandy Anderson, Amy Burt, Betty Jones, and Josh and Sarah Mandell, you offered suggestions that made the story better. Thank you so much. Olena Atkins, Tressa Sager, Ashleigh and Victoria Simmerson, and Wendy Wilken, thanks for all your pimpin'. You're my number one cheerleaders! Shannon Lewis, thanks for music and Pinterest suggestions. You helped with writing inspiration. Thanks to all the readers who sent me kind notes and read my other books. I appreciate you all! And, thank you to my family and friends, your support and love means the world to me.

Made in the USA
Charleston, SC
09 October 2014